HOUSE OF SCARABS

HAZEL LONGUET

Novel Experience

Novel Experience

A Novel Experience book.
First published in Great Britain in 2018 by Novel Experience

Cover design by Hazel Longuet

Edited by Briar Rose Editing
www.briarroseediting.com

www.hazellonguet.com

This book is dedicated to:

Micky Yandall, *who's always believed in me and pushed me to be my best self.*

Ivy Longuet, *who showed me the merit of undying kindness.*

I pray our shared DNA gives me just a sprinkle of the magic you both share.

PART ONE
THE MEETING

BLACK CATS BOOKSHOP

The old-fashioned bell tinkled a welcome as Ellie pushed open the door. A Siberian-like blast of cold air followed her into the bookstore.

Black Cat Books had a subtle, old-world charm. Rounded mullioned windows looked in on a room with exposed stone walls, covered with shining mahogany bookshelves that bulged with books. Deeply hewn alcoves housed an eclectic mix of antique Asian and African statues of cats. A huge inglenook fireplace with a crackling applewood fire dominated one wall. Deep, cushioned sofas upholstered in jewel-coloured velvet surrounded it. The store beckoned people in with its warm honey glow and then encouraged them to linger with its cosy seating and enchanting décor.

Ellie glanced around for a moment, rubbing her hands together to get the circulation moving and stamping her feet. Ben rushed in behind her, saying, "I locked the bikes up as you asked, but I can't see the need. We're in the middle of a tiny village in England, not downtown Manhattan." He walked over to the fire, putting his hands towards the flames. "Brrr. Thank God for some warmth. I'm a human popsicle."

Ellie turned with a stern expression and said, *"Bil Arabi min fadlak*. In Arabic, please."* Cursing under his breath, Ben repeated the statement, only to be corrected by Ellie.

As he moved around the store, Ben figured it must have once been a house. One room led to another, each of differing heights, some down steps and others up them. It was a warren of a place. A tiny corridor opened into a pint-sized room, just large enough for shelves and a deep mahogany and leather campaign chair. It was lit by a hundred twinkling lights embedded in the ceiling. The book collection here focused on the legends and myths of ancient Egypt. Ben settled in for a rummage.

Ellie, sighing, took the twisting stone staircase to the first floor and found a charming tea room that appeared unchanged from the eighteen-hundreds. There was a vast selection of cakes under glass cloches: colourful cupcakes, lardy cake, fruit cakes, roulades, deep Victoria sponges oozing with cream and jam, huge scones, coffee and walnut cake. The choices were endless and tempting. As she'd used at least a thousand calories on the ride over, and a bookshop specialising in mythology and legends held no interest for her, she decided to enjoy the refreshments and wait for Ben.

Uncertain whether to sit or go to the counter, she searched for someone to ask. A man bustled through a hidden door, disguised as part of the shelves of tea caddies that covered the back wall from floor to ceiling. Beaming at her, he put down the tray of flapjacks and came around to guide her to a table.

"Hi there. Sorry I wasn't here to welcome you, but I had to take these out of the oven. Gerhard, the shop's proprietor, had to pop out. Have a chair over here by the fire. It's a blisteringly cold day today, isn't it? Now what can I get you, poppet?"

Taking the seat he offered, Ellie's eyes wandered across the display of cakes. "I'm drooling - I'd love them all but as that's not possible, which do you recommend?"

"Everything's possible at Black Cat," he replied, his eyes twinkling. "I'll prepare a taster plate with a sample of each of them and then you can decide which to have. I recommend the house tea as the perfect accompaniment. It took a while, but I've at last created the perfect blend to cut through the sweetness of the cakes."

Smiling up at him, Ellie handed the menu back and agreed. "Thanks. That sounds great. You have a huge range for a small village bookshop," she commented.

"It must look that way, but Gerhard's a genius at getting people into the shop. Psychic afternoons, book clubs, themed history lectures, druids meeting – you name it, he does it. The store's used for most activities around here, from birthdays to council meetings. Black Cat's the hub of the village now, and we are famous for my cakes," he answered, straightening his tie. "Yep, it's always busy."

After two hours of obsessive digging around, Ben had a huge stack of books piled up next to the chair he'd adopted as his own. The store, so small and innocuous from outside, stretched up over three floors and into the attic. It had the best collection of ancient Egyptian mythology he'd seen outside the National Library.

Reality reasserted itself, bringing him down from his history-induced high as he realised he hadn't seen Ellie since entering the store. "Jeez, she'll be mighty pissed," he muttered to himself. Then again, she could have found him if she wanted to leave – unless she already had. He wouldn't put it past her. He hurried to the cash register by the door with the books he could carry.

He found the desk empty. As he peered around, he spotted a sign on the wall that stated, "No one home? Please ring to pay," with an arrow pointing at a ship's bell. Dubiously, he rang the bell. A small, amiable-looking man trotted down the stairs, dressed in mustard Harris tweed plus-fours and waistcoat.

"Sorry, sir. I was in the café. Let me take those from you," he said, reaching for the teetering pile.

Ben handed him the books, "I appear to have lost my friend. Have you seen a red-haired woman anywhere in the store?"

"Ellie? She's upstairs, in the café. Quite a baker, that girl. She's made a grand Gateau St. Honoré."

"She's been baking? In a bookstore?" Ben spluttered.

"Well, she got bored and asked if she could help in my kitchen. We've had a fine old time. She's such a sweetie."

"Sweetie? Ellie?" Ben could think of many things he'd call her, but "sweetie" wouldn't be one. "Can you point me towards the café, please?"

After retrieving the rest of his books and paying, he mounted the stairs and made his way to the café. There, he found Ellie with an apron around her waist, serving behind the counter and chattering to a gaggle of old ladies. He stayed in the shadow of the doorway and watched her. This was an Ellie he had only caught glimpses of over the last few months: happy, friendly, and unguarded. Not the stiff-lipped Trojan he'd seen day in and day out as he'd struggled to pick up the complexities of Arabic. She was younger and carefree.

He coughed, and she glanced over, laughing at something one octogenarian said. Seeing him, the laughter died, and her eyes re-shielded.

"Excuse me a moment," she said to the ladies and moved over to Ben. "*Sa'atein ya ragel* – two hours, Ben?" she muttered, "'Pop to a bookshop,' you said. Pop - not relocate."

"*Salam, Salam ya seti* – peace, peace," he said, raising his hands in submission. "I'm sorry. I get absorbed and time just vanishes. I'm a book nerd, so shoot me. I honestly didn't mean to take so long. I'm sorry – *ana asfa*."

"*Inta ragel – ana asif, mish ana asfa.* You're a man, so use the masculine '*ana asif*', not '*ana asfa*'. So, are you ready to go? We've got a long ride home, and it's uphill." She untied the strings and folded the apron. At the door, she said a warm farewell to the shop assistant, thanking him for his baking tips and giving him a quick hug.

"It's a shame you didn't get to meet Gerhard, the shop's proprietor. He'd have loved to meet you both. Anyway, I'm gushing. I hope you come back again soon, even if only to be my sous chef," he said with a twinkle.

Ben held open the door for Ellie, who backed out, still saying her goodbyes. She whirled around to head out and collided with an elderly man carrying a stack of papers in plastic protectors. The papers flew everywhere, and both Ellie and Ben hurried to help the old man gather them.

They reached for the same papyrus, and as their hands touched, a transparent, blue sphere of energy exploded from it. The sphere grew, throwing out sinuous, ghostly tendrils that twisted out and around the three. It brightened into a blinding white light, shimmering and stretching until it surrounded them like a tight skin, a blindfold to the outside world.

The sphere rotated, faster and faster, dizzying its

passengers until they were isolated from everything but each other. Only then did it slow as the tendrils projected a gallery of images: sand and temples, lakes and palms, bee-eaters and egrets, donkeys and shadufs. The pictures accelerated, blurring into indecipherable shapes. They twirled and flashed, exploding into exquisite turquoise prisms, which refracted shimmering beams throughout the sphere.

Ben, Ellie, and the old man stared around in awe as the light display intensified. As it reached its zenith, the light beams merged, forming three wraith-like objects: a scarab beetle, a crocodile, and a cat.

Other shoots flowed from the sphere's floor, fusing together to create three finely formed, transparent chairs. New tendrils unfurled and gently guided each of them to a chair whilst others extended and worshipfully encircled the objects, moving them towards the stunned group, offering one to each of them. They each accepted their object, moving without conscious volition, as if guided by instinct.

As the last of the three accepted the offering, the objects emitted a flute-like note that resonated around the sphere, growing in volume. They shimmered and contracted, becoming smaller and smaller, until they resembled small, glimmering chess pieces. Each person gasped in pain as the pieces sank into their palms and dissolved into their body. The energy from them seared through their veins, surging towards their hearts and engulfing their minds. In that instant, it was as if they knew everything but had forgotten their former wisdom.

Then it was gone – the sphere, the chairs, the images. They were again three people standing outside a bookshop.

GUARDIANS OF THE ANKH

EGYPT

The phone pealed loudly, waking its owner from a heavy slumber. Without introduction, a deep, gravelly voice rasped, "So, it has come to be just as the Deities prophesied. The trio has melded; their quest has begun. We cannot allow it to conclude in the formation of the House of Scarabs, or the consequences would be dire. The council has decided that you will lead the Amenti team. Eurydice, be certain that failure to negate this meld will result in your removal. Do not fight the inevitable! Sadly, there are now no options other than a humane cull. Do I make myself clear?"

"Yes, Tjati. Crystal-clear. May I ask who will serve with me?" Eurydice replied.

"The team is at your door. Make haste and start your preparations. *Salam.*"

The line went dead.

AFTER THE MELD

ENGLAND

They stumbled and glanced around, blinking as they looked to each other for reassurance. One minute, they were wrapped up in a giant energy ball, and the next moment, they were back in the doorway of the bookshop. It'd felt as if they were transported far away, and yet, here they were.

Ben collapsed onto the step. "Jesus Christ! What the hell was that? Did... um, did anybody see what I saw?" Ellie stared at Ben and the old man and, in a state of shock, nodded.

"I did. I... God! We need to discuss it in private - *ja*," the elderly man said. He jerked his head towards Stefan, who stared curiously at them through the glass door. Ben rubbed down his trousers as he stood and nodded his agreement. He stepped to one side to allow the man to lead the way.

"How remiss of me. Sorry, the shock has silenced my manners. I'm Gerhard Webber, the owner of this little shop." He laid a gentle hand on Ellie's shoulder and said,

"Come, my dear – you're shivering. Let's have a cup of tea. You British use it as a cure-all, *ja?*"

As they entered the store, Gerhard turned to his assistant. "Tea for my young guests, if you please, Stefan. We will be in my study. Let's close the shop early. We shall play... now how do you say in English? Ah, yes... we will play truant on this chilly afternoon." With that, he turned towards a shelf and reached for a book entitled *The Secret Room*. The bookcase swung open to reveal a stone staircase spiraling up with a ruby velvet handrail. The lights, as if by magic, illuminated in time with their footsteps.

Gerhard opened the studded, arched door at the top, and they stepped into a circular room of windows, each interspersed with carved gothic bookcases. In the middle stood a cluster of comfy sofas and chairs, into which they sunk. Silence lingered, a great weight hanging over their heads as the shock hit. Gerhard glanced across at Ellie and noticed her pallor. He decided to take matters into his own hands.

"My dear, Stefan will be here in a moment. May I suggest we delay any discussions until he has gone?" Looking at Ellie, he said, "Please don't be offended, *Fraulein*, but you're a trifle pale. It might be wise for you to lie down for a few minutes and catch your breath, *ja.*"

Ellie stared at Gerhard, her large green eyes catching the afternoon rays. Belatedly, she nodded and stretched out across the deep feather cushions.

Ben sat with his head in his hands, going over what he had seen repeatedly, trying to make sense of the impossibility of the situation. No matter how he examined it, nothing made sense. Giving up, he studied their host. At well over six feet tall and lean, Gerhard had the appearance of an elderly country gentleman. He was dressed in cinnamon cord trousers and a tweed jacket, with a spotted handkerchief pointing jauntily out of the pocket. Gerhard peered over the top of his frameless glasses, green eyes studying Ellie with deep speculation. As he looked away, he noticed Ben watching him and smiled, sleeking back his silver hair.

"Gerhard, I'm Ben Ellis, and this is Ellie Bendall. I'm studying Arabic at Ellie's language school. I stumbled onto an interesting blog about your store, so we decided-"

A loud knock silenced him. Pushing the door open with his back, Stefan entered the room and laid out an exquisite bone china tea service. He'd provided a classic English high tea, complete with cucumber sandwiches, petit fours, and a choice of three teas.

"I'll close up downstairs and then I'll be off. Anything else you need before I go?"

"No, that will be all, Stefan. Thank you. It looks sublime. Enjoy the afternoon," replied Gerhard, smiling.

Stefan raised his eyebrow quizzically at Gerhard but withdrew without further comment.

After distributing the tea, Gerhard sat down. Studying his hands, he outlined, in acute yet succinct detail, what he'd seen. "The scent was overwhelming, so exotic and strange. The odour of heat and dust, yet also with a hint of spice and the sweetness of apples. Unlike anything I have ever smelt before," he said.

"It's the smell that made sense," Ellie murmured. "I grew up with it wafting from every coffee shop and street café and rising at night from the garden as my father pondered his finds of the day. It's shisha - an apple tobacco smoked in a water pipe. In fact, everything was familiar - the Nile, the deserts of Fayoum. And yet, it showed things that no longer happen, like the inundation of the delta, where the Nile flooded great swathes of land. That hasn't happened since they built the dam."

"Are you sure, my dear?" Gerhard asked. "It was projecting scenes of Egypt?"

"Positive. I was born and bred in Egypt. I've lived there my entire life. I only left four years ago. My parents and grandmother were Egyptologists of some repute. It was definitely images of Egyptian life."

"But what the hell was it? Did we imagine it? Was it real? Things like this don't happen. I'm a scientist – I work with facts and figures. So far, nothing makes sense," Ben said, rubbing his face with his rough hands.

"No, it doesn't. It's extraordinary and unexplainable, but you've made a valid point. We need to examine what happened to us in, how do you say, forensic detail. Check we experienced the same thing, try to work out what it was and why just the three of us saw it. I assume Stefan didn't, or he would have reacted differently, and I only saw you two within the sphere. So, did either of you see anything different or any details I missed?"

Ellie shook her head.

Ben said, "Nope, but I experienced something like the energy shock at the end but far less intensely when I first met Ellie."

Ellie swiveled her head and looked at Ben. "Yes, I did too. When we shook hands, there was a snap of energy, like a static shock." Ben nodded and scrubbed his hands through his hair.

Gerhard considered this, eased himself from his chair, and with a soft smile, said, "Then I suggest we shake hands to simulate the same result. If you don't mind, *Fraulein*?"

As their fingertips neared each other, an arc of blue energy sparked from each hand, meeting in the middle.

"Wow! That was considerably stronger than last time. Ben?" she said, stretching her hand towards him. Again, as their hands neared, another arc bridged the gap.

"Jeez!" Ben said, flinching away from the contact. "That's a hundred times more powerful than the first time."

Gerhard moved over to his desk and picked up a leather-bound notebook and well-used fountain pen. He returned and settled back into a burgundy Queen Anne chair. Peering over the top of his glasses, he said, "I suggest we note this all down and try to find connectors that may help us understand what precisely is happening here. Can we start with how you know each other? Ben, you said you are attending a course at Ellie's school. Sorry, may I be so bold as to address you by your given names?" They nodded their consent, and he continued, "Ben, how did you first hear of Ellie's school, and what made you go there?"

"I'd applied for a fellowship with the Egyptian Department of Antiquities, and I coloured my application a jot by saying I was fluent in Arabic, which I'm not. I figured I didn't stand a bat's-chance-in-hell of getting the fellowship. It's prized and strongly contested, so I didn't think the over-statement would matter. I was both astonished and morti-fied when they gave me the fellowship. I asked an Egyptian buddy of mine, Sam - who studied with me at Berkeley - for a recommendation for a teacher, and he pointed me towards Ellie. He said if anyone could get me talking in Arabic in four months, it would be her."

Ellie blanched. "Sam! Sam who?"

Somewhat startled, Ben replied, "Sam Gamal. He's an archaeologist of some repute, as you'd put it. He specialises in the funerary rites of Ancient Egyptians. You may have heard of him, if your family are Egyptologists."

"Oh, yes... I've heard of him. He's my ex-husband!"

THREE MONTHS PREVIOUSLY

SCARAB'S REST, ENGLAND

With a deep sigh of relief, Ellie Bendall closed the door on the latest batch of students. As the battered old minibus bounced down the drive, she turned and studied the mill around her. She didn't notice the ancient grandeur others commented on when they first entered her house. Instead, she saw cracks wide enough to absorb a king's ransom. The gentle creaks and rumbles of the old mill reminded her of the endless chatter of a cash register. She flexed her shoulders and marched into the kitchen, armed herself with the last dregs of coffee, and opened the mill's accounts.

"Get a grip, Ellie. It'll work somehow. You know that!" she muttered to herself.

"Watch out, m'dear. Keep talking to yourself, and you'll get an express ticket into The Priory. So, you packed off the gang."

"Oh, my God, Charlie, you frightened me half to death!" Ellie said, clutching her chest. "I wish I could afford The

Priory, but it'd be the national health psych ward for me. Did you see them leaving as you arrived?"

"See them? They almost drove me off the bloody road. Ellie, it's time to find a new minibus company. They're cheap, but that's all they have going for them. A false economy is what it is!" she said as she put her apron on and gathered the cleaning tools from under the sink.

With a big sigh, Ellie replied, "Well, that's redundant for now as we don't have a solitary booking. To be honest Charlie, I'm more than a bit worried about it. We may need to slow the restoration programme." She pushed back her long titian hair impatiently and poked her finger at the accounts. "You know, no matter how often I study these figures, I can never make them add up. It's so frustrating."

Charlie put her arm around Ellie's shoulders. "Hon, you shouldn't have to face this on your own. Scarab's Rest is a family estate. If it were me, I'd be onto my parents super quick-like. You've carried the weight of this around your neck for three years, and it's consuming you."

Grimacing, Ellie pushed away from the large farmhouse table. She paced to the window, cradling her coffee between both hands and stroking the side of the cup. "You know I can't do that, Charlie. They wanted us to 'dispose of it'. Scarab's Rest means nothing to them. Mind you, other than the damn funerary rites of the Ancient Egyptians, I'm not certain what they care about. Not me or my happiness, that's for sure." Looking back at Charlie again, she took a deep breath and said, "If I mention I'm experiencing problems, they'll try to force me to sell up, and that's something I will never, ever countenance. Nope, something will turn up, and if it doesn't, we will just need to tighten our belts."

"Hmm, tighten them much further, and we'll be singing an octave higher. Anyhow, standing here gassing won't get those beds stripped, so I'll get started. Try not to worry, hon," she said and patted Ellie's shoulder as she bustled past.

Watching her go, Ellie thanked the powers-that-be for nudging Charlie into her life, like a blazing comet across her personal sky. She was always brutally honest, always supportive, and infinitely practical. Although only eight years older than Ellie, Charlie soon become her mother figure. Knowing she had someone in the country to turn to was deeply reassuring when she was used to having no one. Charlie had long ceased to be Scarab's Rest's cleaner in Ellie's mind.

Grabbing her waxed jacket and shoving her feet into her muddy Wellingtons, she shouted up the stairs, "I'll be in the garden. I want to check on the stable conversions." She unlatched the door and took the path to the left, stopping to deadhead the lavender bushes as she studied the house that had been in her family since 1086.

She'd loved the mill for as long as she could remember. The castellated turret, the golden limestone walls, the leaded windows which sparkled like facetted diamonds, and the stone humpback bridge that provided the only access to the house. The mill and its surrounding gardens and outbuildings had felt like an enchanted, picturesque playground to her. She'd swum in the river that originally powered the mill with her grandfather, and they'd often used the derelict water wheel as a diving board.

Since inheriting the building in a state of near collapse from her grandmother, Ellie had been fighting every day to stop its accelerated slide into ruin. Her predecessors extended the tiny watermill over the generations, adding on larger living quarters, storage barns, and more land. At its peak, the estate had grown into a resplendent house with over a thousand acres of land. In just three generations, that all changed.

Scarab's Rest had deteriorated until just ten acres remained. The mill had fallen into a gentile shabbiness, many of the outhouses and barns were in ruins, and the estate provided no income to cover the increasing maintenance costs. Ellie poured every penny she had into regenerating the house: the inheritance from grandparents, her life savings, her divorce settlement, and the earnings from her residential Arabic courses. Despite this, although she'd re-roofed the house, she still needed to find the capital to renovate the West wing and finish converting the outbuildings into accommodation.

Ellie skirted the house and entered the rear courtyard. "Shannon," she called. "Shannon, are you in there?" She slammed to a standstill and stared open-mouthed at the keystone reinstated above the main barn door.

"Hey, Ellie. I was just cleaning up for the day," the builder answered, drying his hands as he came out from the scaffold-wrapped building.

"Shannon, you genius. I could kiss you! The keystone's amazing. Where did you get it? It matches the others perfectly."

He tilted his head to one side and peered through his windswept grey fringe, his blue eyes alight with a wicked twinkle. "Hmm. I'd not be stopping you, should you so wish."

"Shannon..." she warned.

"Oh, Ellie, don't be fussing yourself. I am only joshing with ye. I found the stone in the wee river when I was excavating the wheel base. See the *golach*, just like the others?"

"*Golach?*" she asked.

"Um, the wee creepy crawly your family's so fond of," he replied.

Staring up at the large bug in its prominent position, she said, "It's the scarab beetle from our coat of arms. We always have it in the keystone above the door of our buildings. Not sure why, but it's tradition. Thank God you found it. I was wondering how I would afford a stone mason to carve a new one."

The wind picked up, and with a shiver, Ellie moved inside and peered around the immaculate building site. Shannon always left it clean and tidy at the end of the working day.

"How are we doing, Shannon? Are we on schedule? I'm worried about cash-flow. There're no courses booked, so we may need to call a halt at the first fix stage, or we complete half the units. That might be more sensible as I could then rent them out and get cash to fund the others. What do you think?"

"Aye, there's pros and cons to both, to be sure. I dinnae think it makes sense to stop in the middle, so probably better to finish half, but let me have a wee think t'night."

They moved around the five units, each designed with two bedrooms and an open-plan kitchen and lounge. Ellie planned to convert one barn into a refectory that would double as a large conference room for the language school. She hoped to rent out the accommodation suites as holiday lets when not in use by the school to bring in some much-needed cash.

After discussing other building logistics, she left Shannon and returned to the mill.

"Is that you, Ellie?" called Charlie from upstairs. "I might have found a solution to some of our financial woes."

Sweeping down the spiral stone staircase like a modern-day Scarlett O'Hara, she stopped dramatically just short of the bottom and presented her hand to Ellie.

"Why, Miss Ellie, I do believe you owe me a large kiss. I've just booked a GEN-U-INE Yankee gentleman for a four-month intensive course," she said in the worst Southern American accent Ellie had ever heard. "Before you throw a hissy fit, I know that the minimum course size is six people, but we are desperate, and he's willing to pay for all ten places for four months. That's full occupancy! Our costs would be miniscule as we'd have one person to feed and no need for the minibus," she said. "Go on, admit it. I am a genius!"

Ellie turned her back on her friend and said, "Damn it, Charlie. The rules are not just for profit but also to protect my privacy. They stay in my home, and one-on-one is way too intimate. Other course partners enable them to spend their off-time with each other and give me some peace. I appreciate the gesture, truly, but I can't be on my own in this house for four months with a strange man. Do you have his number? I'll call him and cancel or ask him to round up classmates since he's paying for the places."

Charlie stuck out her chin. With a determined glint in her eye, she said, "Ellie, aside from showing a decidedly bad grace, you are being stubborn and timid. I'll not let your pathological fear of men stop you from grabbing this offer. It's bloody lucrative, and God knows we need the money. I knew you'd be like this, so I told him to wire the full course payment to the school's account. It's probably there already. He's arriving the day after tomorrow, and in the meantime, see if you can round up any other students to fill the free places!"

Ellie pivoted away, walking towards the kitchen. Charlie prowled after her and grabbed her hand, pulling her to a stop. She lifted Ellie's chin, forcing her to make eye contact.

"Ellie, we don't have a choice! The school needs his dosh. Maybe we could use some of the cash to finish one of the accommodation units and then he won't be in-your-face. You might be mad with me now, but you will thank old Charlie in the morning, once you've had time to think on it."

"Don't bet on it," Ellie grunted, slamming the kitchen door behind her.

AFTERMATH

Putting the phone down, Ben smiled. *Sam saved my bacon, which isn't the best expression to use for a Muslim,* he thought.

When was he going to learn to think before he did something so stupid? Why on earth had he written on his application form he was fluent in both written and spoken Arabic? How could he pick up a language in only four months?

His only consolation was that Sam thought if anyone could help him, it would be Ellie. Her assistant, Charlie, had negotiated a damn hard deal, stating that Ellie never did one-on-one courses. It'd taken all his negotiation skills, a bucketful of flirting, and a huge amount of cash to get the deal approved, but approved it was – with the proviso he didn't answer a call from the UK until he arrived. Odd clause, but frankly, he'd have agreed to anything at that point.

Nothing could be worse than getting the prestigious Hawass Fellowship only to be caught as a liar and cheat.

England

Charlie may think she's smart, but I'm smarter, Ellie thought as she dialed 1471 to get the last incoming caller ID. *There's no amount of money that would make me live with a strange man for four months. What was Charlie thinking?*

She'd had enough of men to last her an eternity. Her job meant she had to work with them occasionally, but she never willingly spent time on her own with one. Retrieving the number, she jotted it down on a pad and then, with a deep breath, dialed it. The number rang and rang, unanswered. She dialed again and again, repeatedly, with no success.

"Damn it all to hell!" she shouted at the phone as she slammed the receiver down. The American was coming whether she liked it or not.

BEN'S ARRIVAL

Ben studied the passing scenery from the taxi's window - lush pastoral scenes, green and glowing in the hazy afternoon sunshine. He'd been to England many times before but always to the urban bustle of London, to the museums and theatres, so this was new.

Everything buzzed with life and energy. Roadside verges were a blaze of colourful daisies and poppies, whilst the neighbouring woods swayed with an ocean of ferns and splashes of pink foxgloves. Grassy fields were home to black-and-white patched cows chewing the cud. A patch-work of thick hedgerows interspersed with intricate walls, held up by the genius of the farmer's stone selection, which negated the need for mortar. The air smelt warm and fresh, richer than in his hometown of Greenwich Village in New York City.

"Your first time to this part of the world, is it?" asked the taxi driver.

"Yeah, I've never been outside London before," Ben answered.

"Argh, London isn't real England. I can't stand the place

m'self - full of tourists and foreigners. No, you need to come here to the West Country to get the best of England. Can't beat Somerset. We've got top-notch food, you know, what with our cheeses and our cider. And we're a darn sight friendlier too. Ah, lookie here," he said, turning into a wide gateway bordered by large pillars topped with finials of a shield embellished with beetles. "Scarab's Rest."

The taxi bumped its way along the cobblestone driveway and through a colonnade of magnificent mature oaks. They approached an ancient stone bridge skirted with the largest weeping willows Ben had ever seen. As they crossed the bridge and turned to the right, Scarab's Rest came into view, glowing gold in the dappled sunlight.

"That's quite some place," said the taxi driver.

"Isn't it just," Ben replied, staring up at the large building with an imposing tower to the rear. The front of the house was moated by the river and had dormer windows pointing up into the aged terracotta roof. At some point in history, a romantic soul had added a dramatic oriel bay window that came straight from the pages of a fairy tale.

Ben thanked and paid the driver, then walked up to a double-sized, oak-studded door. As he lifted the heavy cast iron knocker, the door swung open to reveal a cherubic woman with a mass of uncontrolled curls and rosy cheeks.

"You must be Ben. We've been expecting you," she said, grabbing Ben's suitcase before he could say a word. "Come in, come in. Get the weight off your feet. You must be knackered after such a long journey. Oh, I'm Charlie. We spoke on the phone."

She showed Ben into a double-height drawing room with exposed stone walls on two sides and a galleried walkway that stretched around the other two. The gallery, heavy with bookcases, was an ideal vantage point to gaze down into the room from the upper level. Oak beams and a white-washed ceiling complemented the golden stone work and the simple, comfortable oak furniture.

"This house is enchanting," Ben said to her in awe.

"Yes, it's gorgeous, isn't it? But it's hell on earth to clean," she replied with a laugh. "Still, I shouldn't complain. How else would I keep this heavenly bod in order otherwise?" she added with a cheeky wink. "I've got your room all ready and cosy. I'll just pop your suitcase up and then bring you a nice cup of tea."

Before he had a moment to protest, she'd gone in a flurry of bouncing blonde curls.

As Ben studied the room, his mental image of Ellie changed from struggling business owner to an affluent aristocrat flirting with commerce. Sam had been unusually vague about Ellie. When Ben had asked him for more details, Sam had mumbled she was his best hope and then closed down the conversation. Now he wondered why his normally verbose buddy had been so strangely taciturn about Ellie Bendall.

THE TEST

Charlie returned laden with a heavy tray of sandwiches, cakes, and tea. "Wow, is that all for me?" Ben exclaimed. "I'll be as large as this house if I eat all that."

Charlie fidgeted. "Sorry – I've never been to the States, but on the telly, the food portions are huge, so I served accordingly."

Feeling guilty he'd embarrassed her, Ben beamed and said, "Ah, that it explains it. Just so you know, I don't pack a gun, I hold a well-used passport, and I can talk quietly – well, by American standards." He winked at her.

She laughed and flashed him her teeth. "And I have excellent teeth, we haven't had rain in over twenty-five days, and I've never said 'gosh' in my life. Anyhow, I'm afraid Ellie isn't around today, but she left you a load of material to get started on," she said, crossing to the table and lifting a mound of books and a large folder.

A flash of embarrassment crossed her face, which she cleared with a deep breath and a lift of her chin. "Actually, Ben, she's rather annoyed with me for booking a solo client.

As I said on the phone, she only teaches groups, and she didn't take the news well. I don't know how to put this, so I'll just spit it out. Ellie's left you pre-class study material with a test, and she said she will only continue with the training if you pass with ninety percent or more."

She laid the books on a small side table and said, "She's given you until nine tomorrow morning to finish it." Her cheeks flushed redder as she continued. "If you fail the test, she will refund your course fees in full and provide a return ticket to the U.S. I am so, so sorry. She's an excellent Arabic teacher. This is all my fault. I shouldn't have booked you without checking with her, but she really needs-"

Ben raised his hand. "Stop, stop. I understand. She's a spoiled old tartar used to having her way in everything. Don't worry, Charlie. I've got a phenomenal short-term memory. It'll be easy."

Ellie whistled a perky tune as she white-washed the bedroom wall in the first accommodation unit. She'd extricated herself from having to spend the next four months with a strange man, and the world was a whole lot better than it'd been yesterday.

"You're wrong, lassie," Shannon said from behind her.

"You frightened me," she said, whirling around with the paint roller dripping in her hand. "And for your information, I am not wrong. Charlie is. She had no right to make that booking without consulting me. There's an order of command for a reason. I own Scarab's Rest, not her!"

"You're wrong and you know it, but you're too damned thick-skulled and stubborn to admit it, just like your old Grannie. Never in me life did I meet a more difficult woman when she got an idea in her head, and you, my love, are the same."

Ellie threw the roller into the tray and moved to leave, but Shannon blocked her exit.

"Don't go running away again. Listen for once. I have known you your entire life, lass and lady, and spent a good part of mine helping your Grannie. You need this client. You're going under otherwise, as sure as bees collect pollen. I know you've been hurt more times than any wee lassie should ever have been, and it's created deep scarring, but don't let fear cast its shadow over your whole life. You have an opportunity here, and God knows you are the first Bendall in a long time with a business head - grab your dream. Restore Scarab's Rest to its former glory."

Ellie stared in shock at Shannon, who flicked a gentle finger under her chin and left, his footsteps whispering softly on the hardwood floor.

Ben glanced up as another cup of black coffee appeared next to him. Smiling at Charlie, he stretched and said with a yawn, "You still here? What time is it?"

"Gone three a.m.," she answered.

"Don't you have a home?" he asked.

"I'm here with you till the bitter end. It's my fault, and I will help in any way I can. Although, Arabic grammar is not my forte. Far from it."

"Did I say this would be easy sometime in my stupid past? Jeez - this stuff is so complicated. She's determined to get rid of me, isn't she?"

"Yep."

"Then let's blight her opportunity. Ready to test me again, partner?"

"I'm all yours," she yawned.

Blinking at the screen in disbelief, Ellie registered the test result from her computer upstairs.

"Ninety-seven percent - you did it!" Charlie shrieked at Ben. She grabbed him and whirled him around just as the grandfather clock in the atrium struck nine clear chimes.

"Nope, Lady Charlie," Ben said with a deep bow from his waist. "*We* did it. What a dynamite team! You've shown me I *can* crack this language, and thanks almost whole heartedly to you, I will." With that, he planted a loud kiss on her cheek and swung her around until they collapsed in a fit of giggles.

Lifting her head from the keyboard, Ellie peered at the screen again. She heard screams of excitement from down-stairs and flopped her head back down in despair. *The gods are against you, Ellie,* she thought to herself, *as always.*

Five minutes later, a jubilant Charlie knocked on the door. Without waiting for an answer, she entered and deposited a tray on the desk. Finding Ellie slumped on her keyboard, she pinched her between the shoulder blades and bustled around the room, tidying as she went.

"Ouch! Was that necessary?"

"Sorry. Did it hurt?" Charlie replied innocently. "I was just testing to make certain you hadn't died from a case of the terminal grumps. Glad to know you are still alive and well."

"For your information, I was practising dhyāna medi-tations."

"And I have been polishing the floor with a broom up my ass whilst singing 'Yankee Doodle Dandy' with our guest. Move your bum, girly. You've got a student to teach downstairs, who, I might add, just passed with ninety-seven percent," she boomed into Ellie's ear. "Here's your breakfast. Eat, wash, and come greet our visitor. And pronto!"

THE FIRST MEETING

Ellie shrugged into a charcoal grey poloneck and matching tailored trousers, then searched for something to tie back her hair. She yanked open drawers and rummaged until she found a bobble.

These cupboards need sorting, she thought as she pulled her unruly mane into a severe ponytail.

Turning to inspect herself in the full-length mirror, she twisted from side to side and smiled at her spartan appearance. She took a deep breath, smoothed the invisible creases, and moved to the door, ready – albeit reluctantly – to face her foe.

Shifting as the kitchen door opened, Ben stared at the woman who entered. She was not the dried-up old spinster of his imagination. Facing him across the kitchen island was a titian-haired beauty of around thirty, with glowing peachy skin, generous rosy lips, and a voluptuous figure. Long black eyelashes shielded her eyes as she glided towards him.

She hesitated for a moment before taking a deep breath, extending her hand, and glancing up at him, her green eyes guarded. As they reached across the island to shake hands, Ben noticed her eyes had amber crescents, which curled around the pupil on the outer edge of each iris.

Then their fingers met. A blue spark arced between their hands, fizzing as they touched. They jumped back as they got a huge static shock.

"Ouch..." she said through gritted teeth as she shook her hand in the air. "Sorry. You must be Ben. I'm Ellie Bendall. Welcome to Scarab's Rest."

"Figured out who I was when you felt pain, eh?" Ben replied with a grin.

"Not precisely, no," she said. "You're the only man in my house. It made the deduction elementary."

Cold. No, icy, Ben mused. *Arctic fronts are warmer. I'm going to need a heavy dose of charm.*

"Your eyes are amazing, Ellie. Heterochromia is rare; it occurs in only one percent of the population."

"Heterochromia?" she asked with a frown.

"Sorry. I'm so interested by it, I forget others aren't. It's a variation in colour of the iris, i.e. green eyes with amber crescents."

"Fascinating," she said pointedly.

"Well, having the same condition, I'm always excited to meet someone else with it. I've seen people with two different coloured eyes or splotches of a colour on one of their eyes, but until today, I've seen no one with two matching crescents other than myself. What're the chances of us both having the same coloured eyes and patterning? A fraction of one percent – that *is* fascinating!"

"Ben, whilst most women may be flattered by your over-stated charm, I am not. I want to be unequivocal... you are a student in my school. Should you step over that delineation, I will not hesitate to cancel your course, which Charlie assures me is of the utmost importance to you. I hope I've made myself clear."

"Crystal-clear, Ms. Bendall. You've an over-inflated ego. I am here to learn Arabic and only Arabic. I like women as much as the next man, but my taste goes for warm and friendly, rather than glacial and arrogant. Sorry to disappoint you." Standing, he pointed towards the door and said, "I've paid your school a packet for my tuition and would appreciate if we could start. You are late."

THE CATCH-UP

"*Habibti azayik? Wahashtini habibti.* Darling, how are you? I missed you. It's me, Mama Aida. My Elena, can you hear me?" an old, croaky voice shouted down the line in Arabic.

"Mama Aida! Yes, I can. No need to shout. It's so good to hear your voice. I've missed you."

"*Al Hamdulillah, Al Hamdulillah.* Praise be to God. Elena, *habibti,* speak. Something's wrong. It's in your voice, my darling. Is it that wretched man? Is he harassing you again? Oh, I knew it! Didn't I tell you 'marry in haste, repent at leisure'? That's it. I'll get the Omda to book me a flight, and I'll come to you."

"Mama, calm down. I'm fine. You don't need the Omda. I haven't had any contact with Sam since the divorce. I'm just tired and a touch over-wrought. It's work stuff, I promise."

Ellie smiled to herself at the thought of Mama Aida rushing as fast as her little old legs would carry her, black galabiya flying, to the local Omda, the government-appointed village mayor, to get him to book her airline tickets. The tiny hamlet of mud houses she lived in had only gotten electricity two years before, and the Omda was a village elder of around seventy who couldn't speak English and had never seen a computer, much less used one. He'd won the appointment as he was the only person universally respected in the village. He was a wise, stern but kindly old man, but air-ticket agent he was not.

"My Elena, as Allah is my witness, and may He burn out my eyes if I lie, I sensed your unhappiness deep in my heart. A shadow blotted out the sun today, and I said to myself, 'Aida, your little Elena needs you.' So, I went to the market and I called. Now tell me all about it, my little one. Mama Aida has the answer, you know."

"Yes, you always have," Ellie said with a long sigh. "It's silly, and I shouldn't let it get under my skin, but this student has an uncanny ability to just wind me up the wrong way. It wouldn't matter if he was just one in a class, but he's on his own with me for four months, and he's driving me to distraction and back in a hurry."

"He? On his own? *Ya*, Elena, your reputation! Do you have a chaperone?"

"Mama, it's not like that here in England, I told you. Anyhow, I've moved into one of the accommodation units. It's more a building site than a house, but that's better than living under the same roof with him."

"Why did you accept a solo male student? Didn't I always tell you men bring us nothing but hardship and heartache? Didn't that terrible man prove my words true? Why am I on my own? I had plenty of offers. It's better to find your own way in life, to depend on yourself. Men grow with a good woman's love, but women wither. It's a common truth, Elena, *habibti*."

"I didn't accept him. I would never have accepted him.

Things are a bit tight at the moment, so when he called and offered to pay for a full-time, ten-person course for four months, Charlie accepted, and I'm stuck with him. I've tried everything to wiggle out of it, but he's too smart."

"*Yanhar esswed*. What a black day. A maid decided your business's direction. Are you crazy? Did I teach you nothing, girl of mine?"

"She is not a maid. She's a friend of mine, and she was only trying to help."

"If it has four legs, pulls a cart, and brays, it's a donkey. She cleans your house, so she's your maid. Where did I go wrong? I tried so hard to raise you well, when your mother was more interested in old, broken pots. I was there loving you, teaching you. I failed! Oh, what a black day. A black day," she wailed.

"Mama Aida – stop! You raised me with more love and more human insight than anyone could ever hope for. I'll be fine, really. I promise. It'll be okay. Calm down. Please don't stress your heart. Please..."

Aida replied with new vigor, "Elena, my darling, I've been saving, and I have just over five hundred dollars. I'll invest it in your school, and you can pay me back when God grants your school sunshine days. Then you can get rid of this male parasite. *Al Hamdulillah*, we have a solution. God be praised."

Smiling gently at Aida's offer, Ellie declined as tactfully as she could. She ended the call with a promise to call Aida at her neighbour's house the following day on the only telephone line in the hamlet.

Egypt

Aida returned the handset to the boy running the tiny kiosk in Abusir. The telephone line was stolen from the nearby exchange and rented out by the call. The dusty streets swarmed with children and cars, sheep and water buffalo, all bustling to get home as the sun set. The hawkers selling homemade flatbread and the stall owners selling street food called out to attract the passers-by, but the cacophony of car horns blasting and brakes squealing drowned them out.

Through this chaos, she plodded back home, not feeling the two miles. She rolled her prayer beads through her fingers in an obsessive and worried manner. She chewed her bottom lip and muttered passionate entails to God to protect her ward, her heart's child.

Aida had been with Ellie's family for over sixty years and had been Ellie's nursemaid, then her nanny and, to all intents and purposes, her mother. It was Aida she'd run to when she'd woken from a bad dream. It was Aida who'd guided her through adolescence with all that involved, and Aida who'd provided stability and love throughout her childhood. Though only the house help, she'd been more knowledgeable and wiser, more curious and self-aware, and infinitely more compassionate and loving than anyone else in Ellie's sphere.

Now she was suffering from Ellie's self-inflicted exile from Egypt. Fast approaching eighty-two, her eyes failing and her limbs weakening, she felt the loss of her life's one love. She desperately wanted her to come home, but she was deeply proud of Ellie's success with the house renovation and the establishment of the school.

Despite Ellie's pleading and bullying, Aida refused to move to England. Her bones formed from the sands of

Egypt and would return to those sands, not the cold, wet mud of a country unknown. Yet, if Ellie needed her, she'd go. She'd have to go. Her vow was sacrosanct.

"My Elena, my sweet girl, I'll find a solution. I'll not let them hurt you again..." she muttered as she continued her long walk home.

AN OUTING

"I'm bored. I've been here for two months and barely left this house. 'You'll practise immersive language courses' – that's what the brochure says," he said, waving it in front of her. "Come on, Ellie. It will be fun, and where better to practise the academic Arabic I need? I'm the top of the class! Don't I deserve a reward for that?"

"You're the only one in the class, so you're also bottom," she answered, slamming her coffee cup down and opening the newspaper with a snap.

Charlie reached across them to clear the breakfast dishes. "Ellie, he's right. Normally, you'd have had a shed-load of outings by now. Give the guy a break." Turning her back on Ellie, she gave Ben a cheeky wink.

"So, whatcha say, Ellie? We could take the bikes. It's only a couple of villages away. If we use the cycle path next to the canal, we'd cut a click or two by going cross-country. Please. I'll let you test me on grammar the whole ride," he said, trying to tempt her.

Raising her hands in surrender, she said, "Okay, pass today's test and we'll go. I've put the Bible in Arabic on your desk. If you can read me Genesis and Exodus without making a mistake, you're on. Otherwise, we stay and study."

Lifting his eyes to the heavens, Ben lurched out of his chair. "Fantastic. Nothing like a little Bible studies to cheer a guy up," he grumbled.

How in the name of God did he pass that test after only two months? Ellie wondered as she puffed along the cycle path. He was the most talented student she'd ever taught. He absorbed information with almost no effort. Normally, she'd be happy teaching someone of his abilities, but Ben Ellis was easily the most arrogant and insufferable man she'd met. He was her antithesis in every way.

British weather certainly adds a little drama, Ben thought.

The day had started with a beautiful misty morning, the vapour hanging in the folds of the countryside that wrapped around Scarab's Rest. As the sun peaked over the horizon, the mist had taken a golden hue, and Ben had watched a deer grazing peacefully in the front paddock. By nine a.m., the sun burned off the mist, and the day promised to be an autumn spectacle.

When they set out, just after lunch, it started to drizzle. Now, from nowhere, the wind had picked up, and an Arctic gale was sweeping the Kennet and Avon Canal.

"Do you know any songs?" Ellie shouted breathlessly over her shoulder.

"You want a sing-a-long? Wow, you're embracing the

spirit of an outing, Ells. I do a fairly good rendition of 'My Way'."

"I've told you repeatedly not to call me that, and lord preserve my ears from the torture of your voice. No, I want you to translate it," she replied.

He crooned the entire song, mimicking Frank Sinatra, in perfect Arabic. Ellie groaned and surged forward to escape the final deafening chorus.

With a smirk, Ben noticed Ellie lift herself from the bike's seat and use her full body weight to push on through the wind. *How could such a cold, difficult woman come in such a siren's body?* he wondered for the hundredth time.

The weather didn't dent his enthusiasm. It felt good visiting Black Cat Books at last. He'd started to read about it six months ago on various blogs. It was Ellie's proximity to the store that had sealed the deal, killing two birds with one stone. He'd learn Arabic *and* visit the famed bookshop.

For such a remote business, it sure got a whole heap of publicity. It seemed to be everywhere: on Facebook; first return on Google searches; and reviewed by every blog related to Egyptology, mythology, and Wicca. Ellie interrupted his train of thought by throwing out phrases for him to translate as they cycled on towards the store.

"This weather looks changeable. I think we should do a flying visit and get back home before the heavens open," Ellie said.

She stared up at the blanket of grey clouds overhead as they rounded the corner and saw the bookshop. Built of the local honey-gold Bath stone, with two mullioned windows that projected a warm glow out into the gloom of the day, it looked like a perfect refuge. Two large black cats hewn from granite stood guard outside the door.

Ellie passed her bike to Ben and stamped blood back into her feet. "Lock the bikes up over there, please."

"Do we need to lock them? Ben asked. "We haven't seen a soul since we left the house."

"Yes," Ellie answered, disappearing into the warmth of the shop.

CONFUSION

"So, that's how we ended up here," Ben concluded.

Gerhard, who'd been listening with closed eyes and jotting down notes every now and again, straightened in his chair and stared down at his notebook.

"So, to summarise," he said, pointing to the jottings in his book, "first, you had an overwhelming desire to focus on Egyptology. Second, Ellie's ex-husband, an old friend of yours, recommended her to you. Third, you went to her school because of its proximity to my shop, which you'd seen mentioned all over the internet. Is that right?"

"Yes, I guess so," Ben replied, "except I didn't know Ellie was his ex-wife. I knew he'd married. I'd even got an invitation to the wedding but couldn't attend as I was on a dig in Cusco and caught Typhus. But he'd always called her 'his Elena', and I didn't connect Ellie with Elena. I'm sorry," he said, turning to her. "I had no idea."

She looked down at her hands clenched together. Tears

welled in her eyes, magnifying the vulnerability. She shook her head slightly. "It's not your fault. How could you know?"

Gerhard stood, moved stiffly to his desk, and sat down at his computer. He opened a complicated spreadsheet, scrolled down the long list, and asked Ben to name the blog sites on which he'd seen the reviews. Ben named the few he often visited and the search strings he'd used to find others on Google.

Gerhard checked the names against his data and then he opened each of the web pages and searched for "Black Cat Books". Finally, he asked Ben to sign into his Facebook account and review the advertisements presented on his feed. All the searches came up negative. Black Cat Books was nowhere to be seen.

"This is odd. I've not placed an advertisement on Google or Facebook, and I can find no reference to any review about Black Cat Books on any of the blogs you've highlighted. You're sure it was my shop mentioned, *ja?*"

"Absolutely. They all covered the store, with photos and even the address. That's how I knew it was near Ellie's as you're both outside of Bath. I don't understand. You were everywhere I looked," he said, pushing his fingers through his dark hair. "How about you? How do you come to be here? I mean, you're not English, but I can't quite place your accent. Sometimes it has a Germanic twang, but then there's a softness and a roll to some words."

"Ah, how sad," Gerhard replied with a twinkle. "I still have an accent, *ja?* I thought I sounded like John Gielgud. Well, my accent has many influences. My parents were both German, and that was the language we spoke at home, but I was born in Peru and lived there until ten years ago. My wife, Sofia, became ill, and we came to the UK for treatment.

"After her loss, I couldn't face returning home without her. I didn't feel I had a home any longer. I toured around for a while. It was a hard time. I didn't cope well at all, but all clouds pass, as they say. One day, I found myself in this little village, facing this building, and I remembered her dream to open a community-led bookshop. So, I combined her dream with my obsession with magic and mythology, and I created a memorial for my Sofia here," he whispered, drifting into his memories. "She was a beauty, full of Roman fire and fight. *Ja*, well, that is it."

Ellie smiled sympathetically at Gerhard. "So, no obvious link to either myself or Ben. I was thinking maybe the symbols it gave us had a hidden meaning. The scarab is part of my family's coat of arms. Gerhard, does the cat mean anything to you? After all, you named the shop Black Cat Books. Why did you choose that name?"

"It may have symbolism. I'm not sure. My mother gave me an ancient spherical watch, which she said had come from her father's family. It's a beautiful thing, round with a loop on the top for hanging from a belt, I suppose. When you lift the lid, it exposes a dial. It's not very convenient for day-to-day use, but it's my only link to my family line.

"My mother was tight-lipped about her family. She said we'd left them and all they stood for behind us. I know nothing at all about them. My parents changed our name when they arrived in Peru, and I don't even know what our original name was. I've always suspected there's a dark secret hidden somewhere. The watch is all I have to define my heritage, so when I named the shop, well, see for yourself."

The item he showed them wasn't like any watch they'd ever seen. It was more like a pomander, a heavily decorated sphere with interlocking hooks that held the two halves together. Stylised etchings of cats covered the brass-coloured metal, and punched into the middle and top of the sphere were triangular shapes. It was clearly very old.

Ben asked for a magnifying glass and studied the watch intently, turning it this way and that, opening the container and examining the mechanism. With a sharp intake of breath, he said, "I'd say this is medieval. It looks like a Bisamapfeluhr watch, but it can't be. Only five had survived up to World War II, and most of those vanished during the war. None are known to have featured cat etchings. Gerhard, this may be extremely valuable."

"To me, it is priceless, and that's why I called the shop Black Cat Books," Gerhard replied, taking the watch back. He deposited it in a custom-built, moulded and baize-lined drawer, which he locked.

"Okay, so you and cats, Ellie and scarabs, but why the hell did they burn a crocodile into my palm? I have no association with them whatsoever." Ben thought about his parents, with their compulsive consumerism, addiction to the newest brands and latest gismos, and their ultra-modern, minimalistic homes. "Even if we'd had a historical connection, my family wouldn't have preserved it. I'm afraid heritage is alien to my family. Progression is the key word at home. I'm the black sheep of the family, turning my back on the call of the dollar to 'grub around in the dirt', as my father calls it."

"Ah, well, the connection may still be there, even if you are not aware of it. We should explore that line of investigation later," Gerhard said, noting it down in his book. He took his glasses off and rubbed his eyes, squinting across at them. "We seem to be opening more questions than we're closing."

"Gerhard, can you look at me?" Ben said, springing to his

feet. Taken aback, Gerhard turned towards him. Punching the air triumphantly, Ben said, "Yes! I had a hunch, and I'm right. You have heterochromia."

"Yes, I have it, as did my mother. It's a genetic variant, I believe. Completely harmless. Why?"

"You, Ellie, and I all have emerald green eyes, which are rare in the general populace. We also have heterochromia, which is extremely rare. In addition, we all have amber crescents in the same position on our eyes. The chances must be infinitesimal."

Staring first at Ben and then at Ellie, Gerhard shook his head in wonder. "Oh, my! That's off-putting. It's like looking in a mirror. *Ja*, you may be on to something, Ben. This must be significant. I cannot believe it a coincidence."

Ellie reached across and grabbed a petit four. She nibbled on it, flicking at the crumbs that fell. The link between them was unquestionable, but for what purpose? Gazing out the window, Ben noticed that the afternoon was drawing in, leaves were blowing around in a whirlwind outside the store, and the sky was full of dark, ominous clouds.

"I'm beat. Let's sleep on it and see if the cold light of morning will shed any further illumination on the matter. Come on, Ellie. We've got a slog ahead of us. You don't mind if we break off here, do you, Gerhard?"

"No. On the contrary, it's a good idea. May I take your number and call you tomorrow?"

Ellie reeled off her mobile number as she pulled on her outdoor layers.

THE BOUNDARY

Ellie paused in the doorway, peering out at the raging storm. Shivering, she raised her collar and snuggled deeper into her jacket. "Good God, can this day get worse?" she muttered to herself and took a determined step towards the bikes.

The wind howled as they set off. It whipped around their legs, searching and finding every gap in their clothing, chilling them to the bone. Leaves whirled in frenzied swirls, lashing their faces, and the sky was darkening into a moody, dark opalescence. They were both deep in contemplation, and the silence between them sat like an impenetrable wall. The wind's velocity grew more aggressive with each rotation of the pedals. Soon, even though they were on a level path, they had to rise from the seats and use their entire body weight to drive the bikes forward. The noise was deafening as trees groaned under the onslaught. Tiny, sharp shards of hail sliced from the sky, cutting into them.

"Jeez, this is awful. We need to take cover," Ben screamed at Ellie. Ellie gestured that she couldn't hear.

Pulling over, he screeched into her ear, "We need to take cover and ride out this storm."

"Where, exactly? We're in the middle of countryside, and taking cover under the trees would be more dangerous than continuing in the open," she bellowed back at him. Ben searched around in desperation but realised the truth of her words.

They remounted and struggled onwards into the fury. The hail, like little bullets, hammered down, and both were desperate to escape its barbs. They were buffeted around and destabilised as gusts swept from the North, then changed and attacked from the East, only to change again within seconds to another direction. They wobbled and teetered their way along the cycle track, making little headway.

Ben peered ahead and recoiled. A wall of opaque fog swept towards them, belying the laws of physics. Its alien presence was intimidating. *Fog couldn't exist in this wind*, Ben thought. *What the hell is it?* He drew alongside Ellie and gestured forward.

"Oh, my God," Ellie mouthed at him, her words tossed away by the wind.

"We have to turn back."

"No, we'll get lost. I don't know the roads in Freshford. If we carry on, we are on a flat cycle path almost all the way home. Less chance of getting lost in the fog."

"What?" Ben mouthed.

Ellie bent into him and repeated herself, screaming the words.

"What about the canal? We could fall in it!"

"We'll push the bikes. That way, we'll feel the path under our feet."

They struggled on, fighting every step of the way,

creeping slowly towards the encroaching wall of fog. As they entered, it silenced everything – the sound of the wind and the trees and even their own footsteps and breath. It was ghostly and eerie. Ellie shuddered. The fog was more like a hostile presence than a natural meteorological occurrence. It cancelled out all sound and absorbed all light, rendering them almost blind, only able to see the cloying, swirling gloom of the fog itself.

Ellie reached for Ben, touch being one of the few senses left to her. The wind had grown stronger still and was almost lifting them off their feet, yet the fog seemed impervious to it. Ellie felt Ben trying to pull her backwards, but she resisted, certain they stood less chance of getting lost if they travelled onward to Scarab's Rest.

The fog grew thicker and darker until it was a dense, jet-black barrier. A hurricane-like gust of wind caught Ellie unaware, knocking her to the ground. Struggling to keep his footing, Ben fumbled in the dark to find Ellie's hand and pulled her back to her feet.

As they regained their balance and took a step forward, they tumbled down in a jumble of arms, legs, and bikes. The path was a slick lane of ice. Ellie landed heavily on top of Ben, who wrapped his arms around her and held on. She felt his hands sliding around her hips and across her groin. She struggled to regain her freedom, punching and scratching. Ben flipped her over and pinned her down.

"What the hell are you doing? Let me go!" she shrieked, her words absorbed by the fog. His hands continued their investigation, sliding from her hand to her arm and down. Then she felt him take something from her pocket. A faint glow moved towards her, and she saw the screen of her mobile. Ben held her hands above her head with one hand

and used the other to type a message on the phone, which he then passed to her.

This is impossible. We need to call for help. I'm going to let you go. Don't hit me, okay?

Slowly, he eased the pressure and released her. Ellie grabbed the phone and typed:

Try that again, buster, and you will have a bloody nose and more trouble than you'll know how to handle!

Exasperated, Ben snatched the handset and hit the keys manically.

Ellie, we have a bigger problem here. This is not natural. Something is trying to block us. We shouldn't provoke it further. Did you get Gerhard's mobile number?

Ellie felt the creep of claustrophobia as she peered around, trying to infiltrate the wall of fog whilst Ben typed. All her senses were screaming at their sudden sensory deprivation. She'd never admit it to Ben, but she was doubting her conviction to keep moving forward. What on earth was happening? Nothing made sense.

Ben handed her the mobile.

"Damn it!" She realised that she didn't have Gerhard's mobile number; she'd only taken his landline. Panic rose in her throat. What should they do? She wasn't prepared for this. Her world had shifted on its axis, and her perfectly organised and managed life didn't give her any tools for working in this new arena. Her mind flicked through their options; should they continue onward, retreat, or sit it out?

Her mobile lit up. She glanced down and saw the icon for an incoming text message from an unknown number.

Ellie, are you both okay? There's a wall of blue energy through the middle of Black Cat Books, and I can't get through it. It keeps showing me an image of the three of us. I'll come and find you. Where are you?

She read Gerhard's message one last time and then passed it to Ben, biting down on her lip to stop the brimming tears.

Ben read it.

He's right, Ellie. We should wait for him. I've lost my orientation. Let's dig in here.

Without warning, Ellie was swept into a huge bear hug. She went rigid with shock and pulled away, but Ben strengthened his hold. She fought the panic until, to her surprise, a slow glow of peace calmed her, leaving her warm and safe. Sensing her relax, Ben rested his chin on the top of her head and rocked her back and forth. The sweetness of the gesture was her undoing and unlocked her tears. Hadn't she gone through enough, suffered enough? Why was this happening? She wanted her life back under control.

Ben held her, smoothing her hair until she'd sobbed it all out. Lessening his hold, he texted their rough location to Gerhard. Wrapped in each other's hug, they waited for his arrival.

Ellie closed her eyes and rested her head against his chest. His heart thudded a Morse code of comfort. How odd that Ben, of all people, provided such a safe harbour for her. She filed that thought away to dwell upon at a later date.

She sensed a gradual change in the atmosphere and opened her eyes to find the fog folding back into itself and withdrawing. The wind had quietened, and the storm seemed to be moving away. Embarrassed now that she could see Ben, she moved away and stood up, brushing the mud and moss from her trousers.

Gerhard's figure emerged from the final fingers of fog, moving with purpose and vigour towards them. "That was interesting, no?"

Ellie and Ben grabbed the bikes and rushed to meet him.

"After you left, I pottered around the shop, tallied the till, and secured the takings in the safe in the far back of the shop. Then, from nowhere, the wall of the security room glowed blue, like the sphere. I watched it and saw it coming towards me at a walking pace, pushing me back into the store. I tried to get through it, but it was a corporal substance, solid as a real wall and impenetrable. It kept moving until it reached the middle of the shop, where it projected a picture of the three of us within a circular boundary, like a prison boundary, which is when I sent you that note. It was very obvious it wanted us to be together."

Ben thrust his hands through his wildly disheveled black hair. Ellie found, to her surprise, she recognised the meaning behind his instinctual gesture. Ben was feeling out of control. Hardly surprising. Weren't they all?

"Come, I have my car parked just up there. Let's put the bikes in the back, and I can give you a lift," Gerhard suggested.

"So, you think we are being held within a confined area? That we're prisoners?" asked Ben.

Rubbing his chin, Gerhard shook his head. "No, not imprisoned within a specific area. I think we'll find we're free to move wherever we want to go as long as we are together. I think it's bound us together. We can't leave each other, or at least not wander far from each other. However, together, I suspect we are free to move anywhere. It would be expedient to identify the radius of our binding."

"Hang on a goddamn minute. Are you telling me this *thing* has tied us together?"

"Yes, Ben, I think that is exactly what's happened. Very succinct précis of the situation."

"Well, how do we untie ourselves? It's not practical. You have a shop, I've my school, and Ben is going to Egypt soon. We need to countermand this thing."

"That, *mein liebling*, is the question. I believe this sphere has a purpose for us. Obviously, it's something to do with Egypt, and unless I am misguided, we'll not be free until we have done its bidding. Now I don't know about you, but I'm exhausted. I would love to extend my hospitality to you, but my accommodation is limited to just one bedroom. Would it be an extraordinary discourtesy to ask if I may stay at your school, Ellie? I presume you have vacant student rooms, and as we can't stray apart for the time being, we'll need to sleep in the same building."

"No discourtesy at all. We have loads of spare rooms. To be honest, I would love to go home and put my head under a pillow. This day's been trying in the extreme."

Smiling at her, Gerhard, with Ben's help, stowed their bikes in the boot of his Volvo and murmured, "Let's do that. There's always tomorrow."

THEORIES AND THOUGHTS

Ellie awoke as a sunbeam danced lazily across her cheek, the dust fairies pirouetting and swirling in the golden ray. She smiled and nestled down into her pillows, snuggling into the cosiness of the feather duvet. The golden glow of sleepy peacefulness didn't last long as, one by one, the memories of the previous day unfolded, and a grey dread replaced all sense of wellbeing.

Surely, it had all been a dream. Oh, please let it all have been a dream. Didn't soap operas always have a dream scene where the hero wakes up and realises the ludicrous events he'd just experienced were just figments of his sleepy brain? In this situation, a dream would make more sense than the reality she'd experienced.

There was a gentle knock. "Yes," she said.

"*Guten morgen*, Ellie. I took the liberty of making breakfast. It's on a tray. I'll leave it by the door."

"Oh, thanks, Gerhard. Is Ben up yet?"

"Yes, we're having breakfast in the kitchen."

"Okay, I'll just have a quick shower and join you."

She let the glorious hot water pour like a waterfall over

her. Throughout history, so many had achieved moments of profound clarity in showers and baths, but not today. Not Ellie. She found just a modicum of peace. With her hands raised on either side of the shower and her head bowed under the stream, she remembered her grandmother's words:

"What doesn't kill us, Ellie, will always make us stronger."

Oh, Granny, I wonder how much it takes to kill. Sometimes I feel like I'm just a millimetre away from a fatal dose, she thought. Yet again, she did what Elspeth had taught her so well. She raised her head and fixed a smile to hide her festering wounds.

It was one of those crisp, bright, and sunny winter days that help carry the average Englishman through the drudgery of the endless overcast and dreary months. She found the guys reading papers at the old and well-scrubbed kitchen table. The scene of normalcy was jarring. It could be any Sunday morning scene across the breadth of the land, a family enjoying a cosy breakfast over the papers. Except they weren't a family.

Ben glanced up from *The Sunday Times* and beamed. "Hey, Ellie. Did you sleep well?"

Nodding, she helped herself to a strong cup of coffee. "Surprisingly well, under the circumstances."

"Gerhard thinks we should test the boundary today to check it's active and, if so, its size. Are you up for that?"

"Um... yep, sure," she mumbled absentmindedly.

Gerhard took his glasses off, swinging them as he watched her. "I've been thinking about this all night. It seems clear we are bound by an unexplainable force, *ja?*" he said, checking to see she concurred. "And whilst we have freedom to wander to some extent, we have a clear boundary we can't pass. To test this boundary, we need to understand its radius and circumference. We must identify if it's a stationary or a mobile area based on our proximity to each other. To do that, we need a large, empty area out of sight of the general populace. I estimate the radius to be around two or three kilometres, although that's a rough approximation. Ellie, is there anywhere we could use to put the theory to test?"

"I'm not certain off the top of my head. Longleat has a straight drive, but it's only a mile or so long. Otherwise, there are old, disused railway lines that have been converted into cycle paths and a couple of World War II airfields. I'd need to check on a map to be certain." Crossing to the Welsh dresser, Ellie rummaged around in the overflowing drawers, pulled out an Ordnance Survey map, and unfolded it onto the table, smoothing out the creases.

"Here's the Bristol to Bath cycle path, and here's Longleat," she said, pointing towards a large estate on the map. Gerhard and Ben huddled in to get a better look and quizzed her on the various options.

"To be honest, none of them are ideal. The only remote area I can think of would be somewhere on Salisbury Plain, but that's under tight military control. The Fosse Way is super straight. It's an old Roman road, but it's busy."

"Let's use the cycle path. But it would be prudent to do it under cover of darkness to hide any, shall we say, unexplainable occurrences," Gerhard said with a smile. "In the meantime, we should plan the coming few days until we can free ourselves from this little problem. I will need to organise help for Stefan, and I guess you'll need someone to teach your students."

"Ben's my only student, and we can fit our lessons around you."

Ben poured himself a glass of fresh orange juice and bit into a pain-au-chocolat. "My lessons can wait. We should spend our days at your place, Gerhard. We need to research what's happened to us, and there's no better repository of mythical and magical information than your store. Charlie can help Stefan, so the three of us can focus on the problem."

"Hang on one minute, Mr. Ellis. It may have slipped your memory, but Charlie works for me, and she's a critical part of my business. You can't just allocate her willy-nilly without checking with me."

"Jeez, Ellie, don't lose your hair! Your business won't do so well if you're following me around the world for the rest of your life. You can be damn sure I won't be kicking my heels in rural Somerset forever."

Pulling her shoulders back, Ellie glared at him. "I'm not denying it's a sensible move, simply your assumption you can decide what my employee does without consulting me. I'll call Charlie and see if she is amenable." Turning to Gerhard, she said, "Charlie is my housekeeper, but she also acts as my personal assistant, and I would trust her with my life."

"Yep, she's great. You can totally trust her. She livens up this place," Ben confirmed.

"That sounds infinitely suitable, and it would give me a degree of comfort to be on site as Stefan is far better suited to the catering side of the business. I can be on hand to help Charlie if she has any customer queries."

After organising things with Charlie, Ellie and Ben went to the study to gather their laptops and pack up their bags.

"Listen, Ellie, I know you can't stand me. That's been obvious from day one, but we need to work as a team. You've got to put your animosity on the back burner until we've solved this issue and then I will be out of your hair, and you'll never see me again. I didn't ask for any of this. It's no picnic for me either, but if we don't figure it out, we'll be stuck together for a hell of a lot longer. Neither of us would savour that. So, how about it? Truce?"

"I don't dislike you. I have no particular feeling about you, but I agree it would be simpler if we could work peaceably, so okay. Truce."

Ben watched as Ellie ducked her head down and focused on packing her laptop away. Why did she hate men so virulently? Just the other day, he'd seen her prickle like a grouchy hedgehog when the postman had launched a harmless charm offensive. She'd asked Shannon to replace a young, fast but flirtatious plasterer with another, who was past retirement and slow as hell even though it cost her double.

It wasn't all men. He'd noticed that much. She'd been enamoured by Stefan and enchanted by Gerhard's old-fashioned grace. Yet, the only man he'd seen her relaxed with was Shannon, and he was in his mid-fifties and gentler than a newborn faun. Ben decided he'd get to the bottom of it as he threw his mobile office into his capacious and well-travelled brown leather satchel.

TESTING THE BOUNDARY

As it was Sunday, Black Cat Books was closed. So, whilst Gerhard gave an over-excited Charlie training on the till and the reference system, Ellie and Ben focused on trying to dig out information from the plethora of books on Egyptian mythology.

Ellie trailed her finger along a shelf lined with twinkling fairy lights, scanning the ranks of books for inspiration. She paused, pulled out a directory of Egyptian gods, and flopped into a velvet armchair, which was already surrounded with mounds of discarded books. She chewed on a flapjack whilst flipping through the various chapters on the vast number of gods worshipped by the ancient Egyptians, stopping every now and again to note down a word or phrase of interest.

She'd written "Khepri", the name of the scarab that had attached itself to her, in the middle of her pad. Lines shot from the word with random phrases topping them: *creation, renewal of life, pedestal statue - Karnak Temple*. She created similar spider maps for Sobek, Ben's crocodile, and Bastet, Gerhard's cat. Both deities appeared to be linked to warfare and protection. Bastet also wore the mantle "Guide to the Dead".

Following the only trail she could find to Khepri, Ellie searched for more information on the statue in Karnak Temple but found only silly stories of eternal love boosts for people who circled the statue. The rumours appeared to have been created by modern tourist guides to entertain their visitors. Sighing, Ellie attacked the shelves again, searching for other sources that might add some enlightenment.

Ben and Ellie worked diligently until dusk started to pull its cloak over the light of the day, nibbling on leftover cakes from the café as they scoured books. All too soon, it was time to leave.

The trio drove in silence towards the cycle path, each deep in their own thoughts. All they'd found out after an entire day's research was the religious and mythological relevance of the three animals; the scarab, the cat, and the crocodile. They'd discovered no reference to anything like they'd experienced in any of the conspiracy or paranormal websites, which led them to believe it was unique to them. Most of the unexplained surreal episodes on the sites were shared by reams of people globally. Not one site mentioned blue orbs and animating Egyptian gods.

They arrived in a small street lined with compact Victorian terrace houses, uniform in their cloaks of ubiquitous Bath sandstone. The houses fought to express their individuality via an array of gaily-coloured doors. Gerhard looped around, searching for a vacant parking space to accommodate the Volvo, and eased into a gap outside a house with a door of vibrant chartreuse. To ensure they didn't draw attention, they'd arrived as dusk was descending and parked a distance from the cycle path.

"Gerhard, pass me your mobile, please. I'll download the movement tracker app. I've already loaded it onto mine and Ellie's. It'll enable us to plot a starting point, track our GPS location as we move apart, and to gauge our finishing distance relative to our starting point. We should also be able to pinpoint each other in real time on this satellite map."

Gerhard peered at the screen on Ben's mobile and handed his own to him. "It's fascinating what one can do with technology now. My father would have loved this. It would have made his tours around the mountain passes of Peru so much easier - wonderful. *Ja - wunderbar.*"

They ambled along as Ben set up the app on Gerhard's phone. Moving past the Victorian terrace, they followed the road past industrial buildings before passing large council houses.

"I spent time this afternoon planning the best way to plot and gather data to help us understand what's binding us. I suggest we define a starting point on the path and then move out in a triangle formation. You two follow the path in opposite directions, and I'll go cross-country. That way, we should be able to triangulate the extreme boundaries of the bond. To correlate our findings, we need to gather data as we go – any weather or temperature changes, when they occur, and where - by placing GPS flags. We should also gather photographic evidence to examine later. Does that sound practical to you?"

Ben eyed the other two, who nodded their agreement.

"Good. Both your phones have a data sheet where you can enter the details. I've added a shortcut on your home screen. I think once we've reached the limits of the bound-ary, we will know we can't move forward, but can we move sideways? Let's test that. I'll co-ordinate via text message."

They'd reached the gate to the Bristol to Bath cycle path. Dusk flowed into the darkness of night, and a chill curled around their ankles. Ellie gazed around nervously. This was eerier than she'd expected and would only get worse. Steeling herself, she strengthened her resolve. She had to get on with it. Fear of monsters in the dark was all very well, but being tied to Ben for the rest of her life was worse.

The path started with a strong, galvanised steel gate positioned in a peninsula between two hedged roads. Ben stepped over the low cycle barrier. This place was much creepier than he'd expected. Maybe they should have done this in daylight. He knew this would be harrowing. He'd been struggling all day to find a way to spare Ellie. Although she exasperated him, he was protective of her. He didn't like putting her into this position. She projected an icy veneer, but he understood that was what it was: a veneer. Underneath, she was vulnerable. The best he could do was put her on the path that would end in a lit area, but it made him uncomfortable.

He'd studied the maps all day and chosen a perfect start point from which he had the easiest cross-country route, so he guided them towards it. When they arrived, he took their mobiles and registered the GPS starting point. Then he showed them how to enter the climatic and positioning data into the mobile. After they'd both completed a couple of dummy spreadsheets, he was confident they were ready to start.

"Okay, guys, we're good to go, but remember to note every experience down accurately. We don't want to do this again. Oh, and keep your eyes open for any messages. If any of us find ourselves in difficulty, retreat and send the word 'Abort', then we'll re-meet at point zero. Everyone clear?"

Gerhard gave a sharp nod and turned to Ellie. "Take this, my dear. Give an old man peace of mind. Please, *mein liebling*, okay?" He handed her a small canister of pepper spray and bent to place a tender kiss on her forehead. Both shocked and touched by the obvious affection, she accepted the spray wordlessly and slipped it into her jacket pocket.

Typical, thought Ben. *If I'd done that, she would've bitten my head off and spouted feminist protestations of independence. Just typical!*

"Come on, guys," he snapped. "We don't have time for sentimentalities. We've got a mystery to solve." He positioned them in a triangular formation around point zero, with Ellie pointed back the way they'd come, Gerhard facing the other direction, and he towards the open fields. "In five, four, three, two, one, GO!"

Ellie walked back in the direction they'd come. She'd assisted Sam in many digs during their marriage when they couldn't bear to be parted. She'd done all the grid drawings, descriptions, and photos (under Sam's patient and conscientious tutorage) until she'd garnered quite a reputation among his peers for her acute attention to detail. It was this she harnessed now, slipping into the routine like a well-worn body armour, using its familiarity to protect herself against her galloping nerves.

The road had grown much darker in the short time since they'd travelled it. Shadows weaved and slid across the path, and icy fingers of frost crept up her legs, searching for any exposed skin, but Ellie was impervious to the normal elements of a winter's night. She was searching for unexpected details she wouldn't associate with a normal evening on a deserted cycle path.

Somewhere to her right, a pheasant darted out of its cover, hooting in panic as something – probably Ben – frightened it from its night roost. Ellie jumped as the bird flew low across the path in front of her. With a deep breath, she moved on, vigilant for any slight changes.

After a few minutes of walking, Ellie felt a slight shimmer of energy cross her palm. A haze of blue energy sparked and crackled across it, growing in intensity with every step she took. The energy focused on her palm and formed a discernible outline, one she'd seen just the day before, although it seemed so much longer ago to her. She stopped and took a GPS position and noted its location, and she took photos from several angles. The scarab had become fully formed and was moving around her hand.

She checked on the app and saw that both Gerhard and Ben were also stationary. *I guess they have little visitors as well*, she thought as she moved the scarab closer, so she could see it better. "Hey, little fellow. Aren't you a beauty? If only you could tell me what was going on, it would make life much simpler."

The scarab turned to face her as she spoke, as if she were in the company of a sentient being. It was a beautiful thing, not solid, yet not transparent. It gleamed like the palest blue opaque crystal with an outline of striking turquoise. Rising majestically, it stood on its back legs for a moment and then stretched its wings and swept off to circle her head. It brushed against her cheek in the gentlest caress before swooping off, leaving a ghostly blue vapour trail behind as it followed the path. Ellie jotted this down, checked her mobile for any messages, and saw the guys were on the move again.

She searched around for the scarab, but it had vanished. As she walked on, the night became quieter, but the change was too subtle to be definite. Ahead, at the vanishing point of her vision, she sensed a presence, a darkness. Her pulse rose and her body tensed. No matter how hard she looked, she couldn't define the form of the presence, but her body reacted strongly, advising her to turn away.

Her hands became clammy, and her breath caught in her throat as the quiet, dark, ominous presence urged her away. Seizing all the courage she possessed, she strengthened her back and noted down the data and that both the guys were also stationary.

Come on, Ellie. Your body's reacting to your anxiety. There is nothing to fear except fear itself. Calm down and observe. Spectate, don't participate. Breathe.

Ellie tried to talk herself down from the clawing hysteria that grabbed at her throat. She stepped up her stride and moved forward with purpose, attuning her senses to pick up any tiny changes around her. It attacked from the flank, unexpectedly, throwing darts of razor-sharp ice in her path. One barb sliced through her regatta overcoat, narrowly missing her arm. She shied away, pulling backwards instinctively.

"Jesus - that was close."

She took a cautious step forward and then another. Nothing happened, so she took another. The barbs were immediate. They shredded more of her jacket but missed her. As she retreated, she sent a quick message.

Watch out for ice darts. Will test a theory. Don't continue till I come back to you.

Taking off her backpack, she pulled out her spare

bobble hat and tossed it forward into the dart zone. The hat was shredded in seconds. "Impressive! Let's see your worst," she muttered into the darkness, rolling up her sleeve.

It won't hurt me. It's making too much effort to keep us together to hurt me deliberately, she thought, extending her arm inch by inch. The barbs whizzed past, so close that she felt their tailwinds. Not one hit her, although her sleeve was tattered into ribbons.

"Ha, I've got you pegged. You're full of fancy tricks, but you need us for something. You'll frighten us, but you won't hurt us, will you?"

Shrugging out of her overcoat and waterproofs, she stripped down to a close-fitting layer and stowed everything in her rucksack, which she put to one side. She took her GPS location and then peered forward and lifted her chin.

"Okay, buster, I'm coming through, and you will not stop me." Gulping, she stepped forward.

Her pulse beat erratically, like the pounding of waves in a shell, and then came a shower of barbs, careening down, whistling as they flew by. They came from every angle: vertically, horizontally, even from the ground, materialising from nothing. The noise and the sensation were terrifying, but Ellie moved through it without being hit.

At first, she moved with caution, but gradually, she became braver and danced around, taking a video of the spectacle. Nothing touched her. Then, just as quickly as the storm started, so it stopped without a trace. Although thousands of barbs had passed Ellie, there wasn't one anywhere on the path.

ELLIE'S FEAR

Ellie was elated. She felt that at last she understood what she was facing a little better. After texting the guys with her findings, she sped up a little, partially as she now felt the night's chill but also because she felt confident that whatever they were facing wouldn't hurt them. It needed them.

Speeding along, she scanned ahead, waiting for the next smokescreen, confident she could outwit whatever they were facing. What she hadn't expected was to hear the raucous laughter and rumble of conversation from a group of men. She felt her stomach drop. She was exposed on the path, and the group sounded large and drunk. She searched around for anywhere to hide, but she was in an open area with large, rolling fields all around. She saw the outline of the group, numbering around eight, staggering towards her.

"Hey, what do we have here?" one of the group shouted.

Ellie was conscious of her form-hugging leggings and tight, cashmere sweater. She had no options. She had to walk on confidently and hope they were harmless. As they neared, the cat calls became more graphic.

"Tom, look at her. She's just your type. Give it a go."

"Aw-right, darling, fancy something big to warm you up?"

"Come and give us a West Country welcome, babe. Come to papa..."

Her pulse rocketed, her mouth dried, and her body tightened like a bow. Every instinct screamed, "DAN-GER!" She was acutely aware of the group's movements and felt them move in a pincer movement to surround her.

"Don't be unfriendly. Give us a kiss," said a stocky man in his mid-twenties, stumbling towards her. He grabbed her and pulled her towards him. Struggling, she searched for the pepper spray only to realise she'd left it in her rucksack.

The man stunk of stale beer and kebabs and was built like a bear, strength rippling through him as he suppressed her struggles. She kicked with all her might against his shin, but he didn't even register her efforts, anaesthetised by alcohol and the adrenaline of a successful hunt. Sheer terror jumped from Ellie's stomach to her brain. She ramped up her struggles, fighting to save herself. This was real. She was in danger of the worst sort.

She felt the rub of her assailant's stubble against her cheek as he clumsily sought her mouth and shook her head back and forth to avoid his advances. She gasped with shock as he kicked her legs out and threw them both down onto the path. His full body weight pinned her down as he found her mouth and bit down on her lips, thrusting his tongue into her mouth and drawing blood.

His hand pushed up under her sweater and found her breast, pinching her nipple and pulling her bra down, gaining access to the erect nipple. Her attacker's friends whooped and cheered him on, getting him ever more excited. His attack on her mouth became more ardent, and he pushed her sweater up to expose her to his friends, one of whom reached down to pull the other breast free of its cover and then proceeded to kneel and suckle his freed treasure.

Ellie's vision slowed her mind, registering images as if a shutter were closing between one image and the next. Flash - a ginger man jeering down at her. Flash - her original assailant pushing off the second. Flash - his friends holding her down whilst he unzips. Flash - his teeth biting her nipple. Flash - her leggings being pulled down. Flash - a huge penis against her bare stomach. Flash - thick fingers rubbing her most intimate areas. Flash - his tongue circling her nipple, tugging and pulling. Flash - another man, blond-haired, is lowering his trousers. Flash - faces staring down, eager and hungry for action. Flash - a sharp upward thrust and hands everywhere, pulling and pinching. Flash - her assailant heaving up and down, hurting her with every thrust. Flash - a grunt and he collapses heavily on top of her, squeezing her nipples painfully. Flash - "My turn," the blond swaps in, turning her over, pulling her hips up, and thrusting in from behind like a dog on his bitch. His hands biting in everywhere he touches. Flash - the next one slaps his way to erection. Flash - he ejaculates over her face.

Flash. Flash. Flash. Flash. Flash.

Each took a turn. Each had his preferences and foibles. Through it all, they cheered and laughed. Some used their mobiles to take videos of the action for future entertainment.

They left her, throwing down five ten-pound notes and some change, thanking her for finishing their trip perfectly, and walking away laughing and whistling. She laid where they left her, a silent scream tearing her apart.

Realising her state of undress, she forced herself onto her knees and crawled around, searching for her clothes.

When she found them, she pulled them on, crossing her arms across her chest and dropping again to her knees, rocking silently. She was lost inside her head, on another plane. Eventually, the ping of her mobile registered, and she pulled it from her pocket.

Be very careful. It knows our deepest fears, and it will play them out.

She dropped her head to one side and read the message. Numbly, she stared into the distance, seeing nothing. *It knows our deepest fears. No...* She shook her head, gasping, unable to breathe, panting. *It can't be. Last time, it threw random weather events at us. No! It can't be. It happened.*

She'd felt it, every movement, every punishment. They'd burned it into her mind. There couldn't be more to face. There couldn't. Her strength expired, she wanted to be safe at home, to take a shower and cleanse every touch away. Pulling herself into a ball, she mewed, half-crying, half-screaming, unable to release the pain locked inside her.

BEN'S FEAR

Ben walked across the field, stumbling every now and again. He whistled quietly, jumping as a pheasant trumpeted its distress and took flight in front of him. *Keep it together, man. It's just a bloody bird.* The field was dark and silent, stretching out into the distance. He walked for a few more minutes undisturbed.

He heard a rustling and saw the field's ploughed earth undulating. Staring into the darkness, he tried to focus on what was making the soil move.

"Sweet Mary, mother of Christ." Ben shied away from the carpet of seething arachnids that blocked his path. Millions of spiders of every size, colour, and shape clamoured over each other, creating a turbulent wave that tossed and curled at the leading edge. The noise of an ocean of tiny legs scurrying across the grass grew louder, rumbling and resonating like a deep bass; their hairs mewed like an out-of-tune violin as they rubbed against each other. He felt his pulse rocket, and his chest tightened as a wave of clammy terror raced from his neck down to his fingertips and, for just a moment, paralysed him.

The spiders advanced at a frightening speed, flowing across the entire field as far as the eye could see. As they neared, they curled into a grotesque form that writhed and stretched, changing from an army of individuals into a solitary, monstrous creature that towered over him, at least twelve feet high and gargantuan in its proportions. Now every step it took, moved it forward six feet. It covered the space between them in seconds. As it neared, it raised its two front legs and long fangs high over its head, exposing rows of expressionless eyes and a pincer-like mouth.

Ben's legs had turned to clay, weighing him down. He couldn't think or move but felt compelled to stare into its eyes as its eight hairy legs moved ever nearer. As he stared, it shimmered back and forth between its solid entity, never fully losing its form. Stumbling backwards, he tripped over an unseen snake of thorny bramble and landed heavily on his back.

The tarantula jumped the remaining distance and landed lightly, its legs forming a prison within which it trapped Ben, who stared up at its huge abdomen. Instinctively, he scuttled backwards, feeling blindly behind himself. Never taking his eyes off the spider, he searched for a gap in his living cage. His fingers brushed a leg, releasing a flood of spiders that swarmed up his arm. With a guttural scream, he frantically brushed them off and pulled away, watching in horror as they merged back into the leg. What could he do? If he continued searching for an exit by touch, he would risk a swarm again, but if he took his eyes off his nemesis, he would be fighting blind.

Fear numbed his mind, making his thoughts laboured, slowing his desperate search for solutions. He stood gingerly and realised his safest place was directly under the flat, black abdomen high above him.

The spider slowly rotated, and Ben followed suit. Always keeping his eyes towards the front, he watched the fangs probe the ground, searching for him. He stilled his breath and moved as silently as possible, desperate to keep his location hidden. And then it jumped, twisting in midair, and landed in front of him within touching distance. It flicked a leg under his, knocking him down and trapping him. Slowly and malevolently, it bent towards him until all eight of its eyes were only centimetres from his face. He felt the heat from its grasping mouth and a damp, musty, earthy smell.

Without warning, it lifted its fangs and speared him straight through his chest. The fangs didn't deliver venom but instead funneled a myriad of spiders into his labouring lungs, filling them in moments before spilling out and filling his screaming mouth, his nose, and his ears. He felt the writhing and realised they were moving closer together to allow more to enter. The pain ripped through him as they passed down his gullet to fill his stomach and colon. Mercifully, he faded out. Grey to charcoal to black to silence.

ELLIE. The thought screamed through him. *GERHARD.* They needed him. But why? He couldn't remember, but he knew he couldn't fail them.

He forced himself to focus and found he could still breathe. With both lungs pierced and full to capacity with a host of squirming arachnids, he shouldn't be able to. Keeping his eyes closed, he tried to ignore the clamouring mass within him and focus on why he was in a field in the dark.

Again, the thought exploded into his consciousness: *Ellie and Gerhard need me to finish the task. We must know the boundaries. Yes, that was it. We were testing the field that contained them, and last time, it threw a false storm to stop us breaching it. A false storm. False. This is another carefully crafted illusion.*

He focused all his attention on his breathing. Inhaling... and exhaling... in slow, measured breaths. He gradually reclaimed his body. *Thank God for that dippy ex-girlfriend who forced me to learn meditation*, he thought as he used cleansing breaths to clear the illusion. Opening his eyes, he saw the huge body disintegrate back into millions of spiders, which swarmed towards him again. But this time, he stood and thought, *You're not real. Not remotely real.*

The swarm subsided, those closest to him disappearing whilst the rear vanguard became transparent. They withdrew and reformed, advancing again in a pincer formation, trying to surround him. Taking a deep breath, he again denied their presence and moved towards them. His mantra – *you're not real, you're not real* – repeated continuously as he strode forward. Those spiders close to him again disappeared, and a path cleared in front of him.

Taking more deep breaths to maintain his composure, he removed his mobile phone from his pocket and sent a warning to Ellie and Gerhard. He noted down his GPS position and took photos of what he saw. He moved on again.

THE VISION

After a five-minute walk, during which he'd repelled wave after wave of attacks, he stopped in his tracks as a vibrant blue bolt of energy shot from the ground, moving to create a wall that extended out as far as he could see. After a few seconds, the wall rose and curled inward, creating a perfect dome, miles in diameter, that shone brighter than a lit stadium. He approached the wall, sliding his foot forward inch by inch, panting as he eased onward. It appeared highly charged and potentially dangerous. When nothing happened, he slowly reached out with a stick he'd picked up and touched the barrier. It was solid and unmovable. Dropping the stick, he took photos, plotted the location, and then gingerly touched the wall with his hand. It felt as solid as a brick wall and gave a warm tingle.

As he pulled away, the dome brightened. A strand of energy danced sinuously towards him. It split into multiple fronds that wrapped around him, much as an ivy climbs and embraces a tree, gripping strongly and incapacitating him. A frond weaved up his body, circling his neck and opening into a large mesh in front of his eyes that slowly merged into one solid skin and encased his face. He moved his head, trying to evade the skin, but it wrapped tighter with every movement he made.

Think, Ben. Think! Can I still breathe? Yes. Okay, so it doesn't want to kill me. Maybe this is an illusion again. He tried the mantra to no avail. It had trapped him with no way to call for help or warn the others.

The skin changed, subtly at first, fading from cerulean to duck egg until it faded out to white. From the snow-like scene emerged Gerhard, striding confidently, as was his wont, towards Ben. When he was about four feet away, he stopped and turned to face the direction from which he'd come. As if a fog had obscured it and was now peeling away, slowly, a pyramid emerged. It was not a standard pyramid as a child would draw, with four clean, shining sides but a pyramid constructed of several steps. Around it was a temple complex, breathtaking in its beauty, the walls awash with vibrant colours and images.

A cat of vibrant blue ambled towards Gerhard and weaved around his legs, pushing in close and stretching in feline pleasure. Gerhard bent to stroke the cat behind the ear. It purred contentedly and then sat and lifted its paw to clean it. Once satisfied with its work, it extended the paw into a strand of energy that captured Gerhard's left hand and walked him towards the temple. As if watching a film, Ben remained with Gerhard.

The cat took them into a large room. Shafts of light played lazily against row upon row of papyrus and lotus-topped columns. The columns shrieked out for attention, covered with two-dimensional depictions of Egyptian life washed in vivid reds, turquoises, greens, yellows, and whites. Ben tried to study the temple, ever an archaeologist, but the screen continued to shadow Gerhard. He walked farther into a curtain of incense smoke that drifted throughout the building, stirred by the hot, gentle breeze.

Gerhard lifted a long, bronze tube with a scooped-out end. Taking a dried reed, he lowered it into an oil lamp and, guarding the fledgling flame, lit the incense in the censer bowl. He continued on deeper into the temple, swaying the censer as he went, wafting the delicate fragrance in his wake, moving steadily towards the temple's most holy of holies. The temple's spiritual heart rested in this inner sanctum.

Gerhard stopped in front of a large stone altar, as so many high priests had before. On it sat a simple wooden casket with two doors at the front that were secured with hemp cords and a large mud seal. He bowed low in reverence, broke the seal, and untied the cords from around the doorknobs. He eased the left door open, and the right swung out and revealed a bronze statue of the goddess Bastet in her feline form. Gold rings adorned its ears and nose and a silver collar hung around its neck. Gerhard dropped to his knees in front of it and kissed the ground before raising his arms and chanted in a guttural language Ben didn't understand.

The cat leaped up onto the altar and merged into the statue, whose eyes opened with a blue glow. Ben watched in awe as Gerhard dipped his finger into a rose-coloured alabaster bowl at the foot of the altar and then anointed the now animate statue with heavily scented oil. The cat stretched into a regal stance and dropped its head down into a nod of acknowledgement. Gerhard dropped onto one knee, picking up a length of blue fabric.

"*Irtyu,*" he chanted, raising the fabric in both hands above his head before laying it around the statue's neck.

"*Wahdj*," he said, placing a vibrant green swathe onto the statue. "*Hedj*," he continued as he placed a pure white cloth. He finished the ritual by placing a pitch-black cloth around the cat's neck. "*Kem*."

The cat, swathed in the vibrant fabrics, purred. Gerhard bowed formally from the waist and picked up a platter with three tiny pots filled with oil and green and black powders. He placed them in front of the cat.

Ben was conscious of the ritual's importance. *I have to remember each of the elements. I might be the first person in thousands of years to have witnessed this*, he thought. It fascinated the archaeologist in him. He'd read about many Egyptian rituals, but experiencing one in person was priceless. He was so busy surveying the scene, he almost missed Gerhard withdrawing from the altar, walking backwards, cleaning his steps as he went with a palm frond.

Ben's screen shadowed Gerhard as he withdrew from the Holy of Holies into the incense-scented outer sanctum. Gerhard halted and extended his hand. From the gloom, the blue cat emerged, sauntering towards Ben. It stopped just in front of him and jumped up into the air, hovering in front of Ben's face. It looked into his eyes and then gave a sharp nod before turning in midair. It landed on Gerhard's outstretched hand, into which it seemed to merge and disappear. Gerhard smiled at Ben and walked away into the swirling white fog.

REUNION

Ben found himself back in a dark, barren field. Shaking his head to clear his mind, he grabbed his mobile and started to diarize as many of the events and details as he could remember. Lost in his academic endeavours, a screaming in his head startled him.

ELLIE.

He felt his heart constrict. Flinging everything into his rucksack, he ran back towards the cycle path. The darkness hindered him as he stumbled over half-frozen clods of ploughed soil. Picking himself up, he ran on, jumping over ditches and hurdling low hedges in his desperation to reach her. The darkness suffocated him, and he jumped as a hunting owl let out a piercing screech. Something had happened, and he needed to get back to Ellie. Gasping for breath, he reached the relatively easy terrain of the cycle path and sprinted towards Bath.

He heard her before he saw her – a haunting keening, quiet but savagely emotional. *God, I'm too late.* He searched the darkness and found her hidden in the verge, hugging her knees to her chest and rocking. She didn't have her overcoat on and resembled a pale marble statue peppered with sparkling frost. He tugged his coat off, struggling to get the arms over his gloves, and swept the jacket around her shoulders. She screamed and leapt backwards into the hedge.

"Stay away from me. Don't touch me. I mean it. DO NOT touch me." She scrambled farther into the prickly hedge to move away from him.

Ben crouched down onto his heels and whispered to her, "Ellie, honey, it's me, Ben. What happened? Tell me." He reached out to smooth her hair out of her face, but she jerked away.

"Please don't touch me. I can't bear it. Leave me alone... I'm begging you."

"It's been playing with us again, Ells. It knows our fears and uses them against us." He pushed his fingers roughly through his hair. "Listen, honey, it terrified – no, *petrified* me. But suddenly, I remembered the storm illusion, and I used that knowledge to cancel its power. That's all it was, I swear to you. A delusion based on your biggest fear. Whatever it showed you or did to you happened nowhere except in your mind. You're safe now. Trust me."

"No, you're wrong. They assaulted me. It DID happen. It had nothing to do with the sphere. I have the bruises... here," she said, pushing out her bare arm. Ben glanced down at her pale arm, clear of any lesion.

"Honey, there's nothing there. Your arm's normal."

"No... see here and here. It's covered in fingerprints. There's a bite here," she said, pointing to her forearm.

"Ellie, believe me, there's not. You need to find that belief inside and keep saying to yourself over and over, 'It's not real, not real at all'. Then you will see the true state of your arm. Please trust me on this. I promise you everything you experienced was a projection from the source of the sphere."

She raised her eyes up to meet his but looked away again quickly. "You can't see anything on my arm?"

"Nope. Your arm's clear."

Ellie studied her arm dubiously. She shuddered and dipped her head back onto her knees, swallowing a sob. With a deep breath, she repeated Ben's words, hesitantly at first and then with more conviction. As she inspected her arm, she saw the bruises flicker and start to fade until her arm was completely healed. She stared up at Ben in amazement.

"It didn't happen, did it?"

"No, sweet thing. It truly didn't, but that doesn't make the experience any less horrifying. We still lived through it as if it did." He stroked the hair away from her forehead gently and patted her cheek. "I think you should talk to someone about what happened. Maybe Charlie. It will help to vent some of that emotional charge."

He eased himself up and put out his hand to her. She ignored it and stood up, stumbling slightly before stabilising herself.

"If we've both had these experiences, Gerhard must've as well. We should go get him. I hate to push you, but we need to go together. We can't risk provoking the sphere further. Do you feel up to it?"

Ellie nodded and retrieved her clothing and possessions.

They set off rushing in the direction that Gerhard had headed. Ben had a gnawing need to get to Gerhard as quickly as possible, apprehensive about what they would find once they reached him. He would have sprinted if Ellie wasn't with him. Instead, he contented himself with setting a punishing pace.

They marched in silence most of the way until Ellie asked, "What did you see? I mean, you don't have to answer, but I'm curious. It's probably not my business."

"It showed me the thing I fear more than anything in the world: spiders. And then it ramped it up to maximum horror voltage. Millions of them coming at me in waves that formed into one serious mother. A huge tarantula. Everything I fear. To be honest, it paralysed me there for a minute."

"What broke the illusion?"

Ben stopped for a moment as the truth behind the answer hit him. They did. Ellie and Gerhard. They mattered, and their welfare was enough to make him fight against the hold of the illusion.

"I'm not sure. Nothing, really. I realised the whole thing wasn't real, and that broke the paralysis."

They found Gerhard lying on his back, completely motionless except for his eyes, which were haunted. Running to his side, they sank down onto their haunches. Ellie stroked his hand.

"You're okay, Gerhard. We're here. Now do exactly as I tell you, and you'll be fine. Whatever you've gone through is just an elaborate illusion generated by this thing. I know it's hard to believe. I didn't when Ben first told me, but it's true. You need to believe it isn't happening, and you'll be released from its grasp. Okay?" Gerhard gazed deep into Ellie's eyes, as if searching for something, then he closed his eyes.

Nothing happened for a moment until his hand turned and clasped Ellie's. As his eyes opened, he said, "Thank you, *mein liebling*. I was quite, quite incapacitated." She smiled and placed a tender kiss on his cheek.

From the darkest shadows of the path emerged the blue glow of three figures drifting towards them. The scarab floated up and caressed Ellie's cheek before sinking into her hand. The cat pranced towards Gerhard, leaping gracefully into his chest. The crocodile snapped menacingly at Ellie and Gerhard before sliding into Ben. They were again alone, three figures on a cold, dark, and lonely cycle path.

They made their way back to the car in silence, each trying to absorb and process what had just happened to them. Ellie's hands shook as she opened the Volvo's heavy door.

As Gerhard drove them back to Scarab's Rest, Ben turned to study Ellie. Noticing her pallor, he decided to distract her with details of the vision he'd seen.

"Once I broke free of the spider illusion, I was able to reach the very edge of the boundary. It's completely impenetrable. So, breaking ourselves out isn't going to happen in a hurry. However, I think I was given a clue..."

GUARDIANS OF THE ANKH

"**E**urydice, was I not clear previously? You must dispose of the trio forthwith. Their bands are tightening; their union strengthens. I referred to the seers today, and their prophesy is most disturbing. However, all is not lost. It appears the trio are unaware of their burgeoning powers, and that provides us with a narrow window of opportunity. Once their powers mature, they will become almost invincible. That will not happen – do I make myself clear?"

"Crystal-clear, Tjati. Whilst it sorrows my heart to take such severe action, the team and I have taken steps to complete the assignment in the coming days. Our crystals registered a tremendous and prolonged power surge this evening, which can only indicate another contact with the source. Our mission is imperative, we are committed to it, and we'll not let you or the other Guardians down. Fear not, Tjati. I will undertake my task as is my destiny."

"You'd better, Eurydice. We don't have the luxury of second chances, which, I need not remind you, is because of you. Goodnight, and may God's blessings rain on your work."

"Peace be upon you, my lord."

With a deep sigh, she turned to her unit. "The mission is go."

IDENTIFYING THE BOUNDARY

Gerhard put down the book he'd been studying, took off his glasses, and turned to face Ben and Ellie, who were curled on the plump sofas in the centre of his office. They looked up from their laptops, eyes wide.

"I may have stumbled on something. Have either of you heard of familiars?" he asked, twirling his glasses absent-mindedly.

Ellie and Ben gazed at him, waiting for him to continue.

"In Wiccan mythology, a familiar is a supernatural being that supports the witch. Traditionally, the familiar is an animal and often has powers of their own. Think of a witch's black cat. That's the most normal depiction today, although they can take the form of any animal. Now I am pretty sure we are not dealing with witchcraft here, but each of us seems to have gained a 'spirit creature', for want of a better description. They seem to only come out to stop us separating. At least that's all we can say categorically so far. Based on last night's events, this sphere understands us on a personal level, so it's not much of a stretch to say these creatures can tap into our thoughts and feelings."

A knock at the door stopped him.

Stefan came in, laden down with a tray of mouthwatering goodies. "I know you said not to disturb you, but you missed lunch, and no one's effective on an empty stomach. I've made you some goat cheese, endive, and onion chutney sandwiches and a range of finger cakes. So, no excuse not to eat and work. Coffee and tea," he said, pointing to two elegant silver thermos jugs. "Now dig in. Charlie's doing a grand job downstairs, and she's a hoot to work with, so don't worry about the shop and café. We've got it under control."

"Thanks, Stefan," Ben said through a mouthful of sandwich. "You're a godsend."

Gerhard waited for the door to close behind Stefan. "As I was saying... each of us has our own creature. We know these creatures have powers they can deploy to keep us together and possibly also to aid us. Is it possible they are our familiars? Ben, you researched the significance of the three animals in ancient Egypt. Did anything jump out to support the theory?"

"I would have said 'no', but seeing your cat jump into Bastet's statue and animating it has changed my mind. If we assume that our animals are representations of the gods – Bastet, Khepri, and Sobek – then we could surmise they may have the powers attributed to those gods. Bastet, the cat, represented protection. They linked Sobek, the crocodile, to powers of the army with the ability to cure ills and defend against evils. That leaves Khepri, the scarab, revered as a solar deity and linked to the power of renewal. I can't find any obvious link among the three gods. They were worshipped in different areas and were in their zenith at different times, but that doesn't refute the theory."

Gerhard nodded. "Well, it's possible. Certainly something we should explore. Did you get any further identifying the temple you saw, Ben?"

"I have. It's at the Saqqara Pyramid a few miles outside Cairo. I went further and found the statue of Bastet, the exact one I saw in the sphere. Here," he said, spinning his laptop around to show them.

Ellie leaned in for a closer look. "It's beautiful. Where did you find it?" she asked.

"Closer than you might imagine," he replied with a smile. "It's in London, at the British Museum. It's known as the Gayer-Anderson cat after some dude who donated it to the museum, but get this. They discovered it in Saqqara."

"Gayer-Anderson, wow," Ellie exclaimed. "He was your archetypal expatriated Brit, an eccentric, ex-military chap. Collected anything and everything and lived in a sixteenth-century house next to one of the oldest and most impressive mosques in Cairo. It's a museum now. I loved it there. The roof terrace has the most amazing vistas over the minarets and the skyline of old Cairo. The ancient fretwork screens frame every view. I used to study up there. I miss its tranquility." Ellie smiled shyly at them. "Sorry - bit off track there. Sometimes, I get maudlin about my life in Egypt. The Gayer-Anderson house, well, it was one of my favourite haunts. Anyway - great work, Ben. We should take a trip to London."

"Are you kidding me? Risk all hell breaking out around us in a public museum in London? Animals jumping out of us whilst hosts of schoolkids watch? I don't think so. Far too risky."

"Not if we can have a private viewing," Ellie said with a smile and a wink. "My godfather is the curator of the Egyptian collection at the museum, and he'd let us visit the cat if I asked. He's a sweet old thing, immersed in Egyptology but utterly lost in the modern world. There's nothing he loves more than sharing his love with others."

"I'm not sure it's a great idea. We don't want to be fighting any bitching tarantula around priceless relics."

"I don't suppose we'll be exposed to any horrors as long as we stay together, and even if we are, no one except us will notice anything. As our photos from last night prove. They showed nothing, just dark, empty fields. And if you remember, Stefan saw nothing. I think you can be assured of that, Ben," said Gerhard, bypassing the sandwiches to take an elegant cupcake.

"Okie-dokie. I'll give Uncle Bertram a call and see what I can organise." Ben nodded and Gerhard smiled.

Gerhard stood and pressed a button. He stepped back to allow his desk to rotate around the circular tower, into the weak autumnal sun that streamed through a window on the opposite side of the office. Ellie and Ben watched in fascination.

"How did you do that?" Ben asked.

"I missed the sunshine when I first came to the UK. God knows we have precious little. The sun moves around this room throughout the day, so I designed my desk to follow it. Now I always get to work in sunlight." Gerhard pointed down at the floor. "See, it runs on this rail. A simple solution for an old man's comfort, no?"

Ben shook his head in wonder. The man's ingenuity never ceased to amaze him. Since they'd been working at Black Cat Books, they'd seen so many examples. A rotating bookshelf that hid Gerhard's sleeping quarters was stocked with dream analysis books. A hidden lift within a fireplace carried you from the witchcraft section up to the fireplace of the religious studies room. He'd planned everything with a wink towards humour and a dusting of genius. It created such a unique and quirky environment. Ben wasn't surprised Black Cat Books had become the hub of the village, and Stefan's café only added to the magic.

"I'm not having any success with identifying our restriction boundary. I've calculated it so many times in so many different measures that numbers are floating before my eyes, but still, it's an arbitrary number. It's 2.6 kilometres, 1.616 miles, 12.92 furlongs, 8,530 feet, 517 rods." Ellie rubbed the back of her neck and sighed. "I hate to admit it, but I've come to a grinding halt."

Gerhard turned from his desk and peered at her over the top of his glasses. "Well, those are all modern, western measures. Try biblical measurements, my dear, or even check if the ancient Egyptians used their own." Gerhard smiled at her and turned back to his notebook.

Ellie cursed. She should have thought of that. It was so obvious. She turned back to her computer with determination, and fifteen minutes later, she'd solved the puzzle.

"Yes! I've found it. They used a measurement called a *khet*, and our boundary equates to exactly fifty of them," she said with satisfaction, curling back into the deep, feather cushions.

Gerhard removed his glasses and rubbed his eyes. "We're making progress, my friends. Real progress. Yes, I believe we may break the back of this little problem."

THE DESTRUCTION

"Hey, gorgeous, has anyone ever told you that you have lovely buns?"

Stefan chuckled, dried his hands on the ever-present tea towel, and kissed Charlie on both cheeks.

"Not for a long time. The last Charlie to do so was six feet, four inches with a rippling six pack and much hairier legs than you, poppet. My, he was fine!" Stefan stared into the ether. "Still mustn't get distracted by tales of yore. The focaccia still needs ten minutes, so why don't you head for home? No point in both of us hanging around."

"Are you sure? I don't mind waiting. Really, I don't. Besides, it gives me a chance to sample some of your wares," she said with a dirty grin.

"That's what worries me. You'll gobble up our profits. Now shoo. Go sample some of your husband's instead. You need to work off some of those calories you've been swallowing."

"Hey, bring on the curves! The more, the merrier. No one ever complained about Marilyn Monroe's voluptuous figure."

"There's a difference between curves and podge, my sweet. Now leave a maestro to his art. Shoo..."

Leaving, she leaned back around the door and blew kisses back to him. "Night, hotcake."

Stefan burst out laughing. "Leave the shop door open, honey. I'm expecting Mrs. Trollope to pick up her grandbaby's christening cake," he shouted after her.

"Open - got it," she bellowed back. The doorbell jingled as she left.

Fifteen minutes later, he was taking the flatbreads out of the ovens when the bell went again. "Damnation!" he muttered under his breath. Leaving the kitchen, he shouted down the stairs, "Hi there. I'm just taking things out of the oven. Come on up, Mrs. T."

"We're just having a wander. We're fine. I'll shout if we need you," a slightly accented female voice answered.

Cursing under his breath, he realised he should have asked Charlie to put the closed sign on the door. Oh, well, never mind. He'd go down once he'd stored the freshly baked bread and herd them out of the shop.

Humming to himself, he tore a hunk of the bread and dipped it in extra virgin olive oil. *Not bad, old man.* He never ceased to get pleasure from his baking skills, and let's face it, his days of needing to stay in trim were long behind him. No Charlies, male or female, on his horizon anymore, so he'd take pleasure where he could find it.

He ground pepper over the breads, sprinkled fresh rosemary and drizzled oil, and stacked them into the store cupboard to season overnight. Wiping his hands, he hosed the baking trays to remove crumbs and then loaded them in the washer, which he turned on to run.

He heard the noise before he saw anything – a whooshing roar followed by crackling and pops. It sounded wrong and dangerous. He rushed out of the café, down the old, worn wooden steps, and stopped in his tracks.

A wall of fire danced along the shelves and fondled the ceiling. He stared in horror, realising flames blocked every exit. Turning on his heel, he ran up the stairs, to the top floor. There was no way to get to the guys in the office, but he could call from the storeroom's internal line. His fingers shaking, he dialed the extension number.

"Gerhard, call the fire brigade. The ground floor's an inferno."

"What? I don't understand."

"We're on fire. I'm in the stockroom. I can't get out, but I'll barricade the door with wet towels to stop the smoke. Call them - hurry."

Gerhard stared at handset. "My God, the shop's on fire!" He shook as he told them. He dialed 999, fumbling in his haste. Nothing. The phone was dead. "Ellie, call the Fire Services from your mobile. *Schnell! Schnell!*"

Ellie grabbed her mobile and dialed. She stared at the handset. "There's no coverage. It hasn't got reception. Ben, you're on a different network. Call 999 and ask for Fire."

Both Ben and Gerhard reached for their phones. Ellie ran to the door and looked down the stairs. The smoke was drifting up towards her. She slammed the door, took off her fleece, and poured the cold tea and coffee over it, then rolled it into a thick twine, which she wedged across the bottom of the door.

She turned to see both men staring at their mobiles, Gerhard repeatedly shaking his head.

"I don't have a signal."

"Me neither..."

"I've checked the staircase. There's no fire, but smoke is rising. Gerhard, does Stefan have a mobile?"

Gerhard shook his head, his eyes welling. "No, he doesn't believe in them. He says he's always here or at home."

"Is there any other way out of the building?" Ben asked.

Gerhard shook of his head.

"You mean we're trapped in here with no way of calling for help?" The realisation hit hard.

Ben felt an icy calm descend over him. He flicked through solution after solution as his mind assessed their viability, only to discard them. Ellie rushed to Gerhard's side and hugged the man who'd withered and aged, tears pouring soundlessly down his high-boned, finely sculpted cheeks.

"It's okay, Gerhard. We'll find a way. Maybe it's just an illusion again. Let's try to cancel it."

"No," said Ben firmly. "It's no illusion. Stefan saw it."

He was silent for a moment, deep in thought. Ellie caught the birth of the idea in his eyes, which brightened and focused.

"I think it's time to test your theory of Familiars, Gerhard. If they are here to keep us together, then it stands to reason they don't want us served up as KFC specials. Let's use them to protect us."

Gerhard didn't register Ben's words, but Ellie did and realised the potential merit of the idea.

"How do we call them? We don't know what language they speak. Hell - we don't even know if they understand us."

Acknowledging the validity of Ellie's remark, Ben felt a bubble of panic rise into his chest, but the desire to protect Gerhard and Ellie tamped it down, and his mind cleared.

"If we send them a clear mental picture of the fire and an image of us perishing in it, well, my guess is that they'll solve the rest. Of the three, Bastet might be most handy with her protective skills, but we need to get Gerhard to call her forth. Can you reach him?"

They both shot worried glances at the husk of the man devoid of his trademark vitality.

"I'll try. He's in shock, but I'll try. In the meantime, try to get in touch with Stefan and make certain he's okay. Tell him to fill in the cracks around the door to stop smoke ingress and whatever he does, not to open any windows. It'll create a wind tunnel and feed the flames."

"Got ya."

"Gerhard. Gerhard..." She stroked his face. "If you can hear me, blink your eyes. Gerhard, sweetie, you need to come back to us. The only way to save ourselves and Black Cat Books is for you to call your cat - Bastet. You need to do that for us, okay?" She continued to stroke his cheek.

"Oh, for God's sake, we don't have all day." Ben leaned across her and slapped Gerhard's face with all his might.

"Ben! Have mercy on the man. He's in shock."

Gerhard's head shook, and he turned to them.

"When a person's in shock, they need a jumpstart, Ells, not mothering. Now, Gerhard, you need to call Bastet. You need to visualise the fire and all of us dying in it and scream her name. Scream it mentally, that is. Do you understand? She's our only hope. Call her - NOW."

He turned and picked up the phone to call Stefan on the internal line.

"Are you okay? Ellie asked.

"Don't worry about an old man, my sweet. Ben's right. We need to call our creatures. Let me focus, and maybe you can call yours."

They closed their eyes, blocked out Ben's conversation, and screamed their dieties' names. The tingle in their hands warned them of the emergence. They opened their eyes and saw the glowing blue creatures, which jumped from their outstretched palms. They shimmered as a field of blue energy circled the trio, closing at the top and bottom to create a perfect sphere.

"We did it," Ellie gushed, punching the air. "Now let's show them a visualisation of extending the field to protect the rest of the shop and Stefan."

Gerhard shook his head miserably. "I don't think they care about anything except our survival."

"Well, we won't know if we don't try. Come on." They both focused on pushing the boundary out, stretching it to protect the upstairs of the shop, both knowing it was too late to preserve the ground floor.

Ben ended his call and watched them curiously, each face contorting and grimacing as they played mental gymnastics.

"What are you doing?"

Ellie explained but with disappointment when the field remained resolutely spherical, unchanged by their efforts.

"Stefan's panicking. The smoke is getting thick where he is. He wants to go out the skylight onto the roof, but I explained the dangers to him of opening the window, so he's staying put."

Gerhard stood up and said, "Come on, we must go to him and get him into the sphere."

"That's lunacy. We'd need to go through the fire to reach him, and if we do that, it would be better to raise the alarm, so the trained fire fighters can rescue him," Ben argued.

"We have no time. The nearest station's in Bath, a good fifteen minutes away. If the smoke's thick now, he'll be dead by then. We really don't have a choice."

"And you're *that* confident in the power of this sphere

that you're willing to risk all our lives in something that's – let's face it – untested?"

"We don't have any other choice. I can't sit here and let him die. I simply can't."

"Nor can I," Ellie added.

Ben studied the two determined faces in front of him. "Okay, if we do this, then let's try to minimise our losses." He closed his eyes and Sobek appeared, jaw gaping open.

"I'll go on my own. I'm the strongest and fittest. This tower is stone, so it should survive the fire. You stay here. I'll be back."

"Hang on a just a minute..."

"I can't accept that. It's my shop - my responsibility."

Ben ignored the protests and focused his mind on creating a sphere to surrounded himself. Sobek wriggled off his hand, and the large sphere surrounding the three of them contracted to surround just Gerhard and Ellie, whilst a new one unfolded around Ben.

"Guys, grab the laptops and anything precious, like your watch, Gerhard. If they're with you, they should escape the ravages of the fire. Close the door behind me and block the bottom again. I'll be back as soon as I can with Stefan."

"Ben - please, don't. We should stick together."

He smiled at Ellie and winked. "See you, Ells." He dashed out the door, slamming it behind him.

The stairs had become thick with smoke, but within the sphere, the air remained clear. He pushed open the door at the bottom to an inferno that whipped up the stone stairs, catching the red velvet rope handrail in curling, racing flames. He jumped backwards, shocked by the extent of fire. The internal structure of the shop was unrecognisable. Flames roared, jumping from one location to another like a voracious, hungry animal.

He took a deep breath, swallowed, and stepped forward. He closed the door behind him, confident that the stone staircase and tower would protect his friends. With his heart beating crazily and his palms laced with nervous perspiration, he stepped into the heart of the beast.

He gasped with relief when he realised that the climate within his sphere remained unchanged, despite the external furnace. The smoke made it impossible to see the route to the main staircase, so he closed his eyes and visualised the route. When he opened his eyes, he saw the crocodile's blue haze drifting farther into the flames. He followed, climbing over collapsed, flaming bookcases and tables and around husks of sofas. The staircase was a snarling shaft of angry flames, burnt through in places, blackened everywhere.

Jeez, they don't look strong enough to take my weight, he thought. *Oh, well. In for a dollar, in for a dime.*

He focused, and the sphere lifted from the ground to float up the stairs.

At the top, the door was badly charred. Ben searched around. If he opened the door, the flames would engulf the room in seconds, but if he didn't, Stefan's prospects were gloomy. There was one skylight in the room, but it opened onto a roof with an acute pitch. Stefan wasn't the most athletic man, and Ben himself wouldn't fancy scaling that roof. Anyway, opening the window would feed the fire and might even blow the door.

Coming to a decision, he shouted to Stefan to turn the desk to the wall and to hide in the foot-well between the wall and the leg board. He hoped the fire would spread over the ceiling, giving him a chance to leap in and reach Stefan. He waited for Stefan to acknowledge his request.

"Stefan, did you hear me?" Silence. "Stefan?" The silent pause was eternal.

Shoot. Either he can't hear me through this damnable sphere or... jeez, Ben thought.

"STEFAN!" he tried one last time.

Okay, Ben, this puts a whole new spin on things. Think, man, think. His choices were limited. He reached for the handle and pushed, raced through, and slammed the door shut against the surging flames.

Spinning around, he saw Stefan collapsed on the floor in the furthest corner of the storeroom. He'd cleared a space of all stock, presumably as a fire break. He was slumped, half-sitting, half-lying, on the floor. The room was thick with smoke.

Ben rushed to his side and tried to pull him into the sphere, but it moulded itself against Stefan like a rubber surface through which Ben could feel and touch but couldn't permeate. Ben gave up and visualised Stefan within the sphere with him. Nothing happened. He tried again whilst trying to feel for a pulse on Stefan's wrist. Stefan opened his eyes and looked at Ben.

"Are you an angel?" he rasped, peering around but not seeing. Ben laughed with relief.

"I'm more often referred to as a demon, but I'll take angel." Stefan didn't respond. "Stefan? Listen to me, man." When Stefan didn't respond again, Ben tapped his hand. Stefan jumped a little and smiled again.

"Just wait until I tell my old dears about this one. It will keep the café gossip active for years. Old Stefan having a guardian angel."

Ben was laughing when the explosion hit.

The room imploded, and a tornado of fire spiraled through the floor. Sound reverberated throughout Ben's body as wood and stone projectiles hit the outer shell and ricocheted away. The sphere flew up before plummeting through a gaping hole caused by the explosion. Flames encircled it, a macabre wrapping that danced across the surface. The fall seemed to last an eternity before Sobek wrestled it back under control and slowed the descent. He landed on the flaming, charred pile of debris that was all that remained of Black Cat Books.

Ben looked down. He was clutching Stefan's hand, complete with a diamond-studded pinkie ring. *Just* his hand.

GUARDIANS OF THE ANKH

Eurydice watched the fire rage through the building, feasting on all the books and galloping ever upwards in its hungry search for more fuel. She watched wordlessly, tears streaming down her cheeks as an explosion rocked the building, bringing down the roof in its wake. Just an old, turreted tower remained of Black Cat Books.

She leaned back further into the shadows as an old lady ran down the street towards the shop. The lady let out a scream, and soon, the street was full of gawkers. Eurydice pulled out her phone and typed a single sentence.

Mission complete - House of Scarabs eradicated.

She slid away unobserved, just a shadow in a dark night.

SHOCK

"Thank you for your hospitality, Miss Bendall. As I explained, it's clear that they used an accelerant in combination with a sophisticated remote charge to start the fire. That along with a disabled sprinkler system and cut telephone lines make it clear this wasn't an accident. I'm afraid this is now a murder investigation. We'll be in touch." The detective stopped in the doorway, shuffling from foot to foot. "I'm truly sorry for your loss. I met Mr. Morris on many occasions. He was... charming."

Swallowing back a sob, Ellie nodded, teeth gritted to control her grief. "Yes. That he was... that he was, indeed. Thank you, Detective. Goodnight."

She closed the door behind him before huge, round tears escaped, washing her cheeks as she rested back against the door. Stefan was gone. It didn't seem possible, but in the hours since the fire, reality had rudely forced the truth forward. The man, so full of life, a whirlwind of humour and vitality, was no more. Someone had taken him from them. Deliberately taken him. Ended his life, brutally and savagely. She sank down the door onto her haunches, staring at nothing, numb.

With a deep breath, she stood up, straightened her clothes, and went into the drawing room. Ben and Gerhard sat facing each other on opposite cream sofas, like marble statues, fully formed yet vacant. Gerhard's skin seemed tissue-thin, stretched cruelly across his cheekbones. He was as pale as death. He hadn't uttered a word the entire journey back to Scarab's Rest and had registered nothing since. The detective had given up asking him questions and had directed all his queries to Ellie.

Ben's bronzed appearance limited the visual impact of shock, but his eyes were horrifying to observe. He looked like he'd had his soul extracted without anaesthesia. Just a shell remained.

Neither registered Ellie's reappearance. She doubted they'd noticed she or the detective had gone. As she glanced from one to the other, she realised she needed reinforcements. Should she call Charlie? She'd thaw out the arctic circle with a blast of her smile. No, not Charlie. Ellie couldn't face telling her about Stefan yet. A soft rap at the door disturbed her thoughts. Retracing her steps, she opened the door to the gentle face of Shannon.

She fell into his arms, sobbing.

"Hush now, my sweet Ellie bee. Hush now. Tell old Shannon all about it." He rocked her in his arms, murmuring words of comfort as he'd used to when she was a child crying over a grazed knee or a lost teddy bear. "Ah, my wee honey, cry it all out and then you can tell me all your sorrows."

He guided them into the kitchen, warmed by the old AGA stove that had served countless generations of Ellie's family. He sat in her grandfather's carver chair and pulled

Ellie down onto his lap. Holding her, he waited out the storm, smoothing her hair away from the torrent of tears and kissing the top of her head. After a few minutes, Ellie regained her composure and pulled away. She reminded him so sorely of Elspeth, her grandmother, heartbroken but determined to fight on no matter what. The women in that family bore tremendous hearts capable of great acts of bravery and endless love.

Standing up, Ellie moved around the kitchen, preparing a tray of tea. She felt embarrassed by her outburst. "I'm sorry... it's just been..."

"There's no need for that, my child. It'll be a sorry day when you can't take your salty tears to old Shannon. Now tell me what's happened. I was letting the dog out when I saw a police car draw away." Sitting down next to him, she poured them both a cup of strong tea and told him of the events of the previous few hours.

"I don't understand. The three of you are unscathed, yet the shop is just a burnt-out husk? How's that possible?"

"The fire officers who found us said both the door at the bottom of the stairs and the one at the top were high-grade fire doors, and the tower's stone construction saved us from the worst of the fire's ravages. Other than mild smoke inhalation, we're all fine. Stefan was in the main part of the building and barricaded himself in the stockroom. The gas in the kitchen exploded and blew straight through the floor," she said with a catch in her voice. "He didn't stand a chance."

"Oh, Ellie. It's a sad story, to be sure. How is the old gentleman taking it?"

"He's not. I think it's too much for him to take in. I don't know what to do. I feel so helpless. Ben is frozen. Shannon, the police are investigating it as a murder because both the fire system and the phones were disabled."

"A murder... But you were all in the building, so who were they trying to kill?"

"I guess that's something the police will try to find out. God knows who'd want to kill any of us," she replied, pushing the hair that had escaped her ponytail away from her eyes before taking a deep sip of her tea.

"Come on, me darlin'. Let's go see what we can do for those poor fellows. Make a pot of industrial-strength tea, and I'll add a dash of my Islay malt."

They worked side by side, their steps choreographed by years of habit, in a comfortable silence. Ellie preceded Shannon into the drawing room, where both men sat, staring into space. Shannon eyed the pair speculatively and focused on Ben. Sitting next to him, he took out his aged silver hip flask and poured an ample measure into a heavy crystal glass, which he placed in Ben's hand before pouring himself a tot and raising his own glass.

"*Slainte*. Here's tae Stefan. May God rest his auld soul."

Ben's head snapped sideways to stare at Shannon.

"Ah, come on now, man. We must toast his soul on its homeward journey. Only right, don't ya think?"

Ben stared at him and then, inch by inch, raised his glass. "To Stefan."

Shannon downed the whiskey, watching Gerhard over the rim of his glass.

"Mr. Webber, I'm so sorry for your loss. I think it's a good night's sleep you'll be needing now. Plenty of time to face your woes tomorrow. I've made you a nice hot chocolate. Drink it down for auld Shannon. That's right, down to the bottom. Good. Now I'll just take off your shoes and put your feet up on this cosy old sofa of Ellie's, and you snuggle down."

Gerhard followed Shannon's instructions like a zombie, lost in an avalanche of shock, and was soon fast asleep on the sofa. Shannon covered him with a thick fleece and turned to Ellie.

"He'll sleep for hours. I put one of my sleeping pills in his hot chocolate. It's sleep that he needs. Now come, Ben. We should leave Mr. Webber to his dreams and retire to the kitchen for more tea."

The three of them chatted in the kitchen for an hour or more. Shannon effortlessly drew Ben out of himself and set the foundations for healing. Ellie wondered at his gentle skill in casting a warmth and security that eased everything in its path. He was a natural and gifted healer. Before leaving, he lifted her chin and looked deep into her eyes.

"Your grandmother was always proud of you. I can't help thinking she's watching from heaven - God rest her soul – and glowing with pride over how you've handled yourself tonight."

He bent and placed a whisper-soft kiss on her forehead and chucked her chin.

"Now get some sleep, my Ellie bee."

THE FUNERAL

The large hole, dark and chilly, called to Ben. He stood among the crowd, all dressed in black, clustered close against the bracing wind, gathered to say their final farewells. He should've been in that hole with Stefan. Not that there was much of Stefan there, but still, Ben felt he'd cheated destiny and was sure she would come and claim a high price for his lack of fidelity.

Looking back, that night seemed such a blur, probably a self-protection device his brain had deployed to limit his stress. He remembered glancing down at Stefan's hand and then dropping it in shock when he realised that Stefan was no longer attached to it. He'd searched desperately for Stefan, but the hand was all that survived of the cheery cook.

There was a vague recollection of Sobek re-appearing and guiding him to the burnt-out bookcase that fronted the door up into the tower. From there, he drew a blank until Shannon had toasted Stefan at Scarab's Rest. There was a Dali-esque surrealism of going from such awful memories to staring down on the gaily decorated coffin.

Charlie had suggested that they forego the traditional floral displays in favour of something that better reflected Stefan's flamboyance. The "old dears" in the village had baked all week to create colourful cupcakes which now dressed the casket. He would have loved the edible patchwork of baked goods. It captured his essence perfectly.

Ellie was concerned about Gerhard. He'd barely registered anything since the fire. He was incapable of acknowledging people's commiserations. So, she stood next to him, shaking the hands of Freshford's extended community on his behalf. She shook a lot of hands; there was a huge turnout for the funeral. That said more about Stefan than the gushing words of Reverend Wakefield.

Charlie, dressed in a vibrant red coat with matching knee-length boots, came up to Ellie and whispered, "I've checked with Mum. The buffet is ready and laid out at the mill. Shall I tell her to expect the first mourners in twenty?"

"Thanks. Yes, that sounds about right."

Charlie leaned across Ellie and kissed Gerhard tenderly on the cheek. "You've done him proud. He'd have loved all this. Can I start the music now?"

Gerhard nodded and patted her hand.

An ABBA tribute band sang the opening notes of "I Have a Dream" as Gerhard threw a billowing cloud of white icing sugar onto the coffin. Ellie, Ben, and Charlie followed suit, and soon, the casket glistened. Ellie ushered everyone away to give Gerhard a moment alone to say his goodbyes.

He stared down into the gaping hole, which echoed that in his chest. How could he walk away and leave his vibrant friend in this desolate place? A solitary tear trickled down his face and splashed onto the coffin, creating a dot of royal icing.

Gerhard's lips lifted at the thought. "I've iced your coffin, my dear boy. Imagine that. Me doing icing." He stared into the distance. Stefan had brought colour back into his life after Sofia died. He was the first person to make him laugh again. "Sometimes, you need not share parents to be brothers. You taught me that, Stefan. I'll miss you, my friend."

He turned and joined the others, who'd led the bemused elderly congregation across the graveyard to the waiting limousines.

The peal of the phone broke Ellie free of her thoughts. She apologised to Mrs. Trollope, who had been waffling about the inconvenience of losing her granddaughter's christening cake in the fire. "I'm sorry. Do excuse me. I must get the phone."

She rushed across the drawing room, dodging mourners, and went into her private study, more for a little peace than privacy.

"Oh, hello there. I wish to talk to Elena Bendall-Gamal, if you please."

"Hi, I'm Ellie Bendall. Who's speaking?"

"Elena, it's Bertram, my dear. You know I can't abide shortened names. Why shorten your beautiful name? Elena has such a glorious ring to it. It's Greek, you know. Means 'shining light', and you've always been your old godpapa's shining light, so it's appropriate too."

"Uncle Bertram! It's so lovely to hear from you."

"Why, weren't you expecting my call? My assistant told me you'd asked me to phone you."

"No. I mean, yes, I was expecting you to call, but still, it's always wonderful to hear from you."

"Ah, yes, I see what you mean. I don't have time to chitter-chatter. What do you want?"

Used to her godfather's rather direct manner, Ellie cut to the matter in hand. "Uncle Bertram, I have a student at the school who's a dear friend of Sam's…"

Bertram interrupted her. "Yes, Sam. Wonderful boy. Don't think I didn't notice you've dropped his name. Elena, you were settled with a good man. Every woman needs a strong man to care for her. I worry about you on your own at your age. You need to go back to Sam, apologise, and beg him to take you back."

"Uncle Bertram, please, let's not go down that path again. I'm no longer married to him, and I won't be again. I am perfectly capable of caring for myself, as are all women, contrary to your archaic beliefs. Anyway, this friend of Sam's is going to Egypt on a prestigious fellowship, and he has to write a paper on an Egyptian artifact. So, he's chosen your Gayer-Anderson cat, and I was wondering if I could tie in a visit to you with an opportunity for Ben to have a close-up look at the cat. Could you organise that?"

"Yes, of course. It would need to be next week as I am giving a lecture in Munich on Thursday. How about the following Wednesday? Could that work?"

"That's brilliant. Would you like a little company in that rambling old mausoleum of yours?"

"If by that, you mean can you and your companion stay with me, then by all means, yes. But take me as you find me, darling girl. I'm in the middle of a new book, so my research has taken over the house a tad."

As Bertram's house was constantly overfull and chaotic, Ellie could only imagine the state it must be in for Bertram to have noticed its disorder.

"That's great. Thank you. There will be three of us as I have a friend staying. You'll love him. He's an older gentleman."

"Hmm, sorry, what was that?"

She'd lost Bertram's attention, so she said goodbye and put the phone down, circling the date on her desk diary. She gazed out the window at the fast-flowing river and wondered what would come next.

LONDON BOUND

Ellie closed the door behind the detective.

"What did he want?" Charlie asked. "I'd have thought they'd spend more time investigating who killed Stefan than bothering the poor victims. Typical of modern police - anything for an easy life."

"Have you finished? He was here on my invitation. I want to take Gerhard away for a change of scene, and I wanted to check that was okay and see what progress they'd made."

"And what progress have they made? If any..."

"Well, we're officially cleared of any involvement. They found that both the front and back doors were jammed from the outside. They've also found other people who experienced mobile network failure at the same time, so they suspect that they deployed a blocking device. It seems whoever did this was both sophisticated and determined. It required premeditation to have all the equipment to hand."

"And..." Charlie prompted.

"And they have no idea who it was or what their motivation was. They left nothing behind, and the charge used was widely available. Detective Enson's been really supportive, but I feel he's more worried about the case than he's letting on. He asked me to install security equipment here, and he seemed pleased that the three of us would be away for a while."

Putting an arm around her boss's shoulder, Charlie walked them into the kitchen. She busied herself making tea and feeding crumpets into the antiquated toaster.

"So, you're taking them away for a bit, are you?"

"Yes. Well, to be fair to Ben, we need to move on with his lessons. I thought a visit to Uncle Bertram would be a good change of scenery for both him and Gerhard."

"I should say!" Charlie scoffed. "Bertie's definitely a change of scene. Are they ready for him though?"

"Ah, come on, Charlie. He's not that bad, and he's a great contact for Ben. Plus, I think Gerhard may light up a little when he gets an eyeful of the library."

"Well, if you like misogynists, then Bertie's a doll. Christ, Ellie, he thinks women are for bedding and breeding. He told me that my husband needed to deploy a firm hand with me. A firm hand - I ask you!"

Ellie acknowledged Charlie's point with a wry smile.

"I'd love to see Dave try. He'd be hospitalised within seconds. No, honestly, he's just an old bachelor with no anchors to the modern world. He lives in ancient Egypt most of the time - at least in his mind. But he has a heart of gold. He's always been there for me."

"Okay, well, I'll take your word for that. When are you off?"

"Day after tomorrow. We might be away for a while. Stay home whilst we are away. I don't want to take any unnecessary risks. Consider it time off on full pay."

"Well, okay, but you make certain you take care of yourself. Now stop sitting around in my kitchen, making a mess, and make yourself useful. Take this tray to the boys. Off with you..."

❧

"Is that all the bags, Ellie?" Ben asked, closing the boot of Gerhard's Volvo.

"Yes. I'll just grab the hamper from the kitchen, and we are good to go."

"Cool. Don't forget to set the alarm. Are you up for the drive, Gerhard, or would you rather I drive?"

"I can drive as long as someone navigates for me," Gerhard replied, folding himself into the driver's seat and fastening his seatbelt. "Explain again where in London Professor Montague lives?" he asked Ellie as she settled herself in the backseat.

"He has a house in Lansdowne Crescent. It's close to Portobello Road - where the antique market takes place."

They navigated the country lanes before joining the larger A303.

"So, you know Bertram well?" Ben asked Ellie.

"Yes, we're very close. I used to love to stay with him when I was younger" she replied. "He's quite a character. He echoes around a huge old place. It was his parents', but he lives on his own these days. I have to warn you it's normally shambolic, dusty, and cold. Bertram's oblivious to anything that isn't three thousand years old, so he doesn't notice."

"It's most generous of him to extend his hospitality. I dare say the dust will bother you far more than Ben or I," Gerhard responded quietly, adjusting his rear mirror.

The journey seemed endless. Despite Ellie's best

efforts, Gerhard wouldn't be drawn into any meaningful conversation, and Ben seemed content to watch the countryside flash by. Ellie gave up and instead issued navigational instructions when needed and spent most of the journey revisiting recent events.

So much had happened. It felt like a picture that was shattered and blurred. They had the pieces but no idea how to put them together to create a clear and logical image. What had seemed an interesting puzzle had rapidly changed into a life-threatening quest.

She'd kept the detective's fears away from Ben and Gerhard as much as possible, trying to give them time to overcome their grief and guilt, but she needed them to come back to her. She feared their lives depended on it.

"This is some prime real estate, Ells," Ben said as he stretched his long arms and legs.

"Gorgeous, isn't it? Although, the old place needs a lick of paint. Still, it's good to be back. It's home away from home."

"Ellie, I was wondering if you could point me towards a good off-license. I'd like to get a gift for the professor. What's his favourite libation?"

"Oh, don't worry. He's flying home tonight, so we have time. Just wait till you see his library, Gerhard. It's magnificent." She grabbed her bags from the boot, whirled around, and bounded up the stairs with the keys dangling from her teeth. "Come on, you two. Hurry up."

Ellie opened the door and stepped to one side to allow the guys into the spacious hallway. Ben whistled through his teeth as he walked in, glancing up the sweeping staircase adorned with family portraits to the galleried landing above. Dumping the bags on the black and white chequered marble tiles, he looked around appreciatively. Ellie picked up the post scattered across the floor and added them to the mountain of junk mail on the console table.

"Welcome to Mandersley," she said. "I'll show you to your rooms and then give you the grand tour."

Gerhard followed her up the stairs, studying the surroundings with more interest than he'd shown since the fire.

"Are these ancestors of the professor?" he asked Ellie. "They all have an underlying resemblance to each other in the eyes."

She stared up at the pictures as if she hadn't noticed them before. "Uh-huh. They're grisly, aren't they?"

"It must be wonderful to be able to trace your family back so far, to know your heritage, *ja*?"

"I haven't ever thought of it, really, but I guess so. I can trace mine back to 1086, when we set up Scarab's Rest. Well, on my mother's side, anyway. Uncle Bertram's family owned the estate that this house was built on, although he descends from a younger son, so the family wealth didn't go down his line."

"Um, it looks like they really suffered, poor things," Ben said with raised eyebrows.

Laughing, Ellie replied, "This is poverty compared to the main line of the family, believe me. Still, Uncle Bertram's comfortably off – enough that he could follow his heart when choosing his profession rather than chasing a purse. This is your room, Gerhard," she said, flinging the door open into a large room with two huge shuttered windows.

Ellie ran forward and opened the shutters, engulfing the

room in weak afternoon light. The room was decorated with exquisitely painted Chinese silk wallpaper showing lush greenery, bright flowers, and swooping birds on a sunny yellow background. A canopied four-poster bed and vast, white marble fireplace dominated the room.

"I'm afraid Uncle Bertram hasn't installed central heating, but the gas fire soon warms up the room. It's an antique, but it takes off the chill. Is this okay?" she asked Gerhard.

"My dear, this is more than okay. It's superb. Time has stopped, no?"

"I don't think it's been redecorated since they built the house, so I guess it did - kind of. Well, I'll leave you to settle in and show Ben his room. I'm next-door."

Ben trooped out behind her. "He seems a bit perkier. It was a good idea to get him away."

"Yes, thank God. Here's your room. It's not so grand, I'm afraid," Ellie said, opening the door into a smaller proportioned but still large room. The white walls were paneled with gilt trim, and another four-poster bed filled the room. Ellie patted the white comforter, and a cloud of dust puffed up into the stale air. "Dust is *de rigueur* in this house," she sighed. "I'll see if I can find you something a little cleaner."

Ben watched as she walked over to the chest of drawers, opened the deep bottom drawer, and removed another large comforter and sheets. "You certainly know your way around the place."

"It's my home away from home. I spent every summer between here and Scarab's Rest, and after my grandfather died, my grandmother and I spent every Christmas here."

"What about your parents? You don't mention them much."

"Oh, they were always preoccupied with some dig or the other. They didn't have time for the frivolity of Christmas or holidays." The words were said carelessly enough, but Ben heard the pang of sadness behind them. Bertram couldn't be too bad a dude. He seemed to have provided a degree of stability and warmth to Ellie's childhood.

"The bathroom's across the hall. The plumbing is a bit temperamental, so be careful. I'll unpack and then we can look around," she said, withdrawing from the room.

Fifteen minutes later, Ellie led them up to the top floor of the house. "I can't wait for you to see this," she said, linking her arm with Gerhard's and sliding open a door. "This is my favourite room. Welcome to Bertram's library."

Gerhard and Ben stared in disbelief. The library encompassed the entire top floor of the house. Half-pavilion, half-room, the library was a monument dedicated to the worship of books. The rear third of the room was a domed glass pavilion with a double-height glass wall constructed of elaborate arches. Interspersed between them were roundels of stained glass, each showing a famed author reading one of their own works; Shakespeare, Chaucer, and Plato rubbed shoulders with Sophocles and Dante. Mantling the entire panorama was a pyramid in vibrant blues and greens flanked with the motto "*sapienta, scientia, fides*".

"Wisdom, knowledge, and belief," Ben translated under his breath.

Ellie went up to a glass reading table supported by large barley twist crystal legs, which ran the full length of the window. "I spent more hours than I care to remember doing research for Bertram at this table. A distant relative of Bertram's spent a king's ransom on landscaping the gardens and was furious that the view was ruined by the old wooden library table, so he threw it from the window and commissioned this. Seems Bertram didn't fall far from the tree." She turned to admire the view over the heavily wooded gardens beyond.

"Did you do a lot of research for Bertram?" Ben asked, intrigued at the thought of a young Ellie ensconced in this mahogany-encased monument to knowledge.

"Yes, although I often sneaked out to enjoy the bustle of Portobello Market." She smiled, lost in memories. "This room is so cosy when the fires are roaring on a cold winter day," she said, trailing her hands along the friezes of autumnal fruit on the large marble fireplace, which was mirrored by a twin on the other side of the room. Ellie stared into the large gilded mirror that topped the fireplace, reflecting the weak autumn sun around the room. "My grandmother would make afternoon tea, and we'd settle down on couches and play charades. Bertram always insisted we could only guess characters that had lived at least one thousand years before. They were happy days."

Gerhard was wandering around the room. Books were everywhere, the shelves full to bursting with leather-bound tomes and humble paperbacks. Books were piled high on the side tables and in messy groups around chairs and sofas. The library had the light atmosphere of a well-loved and much-used room.

"This is quite some room, Ellie," Ben said, running his fingers along the long mahogany shelves.

"Yes - it's a real library. A room that has evolved with the tastes of a long line of book-lovers. I always hate those pristine libraries you see in stately homes, where the shelves are so perfectly coordinated that you know no one has ever taken a book from the shelf. This is a room to rummage in and then to sink down and lose yourself for hours. I love it - *wunderbar, ja erstaunlich.*"

Ellie smiled. She'd hoped the library would release him from the fog he'd been in since the fire, and it seemed it might already be working its magic.

"It's fantastic, isn't it? I've always loved it. It looks like Bertram has been wreaking havoc. Every time I visit, I organise the room, and invariably, every time I return, it's in chaos again. He's a human mess creator." She leaned down and lit the fire, which roared upwards in a pleasing glow, and then turned and lit the other. "There. That should warm the room nicely. Why don't you two hang around here, and I'll rustle up tea and crumpets? I won't be a mo."

After she left, Ben turned to Gerhard. "I'm glad to get you on my own. I've been thinking about the Gayer-Anderson cat, and I have an idea, but it must stay just between you and I."

Ben sank down into one of the leather chesterfield chairs next to the fire. Once Gerhard took the other, he laid out his complex plan. Gerhard listened intently, eyes raised at the audacity of Ben's idea and occasionally adding a twist of his own.

"You realise, my dear boy, I dabble in magic and illusion. I can add to your idea." They fine-tuned the plan, and when Ellie returned with crumpets dripping with butter, she found them reading quietly.

BERTRAM

The three wasted away the rest of the waning afternoon in the library, Ellie tidying and Ben and Gerhard exploring the depth and range of the collection. They were in the middle of a good-natured but heated debate on the merits of an organised library when they heard the front door slam and "Elena!" bellowed at considerable volume up the stairs.

"It's Uncle Bertram," Ellie explained somewhat unnecessarily to the men. "I must run down and greet him. Wait here, and I'll bring him up to say 'hello'."

"Elena - where are you, my girl?"

"Coming, Uncle Bertram," she shouted as she ran from the room, reminding Ben of an elegant young colt.

They didn't need to wait long. A huge man with white, bushy hair and dressed in a dark twill suit, matching waist-coat, and claret bowtie bounded into the room. "Ah, we have company! How divine. This young buck must be Ben. Elena informs me you are a Yank – well, never mind. I'll try not to hold it against you. How do you like my little library?"

One sentence ran into another, barely allowing room for

breath and certainly not allowing for them to respond.

"And you must be Herr Webber. I find it hard to believe Elena invited a Kraut to stay, but I have just returned from your motherland, so I'll stretch my tolerance just this once. Welcome, welcome. Has Elena fed and watered you? Elena, have you tended the needs of our guests? Young women are so frightfully remiss as hostesses these days, don't you find?"

Feeling a little as if they had been hit by a run-away juggernaut, Ben understood why the normally good-natured Charlie took such an intense dislike to the force of nature stood in front of them. But he was oddly charmed by him and understood Ellie's abiding affection for her godfather.

Gerhard stood to attention and took a deep bow from the waist. "Professor Montague, it's indeed a pleasure to meet you, and I would like to extend our gratitude for your hospitality. I completely understand your apprehension about our nationalities as I took an age to adjust to having so many Brits in my vicinity, but that's the peril of living in England, I fear."

The room was silent; both Ellie and Ben were shocked at Gerhard's sharp retort. Bertram studied Gerhard, then roared with laughter and slapped him hard on the back. "Excellent response. We'll get on rippingly. What about you, boy? Are you always so circumspect, or have I shocked you into silence?"

"Yanks are rarely silenced, but we do know which battles to fight. I fear you would always outclass me verbally, so I am in the uncomfortable position of listening – something we are not so good at as a nation."

He chortled. "I like them, Elena. Yes, they will do. It's so rare to be able to engage in verbal sparring these days. Everyone is younger and junior to me, and for some unknown reason, I seem to intimidate them. But there really is nothing like it for rejuvenating the mind. Now your mother and father, they are master debaters, but no one comes close to Elspeth, your grandmother. She was a rare creature. Her mind on idle was a thousand times faster than anyone else I knew, and she had the courage of her convictions. No one could out-argue Elspeth. I miss the old goat. I'm uncertain what happened to you, my girl. You pale in comparison. Still, with a little seasoning, you may mature into your intellect."

Ellie raised her eyes to the heavens and reached up onto her toes to plant a kiss on Bertram's cheek. "And I've missed you too, you old reprobate. Now stop intimidating my friends and tell us about your trip."

"I will after I've poured us all a tot to drink. What's your pleasures, gentlemen? Elena, my case is by the front door. Could you launder the clothes within it? Mrs. Tarquin is frightful at laundry. She overdoes the starch; the shirts always feel like suits of armour. Good for posture but damnably uncomfortable."

The next morning, over breakfast, Ben informed them he'd organised to catch up with an old college friend.

Ellie stared at him in shock and was about to question whether this was the right time for frivolities when Gerhard said, "Excellent idea. Good to let some steam out. Ellie, would you be so kind as to accompany me to the theatre? I've booked tickets for a matinee performance of a modern interpretation of *Much Ado About Nothing*. I find Shakespeare so much more accessible when modernised. We all need a change of scenery and mood. Don't you?"

"Which theatre will you be going to?" asked Ben. "I'll make sure I meet my friend in that vicinity and then we can meet up later for a bite to eat."

"Well, as you young people say, 'that sounds like a plan'. We'll be in Shaftesbury Avenue at the Gielgud Theatre. I find myself pleasantly excited at the prospect."

Ellie smiled at Gerhard, happy to see him coming back to life. "It sounds like I have a date with a rather gorgeous older man," she said, winking at Gerhard.

Ellie tucked her arm into the crook of Gerhard's as they walked from the theatre to meet Ben. "That was sublime. I must admit it was a bit shocking to have it transposed into the collieries of Merthyr Tydfil, but once I got over that, it was brilliant."

"Mmm, well, the broad Welsh accent didn't help me understand everything, but it was an unusual interpretation. Ah, there's Ben," Gerhard acknowledged, raising his hand and waving.

Ben sauntered towards them, swinging a bag and smiling cheerily. Ellie couldn't help noticing all the admiring stares he garnered from the women he passed.

"Hello, my trusted friends. How goeth Shakespeare's fine play on this eventide?"

"You are remarkably chirpy. Had a good afternoon, did you?" Ellie sniped at him.

"Um, yes, it was brilliant to catch up with Cindy again. She always entertains me."

"I'm sure she does," Ellie muttered under her breath.

"Watch out, Ellie, or I might just think you're jealous."

"When hell freezes over," she flashed back at him.

"Ah, the lady doth protest too much," he replied with a wink. Ellie studiously ignored him and guided them towards their chosen restaurant. It was one of her favourites – Maison du Campagne.

The maître d' welcomed them into the dark, wooden paneled room and guided them to a table topped with a crisp, white linen tablecloth and surrounded by plump leather chairs. Ellie took a deep breath and smiled.

"I just love the smell of this place. It hasn't changed since I was a child. My grandmother used to bring me here at least once every time we visited Bertram."

They took their seats and accepted the menus from the maître d'.

"Today's special is moules marinière," the maître d' stated with a smile. "Thomas will be your server. I'll send him over to take your orders".

They studied the extensive menus in companionable silence until Thomas arrived.

"I'll have the salmon en croute with the watercress salad, please. And may we have a bottle of your Châteauneuf-du-Pape?" said Gerhard, closing the leather-bound menu and returning it to the elegantly clad waiter.

"Certainly, sir. Which year do you prefer?"

"I'll trust your sommelier's judgement. I'm sure he will recommend the best," he replied with a gentle chuckle.

Once the waiter finished collecting the menus and left the table, Gerhard turned his attention back to his two friends.

"We are facing the calm before the storm, so a little treat is in order. Now we need to decide our course of action for tomorrow's visit. What do we want to achieve, and what questions need answering? Best to go into the meeting prepared and organised. Then we will maximise our effectiveness and be prepared for whatever eventuality our spherical friend brings forth. Don't you agree?"

Ellie nodded. "Yes, it would be good to predict what the sphere or familiars might do. I don't want to explain this whole thing to Uncle Bertram or his colleagues, especially as we don't really understand it ourselves."

"I've been thinking about this a fair bit, and it seems to me that the statue and Gerhard are strongly linked. I fear that the sphere will be activated when the two become close, but remember that only we see anything. So, as long as we school our expressions to remain neutral and try not to talk, we should be able to hide the event from anyone around us. Ellie, maybe you could pretend to faint, and whilst the museum people tend to you, Gerhard and I could observe the reaction of the sphere. No one would question us. They know men are bad in these circumstances. We can always explain away your faint. After all, you have been under tremendous stress recently."

"Because I am the girl, I have to be the one that faints?"

"No," Ben answered, "because Gerhard has the link to the statue, and I'm in disgusting good health, so it would be far less believable if I fainted. As there are only three of us, that leaves you. Believe me, both Gerhard and I know that you'd be the last one of us to faint. But Bertram, well, he sees you as the weaker sex, so it would be completely understandable to him."

Ellie stared at him for a moment and then raised her shoulders in acknowledgement of the truth of Ben's words.

"Okay, fainting lady I am. But don't think I like it."

"We'd never dare to, my dear," Gerhard said, patting her hand.

The return of the waiter closed their conversation, and they all settled down to enjoy the gourmet meal.

THE BRITISH MUSEUM

They enjoyed a lavish and somewhat leisurely breakfast with Bertram, who didn't pay attention to the normal constraints of time. Afterwards, the four hailed a black taxi and joined the maelstrom of traffic congesting the capital's roads.

London, more than many other cities, was a melting pot of creeds, religions, cultures and philosophies. Ben found it fascinating to observe as the taxi took them towards the museum. Looking out the window, he saw shops selling Halal food neighbouring Kosher markets and Chinese wholesalers next to Italian restaurants. It reminded him of New York. Every face told a story of multiculturalism at work, blended with greater harmony than he saw in many European countries.

Ellie smoothed down her skirt and fidgeted with her hair. Ben watched her, thinking she'd be even more nervous if she knew about their plan. He gave her a wink and turned his attention to Bertram, asking a ream of questions about the British Museum's impressive collection of Egyptian artifacts. As he hoped, Bertram then waxed lyrically for the rest of the journey, distracting Ellie's nerves.

"It's an outrage! That philistine stripped the cat of its original patination and decorative history. Do you know when Gayer-Anderson first purchased the cat, it still had its ancient verdigris and flakes of ancient red paint on it? He stripped it – and he called himself a cultured man. Cultured my ass. He desecrated it. Though, to be fair, he did at least make a fair attempt at the restoration of its head. Well, for the time."

Eventually, the taxi drew up outside the imposing museum entrance, and they piled out.

"Morning, Stanley. Please sign in my guests," said Bertram, waving at the trio.

"Good morning, Professor Montague. I'm not Stanley. I'm Rupak. Rupak Pau."

"Well, I'm blowed. What happened to Stanley?"

"He retired four years ago. I'm his replacement."

Bertram peered at him over his glasses. "But I've said 'morning, Stanley' every day."

"Yes, sir, you have – but to me, not Stanley."

"Goodness, man. You can't steal a man's identity and expect to get away with it. You're a security guard. You're meant to enforce the law, not corrupt it. Does your supervisor know you have been impersonating Stanley for years?"

"Everyone knows I am Rupak except you, sir."

"So, you have been fooling me? I fail to see the merit of this extraordinary deception. What did you expect to gain from it?"

Ellie took Bertram's arm and led him to one side. "Uncle Bertram, the poor guy has been trying to tell you, and you've been absorbed in your own thoughts and not realised."

"Nonsense, Elena. I am not an absentminded fool. I am a man of learning and intellect."

"I know you are, and a self-absorbed and forgetful one at that. Stop blustering and just remember the guy's name."

"What is his name?"

"Rupak."

"What kind of name is that? No wonder I can't remember it. Young man, I will call you Stanley from now on. It's a fine British name, and it suits you greatly. Please sign in my guests, my good man."

Shaking his head, Rupak signed in Ellie, Ben, and Gerhard and gave them visitor lanyards. Ellie smiled gently at the man whilst raising her eyes to the heavens.

"Thank you, Stanley. I'm glad we got that sorted out. Have a good day."

"You too, Professor."

Bertram led them through a warren of corridors topped with aluminum-clad service pipes, deep into the bowels of the museum. He barked greetings to the people they passed, who nodded back at him, never quite making eye contact and scurrying away as fast as possible. Ellie smiled. Bertram's bluster had always intimidated people. Most never got past it to realise what a kind-hearted soul it disguised.

Bertram stopped at a door labelled EDA24. He threw the door open with such force, it slammed against the wall and bounced back, nearly hitting him as he exploded into the room. Three of the four occupants jumped, one splashing coffee across the papers on his desk.

The fourth, a blonde woman in her early thirties, looked up. "Morning, Bertram. Do come in. Don't loiter in the hallway like a vagrant."

"Morning, Caro. Martin, do I need to buy you a bib?

You seem inordinately clumsy for someone trained to restore priceless artifacts. To be frank, it worries me. Still, hey-ho, what can we do, eh? Now, Caro, these are the guests I told you about yesterday. Caro is my Assistant Keeper for Late-period Egyptian Archaeology - amazingly talented lass. Shame her training will be wasted when she settles down and starts a family. Still, until then, she's the best I've got."

Caro studied Bertram silently over the rim of her stylish glasses. "You have heard of sexual equality, Bertram - remember? I copied the law and left it on your desk. Several times, actually. Anyway, the way you work me, I have no time to sleep, let alone meet the potential father of this family you have envisioned, unless you are suggesting your-self in that role?"

Bertram flushed and shuffled awkwardly. "No, indeed not. I'm a happy bachelor."

"As am I," she replied, pinning him with her icy blue eyes, "and quite as dedicated to my career as you." She turned to Ellie and with a conspiratorial wink. "You must be Elena. Sorry about that, but someone has to control the old fool, or he becomes unbearable."

Ellie beamed back at her. "I'm delighted to see he's met his match. No need to apologise. You've made my year. Please call me Ellie. Only Uncle Bertram calls me Elena."

Caro pushed her jaw-length blonde bob backwards and slid her glasses onto the top of her head. She had the hearty blushed cheeks, golden glow, and plummy tone that screamed out upper middle-class girl from the counties. Ellie imagined her entering gymkhanas on a palomino mare and enjoying skiing with her old school pals in Gstaad.

Ben's imagination wandered elsewhere, mostly focused on her amazing, svelte figure and clean-cut beauty.

"And you must be the archaeologist as this fine gentleman is far too distinguished to be with the Department of Egyptian Antiquities. So, by a process of elimination, you must be Herr Webber?" Caro said to Gerhard. "Caro Smythe. Welcome to the British Museum. Would you like a tour behind the scenes before seeing Gayer's cat? To be honest, a lot of what we do isn't that fascinating to watch. However, the conservation team and the secret storage areas can be quite interesting."

"'That would be great," Ben replied and Gerhard echoed.

"Good-oh, Caro. I'll leave them with you. I have far more important things to do." Bertram barked the words behind him as he left the room, already studying a paper.

Caro led them through a maze of identical corridors, stopping occasionally to let them peer through windows at the people ferreting away behind the doors. Clad in white coats and face masks, restorers carefully brushed away centuries of dust and dirt from the ancient relics on which they worked. She showed them the laboratories full of the latest technology, where they scanned, X-rayed, and carbon-dated the artifacts.

To Ben's delight, Caro introduced them to one of the country's foremost experts in Egyptian hieroglyphs, Dr. Gillian Shoon, who invited them into her office. The three archaeologists chatted animatedly about Dr. Shoon's latest translation, an obscure plaque found deep in the deserts that seemed to hint at the story of Moses. Ellie watched Ben's face, alight with excitement, as she adjusted her position for the umpteen time. Gerhard had stretched his long legs out and was flexing his toes to restore circulation.

Dr. Shoon glanced over. "Oh, I'm so sorry. You must be stupefied with boredom. I can get a little over enthusiastic on this subject. Caro, rescue these poor souls before those wooden chairs cripple them." She turned back to Ben. "You, sir, can come back again anytime. I like the way you think. Those Egyptians are lucky to have you. Original thought is so hard to find in archaeologists these days."

Ellie raised an eyebrow and followed Caro from the room.

Caro waited patiently outside the door as the men said their goodbyes to Gillian and then gestured down the hall. "So, on to the highlight of the trip. Let's go see our famous pussycat!" She guided them to a large, vaulted door. "I've taken it off display, so you can have a close look in private. Please store your bags in the lockers out here. Nothing personal, but she's rather valuable, and our insurance demands we take certain precautions."

"Quite right too, my dear. One can never be too careful," Gerhard agreed. "There are all sorts of reprobates around. An arsonist destroyed my own dear shop just the other day."

"Oh, my word. That's simply awful. Poor you!" Caro said to Gerhard, who was behind Ellie.

Caro unlocked the door, and they followed her. Sat in pride-of-place on a table in a bland, cream room was the statue. Ellie walked straight over to it and bent down to take a closer look.

The statue wasn't large, only slightly longer than a ruler, but what struck Ellie was its head. Smack bang in the centre, between its ears, was a scarab. *Ye gods*, Ellie thought. As she studied the statue, the scarab moved, raising up onto its back legs, and the cat winked. Ellie jumped back with a shriek, landing in an undignified heap on the floor.

Caro rushed over and helped her up. "I say, are you okay?"

Gerhard pulled Ellie into his arms. "Hush, *mein*

liebling. I'm sorry. I shouldn't have opened the subject." He turned to Caro. "She's traumatised. We lost a dear, most beloved friend in the fire, and we nearly perished ourselves. Ben, can you take Ellie out for a glass of water?" He turned and stumbled into the table, knocking the statue, which swung precariously. Letting go of Ellie, he used his body to block its fall as his arms steadied it. Caro, eyes huge in her pale face, ran to the statue to check it was undamaged.

"Oh, my lord. I'm most terribly sorry, Caro. I'm becoming clumsy in my old age. I'd better take Ellie and leave you with Caro, Ben. It's you who wants to study the statue after all. Come, my dear."

Ellie's eyes flitted from Gerhard to Ben. Something wasn't right.

"Ah, *mein liebling*. Come, come. We'll get a nice cup of tea in the café back there. Sorry again, Caro."

"Don't mention it. No harm done," Caro said with a warm smile. She gave Ellie a pat on the shoulder. "I'd be on my knees if I'd lived through that. Don't be upset. You're doing really well. Go have a drink, and we'll meet up again later."

Ellie was ushered from the room as Ben and Caro discussed the statue's provenance.

The corridor was empty. "What in heaven's name just happened?" she hissed at Gerhard. He shook his head slightly and retrieved their bags, shoving his jacket into his worn, leather duffel bag and pulling her along beside him to the café.

"I could ask the same of you. What was the screech for? You were meant to faint."

"I didn't screech. I exclaimed. It's different."

"That may be, but you didn't answer my question,"

Gerhard said, putting his arm around her shoulder. "Keep up the act. You're in shock, remember?"

"I'm not a girl who swoons. I don't need a man to support me! Too right I'm in shock. That bloody statue winked at me," she hissed, "and the scarab did a jig. I didn't have time to do my fainting scene before you grabbed me."

Gerhard halted and looked down at her. "Ellie, please! Act shocked, and we'll discuss everything later in private, *ja?*"

She studied him. "Okay, but I know something's amiss here, and I intend to find out what."

Ellie munched on an apple and cinnamon slice as Caro and Ben made their way to the table. She watched them chat. Caro played with her hair as she listened to Ben, who, in turn, had a hard time maintaining eye contact and kept glancing sideways at her. Ellie shook her head without comment. It seemed Bertram was at risk of losing his second-in-command after all. She shuddered at the thought of another poor child being raised by two self-absorbed archaeologists.

Caro escorted them out of the private part of the museum and left them to wander around the exhibits, with a promise from Ben that he'd email the report they'd been discussing.

"Spill it, you two," she hissed as soon as they were alone.

"Spill what?" asked Ben nonchalantly.

"Oh, spare me the 'Mr. Innocence' routine. Save it for someone who cares, like Caro! What are you two up to?"

"Oh, do you think she cares?" Ben asked with a huge grin.

"Ellie, my dear. There's nothing to it. I orchestrated a way to touch the statue to see if I got a reaction. Hence the stumble."

"And did you?" Ellie questioned. "Why did we leave the room so swiftly?"

"I got a pulse but nothing more. Undoubtedly, Bastet has a link to the statue, but otherwise, it's of little importance. I fear we must travel to Egypt to learn more. Everything is pointing towards the land of the Nile."

Ellie stared at him for some seconds. "I feared as much," Ellie said with a sigh.

"So, Egypt it is," Ben agreed before extolling the considerable virtues of Caro Smythe.

THE GUARDIANS OF THE ANKH

"That's great news. Yes, well, send her my regards, and maybe we can catch up soon. Bye for now."

Tjati slammed down the phone, jumped up, and kicked at his worn, metal filing cabinet, leaving a large dent in a drawer that would probably never open again. He stalked back and forth like a caged lion caught in the realisation that the House of Scarabs had survived—and worse still, were on their way to the location for the final meld.

"God damn them to hell, where they belong," he spat out as he stared across the square, struggling to control his boiling rage. Every day they survived, they grew stronger and their destruction less likely. Eurydice had failed again, and he doubted her resolve. "Damn her as well. She set this path years ago. I should never have listened to her."

He wheeled around and charged back to the desk with a certainty of purpose and a desperate hunger to be the last Grand Master of the Guardians of the Ankh. After the destruction of the House of Scarabs, he would dissolve the Guardians, who would all drift off into obscurity, and his destiny would be fulfilled.

He tapped out her number, his leg jigging up and down. "Eurydice, meet me at the temple tonight. Your mission failed. The trio live." He slammed down the handset without giving her a chance to respond and immediately dialed another number.

"Hello. It's time for you to be promoted. I have a mission for you."

ARRIVING IN EGYPT

As the door to the plane opened, the familiar smells of Egypt assaulted Ellie. The hot air was fragranced with a unique scent that could only ever be Cairo. Exotic spices, shisha smoke, pollution, and baked ozone combined into an evocative fragrance that brought a flood of memories she struggled to push away. She'd left never intending to return, and yet, now she was here, being forced to face her demons.

She took her first step out, and the heat engulfed her. After the chill of England's winter, Egypt felt balmy.

Her parents were away in Bahariya on an extended dig, so she'd arranged to stay at their villa in Maadi. She was relieved that she wouldn't have to see them again. They were an intrinsic link to Sam and never respected her feelings, conversing about him as if he and Ellie hadn't gone through a heart-wrenching divorce.

She bought a visa at Bank Misr for Gerhard; both she and Ben already had one. They trooped through passport control and were pounced on by persistent porters determined to get every pound out of the unsuspecting tourists who didn't realise the trolleys were free. Ellie barked at them in fluent Arabic, and they dispersed, eager to find easier victims.

Gerhard watched the chaos with fascination. Porters pulled bags randomly from the belt, stacking them in huge piles, forcing people to rummage through a mountain of bags rather than wait for the bags to traverse the belt towards them. Tourists struggled to wrangle bags away from the porters. Tourist police screamed at the airport staff, trying to regain an order that had never existed, and cleaners joked among themselves. The noise was like an avalanche, roaring and echoing as people shouted across the hall.

"It's just like home," he said with a smile.

As they passed through customs control, with nothing but a cursory glance from the customs officer, they faced a massed brigade of people all struggling for the first view of the person they'd come to greet. It was customary in Egypt that everyone came to the airport to meet a person returning from a trip, so every passenger had several people awaiting them. The wall of faces was overwhelming to the average visitor, but Ellie had already warned the guys, so they stepped adroitly through the throng and went straight outside to negotiate a taxi.

Cairo was a seething mass of humanity crammed into too small a space, so the population battled every moment of the day. Cars wrestled for supremacy on the roads. Shops nestled cheek-to-jowl with their competitors and fought for every *guinea* they earned.

The taxi crawled through the crazed traffic. "Look up there on the hill, guys. That's the old citadel," Ellie said, pointing at a fortress with a large, domed mosque at its centre. "Not long till we reach Maadi now. I think you'll like Maadi, Gerhard. It was originally designed as a country retreat for wealthy Caireans in the early 1900s. It was packed with palatial villas surrounded by impressive gardens. It's not so grand now, but there are still glimmers of the former glory in some of the remaining villas, although it has merged into Cairo now."

"How utterly charming, my dear," said Gerhard, studying the Swiss chalet in front of him as he stepped out of the taxi and stretched the travel kinks out of his long frame. "It's a requiem to colonialism."

Ellie smiled at him and turned to settle the taxi bill, ignoring the protests of the taxi driver who was trying to charge ten times the going rate. Gerhard and Ben watched the fierce verbal battle and were bemused when the two foes suddenly beamed at each other and shook hands over the greatly reduced tariff. After many salutations and exaggerated farewells, the taxi driver drove off with a wave.

"There's nothing an Egyptian likes more than a successful and vigorous barter," Ellie said with a grin in response to their raised eyebrows.

"Well, you must be popular here," Ben answered. "You do nothing but barter and argue over everything."

"You are how you were raised, and I, for one, am very grateful for your skills in that area. I'd have been lost without your assistance today, my dear," said Gerhard, ever the peacemaker.

Ellie smiled at him. She led them through a creaky, dilapidated gate, along a heavily scented walkway of evening musk, and up to the ornate doorway complete with grilled peephole. She turned to them before opening the door. "Be prepared. They work in Egyptian funerary studies, and they bring their work home with them. The house is stuffed to the gills with funerary relics. Most people find it rather creepy."

Gerhard patted her hand. "Ben and I are made of sterner stuff, *mein liebling*. We'll be fine."

The house was dark but cool. Wood paneling stretched as far as the eye could see, with matching beams and parquet floors. The furniture was heavy antique oak and appeared Germanic. Every possible surface was covered in clutter; reams of paper and pots, statues, death masks and shards of ceramic scattered wily-nilly, all covered in a suffocating layer of dust. It felt unloved, a place to camp out rather than a home.

Ellie flicked the light switch, but nothing happened. Cursing under her breath, she marched to the window and flicked the curtain. "Damn it to hell! Everyone else has electricity, which means they've forgotten to pay the bills again. Sorry, guys. They aren't terribly reliable. I should have checked before I left. I'll find candles for now and organise for it to be reconnected tomorrow."

After a scavenged snack of crisps, biscuits, and Coke (which were the only edible things in the house), they cleared a space on the dining room table and planned their next steps. Ellie suggested meeting with a close family friend, Professor Mourad Soliman, who was based at the Cairo Museum of Egyptian Antiquities.

"I think he's the best place to start. Most of the people I know have specific and narrow fields of study, but he's more of a generalist. If we share everything that's happened so far, he may be able to shine some light onto it."

"Ellie, I don't agree. He's a scientist—yes, an Egyptologist—but first and foremost a logical, rational scientist, and we have nothing but hearsay and lunacy. If I hadn't seen it with my own eyes, I would never have believed a word. He's bound to throw us..."

Ellie butted in. "I'm not totally without sense, Ben. We won't share the mystical stuff, but we can discuss the three familiars, the Gayer-Anderson Cat, and the vision you saw. We'll wrap it in a story; you're working on a paper on the rituals of ancient Egypt, focusing specially on the deities of Bastet, Sobek, and Khepri. You've appointed me to accompany you here to continue with your Arabic studies, and Gerhard is your uncle. He'll buy that. Anyway, he's a close friend. He'll be happy to help."

"It seems we have a plan, but we need to approach this professionally. I would still like to have my reputation intact after this fiasco, and being linked to this craziness is career suicide, so I'd appreciate it if I could master the helm tomorrow."

Ellie smiled and nodded. "I'd suggest nothing less. I'll run out first thing to get us a few home comforts. I don't know about you, but I'm exhausted. The last few days have taken it out of me, so I will turn in for the night. I'll make up your rooms. Mine is the door at the top of the stairs. Yours are the two rooms to the left."

"Ellie, my dear, just leave out the bedding on the beds. We are perfectly capable of making our own beds."

"Speak for yourself," Ben quipped but quickly reassured Ellie after receiving an unusually disapproving glare from Gerhard.

"It's no trouble, really. I can't let you make up rooms in my home. You're guests."

"No. We are friends, and friends support each other and watch out for each other. You are dead on your feet, so we'll have no more arguing. Anyway, isn't it true that the British think it's rude to argue with their elders?"

Ellie, caught between two contradicting sets of manners, gave in gracefully and took her leave.

The next morning, it surprised her to find both Gerhard and Ben were keen to go with her on errands. First stop, the less than romantically named Road 9, which she remembered as the beating heart of Maadi. It was a long, straight road full of tiny grocers, hardware stores, and primitive little cafés, reminiscent of the old-fashioned high streets of Europe in the forties and fifties. It was only a short walk from her parent's house and gave Ellie a chance to give the guys a little orientation guide.

As they entered the street, she stared around in shock and dismay. It was unrecognisable. The quaint, hand-painted signs of family-run businesses had been replaced with glossy, neon signs of banks, mobile phone operators, and huge café chains.

"Oh, no!" she muttered. "It's changed beyond all belief. I was here only four years ago. How is that possible?"

"Progression happens far too quickly, and often, it's not for the better," Gerhard replied. "I saw the 'westernisation' happen in Peru, and it was almost always a retrograde step, killing the community culture and support we'd all enjoyed. The West has a lot to answer for. Who says these countries need a Starbucks on every corner?"

They quickly gathered their groceries and stopped off in Café Grecco, one of the few original cafés that Ellie remembered, for breakfast.

At the electricity board, Ben and Gerhard gaped at the scene confronting them. The building resembled a condemned squat: filthy, unpainted for decades, and with a tide of bodies surging forward in a battle to get to the barred windows. The process seemed like bureaucratic lunacy. Ellie was logged in at one desk, then joined a mass of bodies surrounding the one window to take cash, everyone pushing and shouting, fighting to get their place at the window. Ellie, well used to the process, fared far better than either one of them would and soon came back to tell them they needed to go to another window to get the receipt in two hours.

In the meantime, they needed to go to another office to book the reconnection. Cats, unkempt and dirty, prowled the halls, searching for dropped crumbs, and Ben caught the scuttling blur of a rodent out of the corner of his eye.

"My God, Ellie, it's crazy. Is it always like this?" Ben quizzed.

"No. Normally, it's worse. They seem to have streamlined the process since I was last here," she said with a grin. "Different, huh?"

"Uh, 'ridiculous' might better express it."

"Don't worry. You'll get used to it in time. It's the way we work here."

Ben noticed that she'd said "we" but didn't comment.

After several hours of traipsing from one location to another and paying copious amounts of *"baksheesh"* ("Tips," Ellie translated; *bribes*, Ben thought), Ellie had managed to negotiate the reconnection of the power. She'd purchased a mobile Wi-Fi service, so they could connect to the outside world, and had organized for them to meet with Professor Soliman the next morning. With every foray back into Egyptian culture, Ellie blossomed, as if breathing the Egyptian air restored her energy and being. Both Ben and Gerhard noticed it.

"She's returned to her spiritual home, and it's charging her," Gerhard stated as if it were an obvious observation. "I've seen it happen with the native Indians in Peru. When they return to their homelands after a long absence, it's as if the earth and air that bore them feeds them. Sounds far-fetched, I know, but I've seen it repeatedly."

MEETING MOURAD

The next morning, after a restorative night's sleep and a cold shower, they set off for the Cairo Museum. Passing alongside the Nile, which ambled through Cairo on its final leg towards the Mediterranean, they watched feluccas glide through the water. They were powered by their billowing white sails, just as they had been throughout Egypt's long history. Young couples strolled aimlessly along the corniche, girls' hands invariably tucked protectively in the crook of the boys' arms in a quaint, old-fashioned gesture.

Ellie pointed out key sights as they traversed Cairo. "You see that conical roof over there?" she said, gesturing to a building on their left. "That covers the old Nilometer, which used to measure the Nile's flood and determined the annual taxation rate for the peasant farmers."

She showed them the grandeur of the American University campus and various heavily protected embassies until they crawled into the now infamous Tahrir Square, scene of the downfall of the former dictator Hosni Mubarak.

The Cairo Museum of Egyptian Antiquities was nestled at the far end of the square. They had to clear multiple security barriers, all protected by armed tourist police, to get close to the grand building. Coated in a faded salmon wash, the domed facade of the museum had a colonial gentility. A buzz of excitement surrounded them as they exited the taxi and negotiated their way to the main entrance, through the persistent postcard and tacky gift hawkers.

In contrast, the museum guards, who were lounging in the shade, fanning themselves with old leaflets, seemed barely to notice the tourists. The tour guides did though and pounced on them the moment they cleared security, desperate to secure business. Ellie marched over to one of the more senior guards and explained they had an appointment with Professor Mourad Soliman. The officer stared up at her over the top of his sunglasses and remained seated, just waving his hand in a general direction before continuing his conversation with his friends.

The trio passed old, granite statues of ancient deities and ponds full of papyrus and water lilies before making their way up the stairs, into the huge entry hall.

Gerhard gazed around in wonder at the mammoth statues and the jumble of precious antiquities that had outgrown the building that housed them. The museum building mimicked the ancient relics it held, with yellowed walls and a liberal coating of dust. The handwritten exhibit descriptions curled with heat and age.

"I could spend days here and still not have seen everything. It's overwhelming," Gerhard said to Ben.

"Yes, it's a country rich in archaeology. It's furnished most of the world's museums and capital cities and still has so much that all the museums in Egypt have more in storage than on show. And, as is obvious here, they have a lot on show. It's an archaeologist's dream," Ben replied.

A man shuffled up to them, wrapped, to the bemusement of the trio, in a thick logger's shirt, sweater, and parka. "Hello. Are you here to meet Professor Soliman? I'm Walid, his assistant."

Ellie confirmed their identities to him in Arabic.

"You speak Arabic. Like an Egyptian too. I'm impressed," he replied. "I'll talk in English, if you don't mind. I get little chance to practice, so I always try when I can."

"That suits me," Gerhard replied. "Unlike my young friends, I can't speak Arabic, and they don't speak German."

Walid led them up the wide staircase and through a huge, heavy door into a long, utilitarian corridor which abandoned all pretence of decoration. He pushed open a door and welcomed them into a grubby galley office barely wide enough to house a row of red vinyl chairs with deep slashes from which foam erupted. At the end of the room was a tiny desk just large enough for the small laptop, desk journal, and phone. There was a hole in one pane of the window behind the desk, through which a knotted tumble of wires and cables poured into the room.

Walid gestured for them to sit and shouted, "Hussein, refreshments for our guests."

A dark-skinned man, also wrapped up for the artic, bustled into the room and asked each of them their preference before picking up the phone and ordering their drinks.

"I'm sorry for the wait, but the professor is chairing his weekly team meeting, and it's overrun. No fear. He knows you are here and is eager to meet you, so he will speed them – *inshallah*," Walid explained.

With that, a man dressed in full butler regalia pushed a

1970s maid's trolley into the room. The trolley held a range of eastern treats and dainty china cups and saucers.

"Ah, Stefan would have loved to see this. He'd have been... how do you say it?" Gerhard asked.

"Enchanted," Ellie replied. "He'd have been in his element."

They shared a sad smile and remained quiet as the "boy", as Walid referred to him, undertook the elegant ritual of pouring the drinks and serving the sweets. Time ticked by, and the padded, green leather door remained resolutely shut. After forty-five minutes, they appreciated why Walid and Hussein were dressed so warmly as the stone floors and walls generated a bone-chilling slow freeze.

"I'd forgotten how cold these old buildings can get in winter," Ellie murmured to them. "It's often colder inside the houses than outside. They are all built to stay cool, and I've yet to come across the concept of heating here. We used to sit in the garden to warm up when I was a kid."

"It's aggravating my rheumatism," Gerhard said in the first complaint Ellie and Ben had ever heard from him. Walid had left them on their own for over thirty minutes, and they had no idea what was happening. Ben had been pacing the floor like a caged tiger ever since and was deflecting Ellie's suggestion they use the time to practise his Arabic.

Eventually, the soundproofed door swung open, and a troop of flustered Egyptians flooded out, looking relieved to be free. Walid appeared from nowhere and was at his desk to answer the intercom, from which a voice barked, "Walid, where are my guests? What are you waiting for? Show them in. Don't keep them waiting, man. It's rude."

Smiling at them apologetically, Walid opened the door

and gestured for them to enter the professor's inner sanctum.

The decorator had clearly not gotten the message when it came to the professor's office, which was in stark contrast to the outer office. Sumptuously decorated with silk Turkish carpets, large leather chesterfield sofas, a walnut desk, and a large meeting table, the room was an ode to opulence. The walls had deep alcoves painted in black, each containing stunning artefacts that were spot-lit from above. A slim and elegant man with a mane of manicured grey hair and a smattering of large freckles across his nose uncoiled from behind the desk and smoothed out his immaculate navy suit.

"Ellie, my dear girl, this is a pleasure beyond my humble ability to communicate in English. *Wahashtini habibti*. It has been too long. Yes, too long. You look beautiful as always, although paler than usual – as if that were possible. I'm so sorry for my tardy timekeeping, but the ineptitude of my team knows no boundaries, and I had to resolve issues before they exploded. Ah, how I wish I'd persuaded you to follow the family business. What a team we would have been. Come give me a hug."

Ellie moved quickly into his arms, and he showered kisses on her cheeks as an old man does on his young nieces.

"Uncle, it's so good to see you. You're as suave as always and ageless - you never change. What's your secret? You could be sitting on a fortune, you know."

"And your ability to make an old man happy never diminishes. Now introduce me to these gentlemen you bring me."

"Professor Mourad Soliman, please meet Dr. Ben Ellis and his uncle, Mr. Gerhard Webber. Ben is taking up a fellowship here with Professor Badri, and he's stumbled across a rather interesting paper I thought you may help shed light on. Ben's been on a crash course at my language academy. He hasn't graduated yet, so he's asked me to accompany him here to complete his Arabic studies."

The men shook hands, and Mourad gestured for them to be seated.

"It seems I owe you thanks, Dr. Ellis. You have achieved something all my begging, bribery, and entreating have failed to do. You've brought Ellie back to us and to Egypt. For that, I'm indebted to you. So, tell me, how can I help you?"

"Well, I've been digging around and preparing for my fellowship, and I came across a fascinating description of a religious ceremony among the private family papers of a contact of mine in Italy. I've read nothing like it elsewhere, and I was wondering if you'd come across references to it or other ceremonies like it. My friend wants me to authenticate the document but will not allow it to be copied, so I've transcribed it here."

Ben handed his description of the ceremony to the professor, who slipped his silver-rimmed glasses on and settled into a poised quiet to study the document. After completing it, he returned to the beginning and reread the sections. His face remained passive, giving nothing away.

Ben fidgeted, his leg bouncing as he waited for any clue as to the professor's thoughts. He glanced across at Ellie, who shrugged her shoulders and frowned at him.

After some time, the professor peered up over the top of his glasses at Ben. "This is fascinating. It's the single most intact description I have ever seen of an ancient ceremony. Where did you say they found it?"

"I didn't say and unfortunately can't, as I'm sure you recall, but a good try, professor."

Mourad acknowledged his words with a wry smile. "Well, nevertheless, it has elements I've seen before but also details I haven't seen referenced elsewhere. If verified, this would be ground-breaking material that the entire Egyptology community will want to access."

"My friend is adamant that this document remains with him alone. He's a deeply private guy and doesn't want to be pestered by viewing requests. He's amenable to sharing my notes, to broadcast the ceremony to the wider archaeological society, but the notes may be met with scepticism if not backed by the original document," Ben replied. "I'm eager to find evidence of where this ceremony took place and any elements we can correlate with known records or evidence. The story has captured my uncle's interest, and he's keen to visit the temple whilst he's here," Ben said, and Gerhard nodded his agreement.

"I'm willing to help but on my terms. I want you to deliver a letter from me to your friend about the potential verification of his document. I will assign one of my team to find some answers for you, if they're to be found. How does that sound, my young friend?" Mourad replied.

"More than fair, but don't get your hopes up. My friend is stubborn as an old mule, and I don't think your request will change his mind."

"Well, that may be, but Ellie will confirm that I can be very persuasive when I set my mind on something, so we'll agree to disagree. Let's shake on it," Mourad replied as he reached across his desk towards Ben.

"Well, that went better than I'd hoped," Ben said as they left the museum having promised to meet with Mourad later in the week for supper.

Gerhard nodded. "But it's wise to not lay all our eggs in, how do you say... one nest. I think we should go visit

Saqqara tomorrow and check if we get any reaction from our familiars."

"Agreed," said Ben. He then narrowly avoiding ploughing into Ellie, who had slammed to a standstill and was staring with wide eyes into the crowded museum gardens. Ben studied the crowd to see what Ellie was staring at and saw the tall, sylph figure of his old college friend, Sam, Ellie's ex-husband.

With a muffled sob, Ellie turned and ran back into the museum, leaving a startled Gerhard calling after her.

SAM

"Leave her, Gerhard! She needs space. She's had a shock. Her ex-husband is walking towards us."

"Oh, Lord, what do we do?"

"Saying 'hello' is the norm, so maybe we could try that," Ben replied sarcastically.

Sam hadn't changed at all since they'd last met. He'd always looked like Michelangelo's David, with curls that played against his collar, but his eyes were the attention-grabbers. They were the deepest brown with glints of gold and glowed with intelligence and an innate kindness. Now they were shadowed with sadness. Despite this, he approached his old friend with a warm smile.

"Ben! What a surprise, *habibi*. What a wonderful surprise. How are you?" The two men hugged, and Ben turned to introduce Gerhard to his friend.

"Sam, may I introduce Gerhard Webber, my uncle. Gerhard, this is Samir Gamal, an old and dear friend of mine from my college days."

The two men greeted each other cordially before Sam

turned to Ben. "Was it my imagination, or was that Elena with you?" he asked.

"Yes, it was. And thanks for the heads up, by the way. You could have warned me that the 'Ellie' you recommended was your Elena. Let me tell you, it caused a few awkward moments there, buddy."

"Ben, I must see her - please help me."

"Your name is toxic, Sam. I can't see I'll ever get her to agree to meeting you, and just opening the subject would get me in extremely hot water. That woman is one tough cookie."

Sam's eyes dropped down and studied the floor. "Elena? No, she's the gentlest woman I've ever met," he murmured, looking up with pained eyes.

Ben spluttered in shock, "Maybe once, although I can't imagine it, but not anymore, she's not. She's a shrew."

Gerhard touched Ben's elbow. "We should go after her before she goes too far. It could compromise us, no?"

"Ben, please, I'm begging you. I need to see her," Sam said, grabbing hold of Ben's shoulders. "Meet me tonight, please. I need to talk to you. You're the only access point I have to Elena. You are my last hope."

Ben stared into Sam's wide, pleading eyes. "Oh, God! All right, but believe me, it won't help you any. The woman despises me. Come to Maadi, Road 9, and we can meet in Café Grecco." Ben gave Sam his mobile number and then hurried off with Gerhard to locate Ellie in the mammoth halls of the Egyptian Museum.

Ellie collapsed against a column in one of the many unvisited back halls displaying fragments of pharaonic pottery.

She'd always preferred visiting the intimate everyday items that reflected the intricacy of ancient Egyptian society. The big-ticket items like Tutankhamun's treasures and the ancient royal mummies captured the tourists' attention, but few, if any, visited the back halls, so Ellie was confident she wouldn't be disturbed.

The shock of seeing Sam out of the blue had rocked her to her core and opened old wounds she'd worked so hard to heal. Without her protective barriers up, it was as if everything had happened only yesterday, and the anguish for her lost life in Egypt was agonising. She wrapped her arms around herself, hugging them close to her, and rocked, trying to ease the familiar tightness in her chest.

How she longed to run back to the familiar security of Scarab's Rest, where she was immune to all this. Where she'd successfully created a new Ellie, one who navigated her way through life with only minor pangs of anguish. But until she could free herself from this bizarre situation, she was stuck here.

Her mobile rang, but she ignored it, knowing she wasn't ready to face Ben or Gerhard yet. The time it would take them to find her would give her the opportunity to re-erect the emotional barriers she needed to protect herself.

"Jeez, this museum is hotter than Hades now," Ben said, rubbing his forehead with his sleeve. "We've been searching for over forty-five minutes."

"A person isn't lost when they don't want to be found, my friend. They are merely absent. We'll find her when she's ready to be found."

Ellie watched Ben and Gerhard enter her hiding hole.

She smiled at them. "Ah, there you are! I was wondering where you'd gotten to. Have you been exploring the museum?"

Gerhard smiled, his eyes creasing as he enthused about the ancient relics he'd seen. *"Mein liebling,* I wish you could have heard Ben. He brought everything to life. Some everyday little pot seems so much more when you understand its place in the temple routines of pharaonic Egypt. There was one cup, so ordinary, yet inscribed with the name of Haremakhet, one of the high priests - fascinating."

Ellie tucked her arm into Gerhard's. "Tell me more on the way home..."

OLD FRIENDS

It hadn't been easy slipping away. Ellie bounced around the house behind a thick screen of false exuberance and seemed determined to incorporate her two companions into her simulated gaiety.

Ben pleaded exhaustion and retired to his room, planning to clamber down the overgrown bougainvillea vine to meet with Sam. He soon realised his folly when the bougainvillea bit back, embedding his arms and thighs with vicious thorns. He cursed as he let go, dropping seven feet to the ground. He dabbed ineffectually at the oozing wounds and muttered, "I look like a bloody escaped convict." He scrubbed his hands against his jeans in disgust and set off for his rendezvous.

He'd agreed to meet Sam in Café Grecco as it was the only place he knew in Maadi. It had been a tranquil haven from the chaos of Cairo, when he'd had coffee there with Ellie and Gerhard in the day. By night, the café was a heaving mass of Maadi intelligentsia, all shouting over each other and competing with the deep rumble of the metro line that ran behind it.

Ben squeezed between expat mums and young, trendy Cairenes to see if Sam had arrived or if there was a spare table available. Weaving between the tables, he spotted Sam checking his watch at a small table in the corner.

"Hey, bud. How's it hanging?" Sam said as he jumped up to hug Ben and deposit the inevitable kisses on each cheek that open all Egyptian greetings. "Whoa! What happened to you, my friend? Have you lost a fight with a rose bush?"

"Nope, a bougainvillea. Who knew they had thorns the size of small daggers?"

"Not you, clearly," Sam replied. "What on God's good earth were you doing embracing a bougainvillea? You've got cuts everywhere."

"It's all your fault, making me sneak out. I had to climb out my bedroom window, hence my present condition," he said with a glide of his hand down his body.

Sam smirked at him. "I don't recall asking you to sneak anywhere. I merely asked an old friend to meet me for coffee. I deny culpability. If you don't have sufficient apparatus to tell Elena you are meeting me, I suggest you get testosterone supplements."

"Seriously, bud, she's one fearsome woman. I was protecting my balls by not telling her I was meeting you. You are her *numero uno persona non grata*."

Sam flopped back into his chair, deflated. Pushing aside an errant buggy, Ben pulled out a chair and sat.

"Seriously, Sam, a little warning would've been nice. I went in blind. She almost turfed me off the course. What the hell happened between the two of you? The last time we spoke, you were all loved up and planning a family. Then I hear on the grapevine you've gone your separate ways. When I asked you for help to find a language teacher,

I didn't expect you to fail to mention the school's run by your ex-wife. Jeez, bud, talk about setting a guy up to fail."

Sam raised his eyes and studied Ben.

"It's not as if you've ever had problems picking up girls, Sam. You're a goddamn Adonis. In college, we had to beat them away from you. Why did you choose her? Why Ellie? She's cold, humourless, and pricklier than a bougainvillea. And boy, are they prickly."

The waiter interrupted them to take their order.

Sam studied his hands, appearing fascinated by the lines and grooves. With a sigh, he wrapped his hands around the chunky white heat of the mug and looked back up at Ben. With his eyes unshielded for the first time, Ben saw how wounded his friend was. The shine of charisma was gone. The laughter that had always lit his eyes, the macho bravado – all of it gone. He was less of the man that Ben knew, less of the Egyptian male, less of a human. It was as if the divorce had carved a chunk out of him, leaving him less Sam.

"I can't answer you. That's a huge part of the problem. I have no answers. We were so happy, so in love. She made life better, truer, brighter. We did everything together – personally and professionally. Then, one day, she'd gone. No letter. No explanation. Just gone. I tried to track her down but got nothing. I talked to everyone, but no one could tell me where she was or why she'd gone. She vanished. I was fraught - I searched everywhere. Left my work. Sold everything to track her down. Then, from left field, I'm sent a divorce petition citing my infidelity and abandonment. Can you believe I was happy to get it? At least I knew she was alive. I fought the divorce, stating my total innocence."

He paused, gazing into the distance, staring at his memories.

"That's when I got the letter. Each character tattooed upon my heart. In the coldest tone imaginable, she told me she didn't love me, realised the huge error of our marriage, and that she could never respect, let alone love a corrupted soul such as myself. She demanded an immediate divorce and rejected any potential fiscal settlement, stating the only thing she wanted from me was a divorce. I worshipped her, *habibi*. She was everything, and if that was the last thing I could do to make her happy, I was willing to do it. Even if it cost me my happiness. To this day, I don't understand what happened."

Ben sipped his coffee, saddened by the torrent of hurt he felt pouring from his friend.

"God, Sam, I had no idea. I'm so sorry. But to be honest, the Elena you love doesn't exist anymore. Maybe she had a nervous breakdown or something, but the Ellie I know bears no resemblance to the girl you've always told me about. She's tough, hard, remorseless, and angry."

His mind flicked back to the glimpses he'd seen of Ellie when she's wasn't aware she was being studied. It was possible Elena was in there somewhere but buried so deeply that it was better to say nothing to Sam.

"What did you hope to gain from us meeting tonight? I'm telling you bluntly there is no way in hell Ellie will ever listen about you. God, the woman hates me nearly as much as you. Sorry, bud. It's hard to hear, I know, but it's true."

"I need closure. I need to understand. It's driving me insane, Ben, and I mean literally driving me insane. Voices talk to me about her. I feel the urge to protect her, even though until now, she's been thousands of miles away. Please, Ben, try to get her to see me, to explain. I'm begging you. I'll leave her in peace. I just need to understand."

Ben glanced across the room at the cheerful young

mums chatting whilst their children wreaked havoc in the café, at the young students laughing at some shared joke, and then back at his old friend whom he'd shared so many carefree moments with. Seeing the empty, broken shell of the shining man he'd once been staring back at him broke his heart. The force of nature that had been Sam tamed and shredded on the flinty, tough surface that coated Ellie. He deserved his answers.

"Okay," he murmured.

PART TWO
GERHARD'S QUEST

THE SERAPEUM

"I still don't understand why we had to meet at such a god-awful time. Who in their right mind gets up at this hour?" Ben said.

"It makes sense to look around before the public is here. We don't want to attract unwanted attention," Gerhard murmured.

Ellie stared out at the passing countryside. The lush green fields were crisscrossed with irrigation canals, the trees dashed with thousands of roosting white egrets, endemic in the agricultural lands skirting the Nile. Today, she grasped her first glow of hope that they may crack this conundrum yet.

The land changed as they neared the Saqqara plateau, desert sands replacing the grasslands and crops. The abrupt change from fertile land to desert never failed to astound Ellie; she could have one foot in rich soil and the other in sand.

Passing through the entrance gate with a salute from the guard, they drove deeper into rolling hills of sand. They passed scattered relics of the pharaohs, crumbling pyramids, solitary columns, and half-standing temple walls. They stopped by a little hut. A sun-dried, wizened old man emerged from a pile of grubby blankets, rubbing the sleep from his eyes, and slipped his feet into tattered flip-flops.

"I've arranged for you to see the Serapeum while I go back and get Professor Mourad. Allah only knows where his driver has disappeared to, today of all days. I will leave you here with Rashid. We should be back in an hour. Rashid can answer all your questions until we return. He can be an old busy-body though, so dismiss him if you want to explore on your own." With that, Walid, Professor Mourad's assistant, scuttled back to the car and drove off in a curtain of whirling sand.

They walked down the gently sloping hill carved into sand dunes that swallowed them. At the bottom of the slope was a huge oak door, pitted by eons of sandstorms, protecting the entrance to the vaulted Serapeum. Their weary guide pulled out a massive ring of keys and flipped through them, searching for the one that matched the door. With a great deal of huffing and puffing, he located it and eased the door open. It revealed a black hole not a single ray of light penetrated beyond the first few yards. A musty smell of antiquity lapped around them, enticing them to explore further.

The guide fumbled around, searching for the lights, muttering, *"Yanhar esswed,"* under his breath.

Ellie laughed. *"Shokran ya basha - khalas delwaati.* Thank you, sir. Please do not let us disturb your rest any further," she said firmly, grasping his arm and propelling him back towards the hut. Perturbed to be frog-marched away from his post by a woman, Rashid pulled his arm free, adjusted his turban, and ambled back to the welcoming embrace of his rumpled bedding.

Ellie found the switch, and the lights flickered on one by one, illuminating the vaulted interior with a soft golden glow. It transformed the black hole into a cavernous space leading off to both the left and right.

"Wow, this place has changed since I was last here. There's a fine line between restoration and reconstruction, and I'm uncertain what side of the line this falls on. I'd heard the Italians had funded the restoration, but I didn't realise it was this extensive," Ellie said.

Huge metal girders, painted to blend in with the golden stone, had been carefully embedded into the sandstone to support the giant vaults. A raised wooden floor led off into the distance, peppered with little glass peepholes that gave tantalising glimpses of the original ancient paving. Subtle floor-mounted lamps threw cones of warm light up the walls and across the soft curves of the ceiling.

To the right was a small anteroom peppered with alcoves for statues of or bequests to the gods. To the left, a small corridor led into a vast complex of arched anterooms running the length of the long sandstone corridor. Each vaulted anteroom held gargantuan sarcophagi, many propped open, thirty tons of rose granite supported by stubby wood posts that separated the lids from the bodies of the tombs. Once home to the mummified remains of at least sixty-seven sacred Apis bulls, each having represented the incarnation of Ptah on Earth during its life-time, the Serapeum resonated with an eerie majesty.

Gerhard strolled closer to one of the sarcophagi, studying the detailed hieroglyphics etched inside the thick granite sides. "They're vast. Must have been difficult to build, Ellie."

"As a little girl, I believed only magic could have transported such huge lumps of granite eight hundred kilometres from the quarry and deep into this complex. It was different here then; it had a gentile decrepitude, a magic. It's a little over-polished now."

"Ah, sadly, my dear, with age, things often lack the romance that the lens of youth provides. To me, this has a magical allure. Remind me again why we've chosen this fine venue as our starting point."

"Major Gayer-Anderson purchased the statue from a local grave robber, who was sparing in his use of the truth. He consistently admitted he found it on the Saqqara plateau but not exactly where. They dated the statue to the Late Period, sometime after 600 BC. Only two places on the plateau were active in that period: the Serapeum and the Abwab el-qotat. Either could be the home of the cat. We started here as Uncle wants to show off the restoration. Plus, he knows it's one of my favourite places. He's a sentimental man."

"Well, then, *mein schatz*, I suggest we are prudent with our time and see if we can find any clues to our predicament in this impressive catacomb."

"Find anything?" Ben asked as the three regrouped.

"Dust, sarcophagi, and plenty of empty alcoves that could have housed the cat or any other offering to the gods," Ellie replied.

"Well, I haven't sensed a thing here. My familiar's gone into hibernation," Ben said. "Gerhard, care to shoot the breeze?"

Tilting his head to the side, Gerhard raised his finely arched ivory eyebrow. "I am not familiar with the idiom, but I, too, sense nothing. There's no evidence linking this Serapeum with the goddess Bastet. Maybe it's time to move on to our next port of call."

BREATHLESS

A deep boom echoed through the chamber. Air sucked at them as if something had triggered a vacuum. Ben sprinted towards the exit only to find it blocked by the solid, thick wooden door. Ben grabbed the large, iron ring handle and tried to open it. He moved the handle back and forth, trying to release the lock mechanism.

"It's jammed somehow. The handle is moving, but the door won't open."

"The wind must have blown it shut. You can get surprisingly ferocious gusts out on these plains. Let's call Rashid," Ellie suggested.

"Shh... hang on a moment, Ells. I saw a shadow cross the daylight around the frame." A ripping sound was followed by a darkening of the frame, as if something had partially blocked the sun around the top of the eight-foot-high door. They shouted for Rashid. The door frame darkened in one-meter strips.

"What's happening? What are you doing? Let us out at once."

"Rashid, in God's name, let us out!"

Mumbled comments outside the door came from more than one person as the final strip of light was snuffed out around the frame. A loud rumble accelerated towards the door, getting faster and louder until it crashed with a huge metallic ring against the door. They leapt back. One crash followed another, booming against the wood and each other, creating the resonance of a massed kettle band playing an homage to the end of times.

Ellie fumbled in her bag and pulled out her mobile. With shaking fingers, she opened Mourad's contact and hit the call button. With the phone to her ear, she mumbled, "Come on, Mourad - answer. Come on." Silence. No ringing tone, nothing. She stared at the screen, dumbstruck, and turned back to the guys, "Oh, my God, it's happening again... there's no signal. Check your phones."

Gerhard pulled his phone from the internal pocket of his tweed jacket and shook his head glumly.

Ben's head shot up as he sniffed the air, "Guys, we have a more immediate issue than nonperforming cell phones. Can you smell that? Gas is seeping into the chamber."

"I don't smell anything," Gerhard replied.

"I do. It smells like strong bleach," Ellie answered.

"Ammonia - I can smell it now. Where is it coming from, Ben?"

Ben knelt down and sniffed under the door. Shaking his head and dusting off his knees, he sniffed the air and moved into the side chamber. "It's much stronger here. I'd guess it's coming in through the air ducts or the climate control system."

"Shit! Ben, it's pumping in under the door now," Ellie shouted.

"Is there any other way out, Ellie? A rear exit or a

hatch?" Gerhard asked whilst shucking his jacket, which he rolled up and wedged against the bottom of the door.

"No, the door's the only way in or out of the chamber. There are small ventilation shafts but not large enough for use. I've explored every square inch as a kid - there's no other way out. Anyone have any idea how toxic ammonia is?"

"Well, I don't think they've gone to so much trouble just to give us the impression of a well-cleaned tomb, do you? It's not like the cleaner thought, '*I'm not in the mood to work today. I know! I'll dupe the boss by pumping bleach fumes into the tomb*'. I'd hazard a guess it's pretty bloody toxic," Ben snapped back.

Ellie scowled at Ben and went to Gerhard's side. "Any ideas, Gerhard?"

He pulled a red spotted handkerchief from his waist-coat pocket and dabbed at his red-rimmed eyes. "None to speak of, my dear one. We need an airtight vessel to avoid these damnable gasses. How airtight would these sarcophagi be?"

They ran down one of the side wings to a large row of sarcophagi. One had an intact lid resting on four wooden posts. The gap between the lid and the sarcophagus was just large enough to allow a body through – a careful body. Both the top of the walls and the bottom of the lid appeared finely finished and as smooth as polished glass.

Ben jumped three feet down into the antechamber in which it rested. The granite behemoth was taller than him. He circled it, inspecting for holes, cracks, or imperfections that could let the insidious gas seep in to them.

"Guys, the air's much clearer down here. It seems the Ammonia is denser up higher. This big fella appears intact and as good a choice as we've got. We'd just need to get inside and then kick those lid supports out. But if we do that, how the hell will we get out again? And who's saying we won't come face-to-face with the gas men if, by some miracle, we're able to get the lid off and escape?"

Gerhard's rake-thin body was racked with deep coughs, and his eyes streamed torrents. He asked for a helping hand and lowered himself down into the antechamber. He didn't answer at once, his hands on his knees, bent as he waited to recover his breath from the coughing fit.

"I'm afraid, my dear boy, we don't have too many other options. Our little guides protected us in Black Cat Books. I see we have little choice other than to trust them with our welfare again."

Ellie clambered down. Her eyes looked like a red eyeliner had vigorously attacked them. "Come on, then. Decision made. Let's jump to it," she agreed.

Ben crouched down, linking his hands to create a step for Gerhard to use to ease himself up the side of the coffin. He grabbed the top edge and wriggled his way cautiously beneath several tonnes of granite lid.

Ellie chewed her lip. "Gerhard, be careful not to hit the wooden posts," she urged.

"Don't worry, *liebling*. I'm good."

"You next, Ells."

"No, hang on a moment. How are you going to get in?" Ellie asked.

Ben studied the area and pointed at a pile of rubble. "I'll go get one of those rocks and use it to climb inside."

"It makes more sense for you to go next, rest on the rim, and reach down and pull me up. You're stronger."

Ben weighed the options and gestured for Ellie to help him with the rocks. Together, they shunted a huge lump of sandstone to rest at the side of the coffin.

Ben clambered up the rock. "Okay, Ellie, give me a bunk up then."

With a grunt, Ellie helped push him onto the sarcophagus. Ben wriggled around, balancing his body on its pivot point and reached down to haul Ellie up. She eased between the gap and dropped inside, landing lightly.

"Guys, take your belts off and pass them to me," Ben said as he wriggled free of his own. "I'll loop them around the support posts, and we'll use them to pull the struts away and drop the lid down into its resting place." After sliding and wriggling along the rim, securing the belts to the struts, he slipped down to join the other two. Pointing at the front left-hand strut, he said, "I'll pull this one first, so we can retrieve the belt and fasten it to the fourth post over there. We must pull the others simultaneously, so the lid lands true."

Coughing slightly, Ellie turned to Gerhard, whose face was in the partial shade. "Ready, Herr Webber?"

He smiled at her and saluted. "Ready as I can be, my dear."

She rushed to his side and gave him a quick kiss on his cheek. Surprised by the unusually affectionate gesture, Gerhard drew her towards him and patted her cheek.

"Together, we will survive, *mein liebling*, for together, we are stronger than our separate parts." He turned to Ben. "Let's do it now, Ben, before the air in here becomes more polluted."

Ben wrapped the belt straps for the first post around his hands and, using his feet as leverage against the walls, pulled with all his might. The post slid across the rim with almost zero resistance and crashed into the sarcophagus. Ben tumbled down onto his rear end with a thud.

Patting the dust off, he said, "I didn't expect that. I

thought I'd need to give it a strong tug. Those surfaces must be super slick." He bent to retrieve the belt. "Righto, Ells, you climb up onto my shoulders and secure the belt onto the last post."

With all the belts secured, they each chose a strut and grabbed the belts. Ben wished them luck and counted them down. "Three, two, one, pull!"

All three fell as the lid slammed down into place and the posts flew down on them. The darkness was absolute, and the boom had deafened them.

"Well, that was spectacular," Ben quipped. "I think it's fair to say the lid is now well and truly closed."

Ellie groaned. "I'm frightened to move in case it slides down onto us," she whispered. "Gerhard, are you okay?"

Silence.

"Gerhard, can you answer me?"

Ellie turned onto her hands and knees, feeling around in the darkness. She moved, easing herself towards Gerhard's corner, calling for him. Her hand patted fabric, sliding up what she realised was a leg. A stationary leg. She eased up the body, shaking slightly as she moved.

"Ben, come over to Gerhard, and for God's sake, turn on your mobile's light."

Ben scurried over, blinding Ellie as he switched it on directly into her eyes. He gasped as the light illuminated their friend.

Gerhard lay sprawled across the bottom of the tomb, one leg stuck out to one side crookedly and one arm under his body. Around his head, the dust had darkened in a spreading pool of blood, which oozed from a jagged cut on his forehead.

"Jeez, Gerhard, can you hear me? If so, answer me, buddy, or squeeze Ellie's hand."

No response. He neither moved nor appeared conscious.

Ellie put her head to his chest and her hand to his mouth. "He's breathing, and his heart sounds normal."

Ben eased Gerhard onto his side and rolled his own jacket up as a pillow, sliding it with care under his head. "We need to stop the bleeding. Head wounds can bleed profusely. Tear off a strip of your shirt, Ellie."

Ellie threw her backpack from her shoulders and rummaged inside, bringing out a small first aid box. "No need. I have bandages and plasters in here."

"Only you, Ells! Well, thank God for your control-freak tendencies," Ben said with a shake of his head.

Ellie ignored him, pulling out antiseptic wipes, cream, and bandages. She turned her full attention to Gerhard, dusting away a smudge of dirt with care from his angled cheekbone. As she worked, she kept up a full, gentle commentary, telling Gerhard everything she was doing and apologising repeatedly in case she was hurting him.

As she cleaned the wound, it was clear the cut was deep. "This needs stitches, Ben. I'm not certain these sticky plasters will hold."

Ben glanced down and nodded. "Do your best, Ellie. We're low on options. To be honest, I'm more worried about his colour. He's deadly pale."

As their ears adjusted to the pressure, they heard the rattle of Gerhard's breaths slowing. Each breath had a large gap between it and the next. Every rise of his chest became more laboured.

Ben pulled Gerhard's shirt to one side and pressed his ear to his chest. "Gerhard, man, stay with us. Fight, damn it. Don't let these bastards win. Come *on*."

They heard a gentle rasp of breath. His chest rose no more.

"NO!" Ellie screamed. "No, Gerhard, no!"

Ben leapt onto him, turned him onto his back, adjusted his head, and gave Gerhard mouth-to-mouth. "Ellie, sing 'Staying Alive' by the Bee Gees. Don't argue; just do it. Now lock your fingers together, knuckles up, and press down, hard and fast, in time to the beat of the song. GO!"

Ellie's anguish paralysed her as silent tears washed her cheeks.

"Ellie, NOW, for God's sake!"

She hummed the tune and did as Ben asked. He adjusted her hand placement and then she pumped down two inches into Gerhard's chest rhythmically in time to the music. They worked, stopping to check for a pulse or breath, and continued again when finding neither.

"Gerhard, buddy. Come on, FIGHT! God damn it to hell. Fight!" Ben screamed in frustration. Ellie worked like an automation, tears pouring, whilst singing the seventies disco classic.

After ten minutes, Ben reached across and stilled Ellie's hands. She glanced up, waiting for him to check for a pulse. "Ellie, sweetheart, he's gone. We've lost him."

She looked up at him, grabbed his shirt, and shook him. "No, we don't give up, not while he's got a chance. Come on..." She went back to giving heart compressions. "Ben, we're his only chance. Keep him breathing."

Ben circled Gerhard's body and pulled Ellie away. She turned on him, kicking and throwing punches. He grabbed her from behind, hauled her to the farthest corner of the tomb, and pulled her down into his lap.

"Ells, I'd do anything to keep him alive, but he's gone.

We did our best, but the force of the post hitting him was too much for his body to absorb."

Keening wails rose from Ellie as shudders racked her body. "No, Gerhard, no!"

Ben just pulled her closer and pressed kisses down onto the top of her hair. They sat with just the noise of Ellie's tears for a long time until her grief quietened down into little hiccupped sobs. Ben rocked them, lost in his own thoughts.

The yellow glow of the mobile faded, eventually tipping them into a deep, velvet black that knew no grey. It muffled their ears as much as it deprived their eyes. Ellie huddled in closer to Ben, burying her face into the arch of his neck.

"Ellie, we still have to face this situation. Okay, we're in here, safe from the gas, but at some point, the people who did this will come and check their handiwork, and we can't be here then." He shuffled a little to find a more comfortable spot. "We need to honour Gerhard by getting to the bottom of this and surviving."

Ellie pulled away as if to study his face. "We need answers and vengeance. I will not lose another person I care for while chasing ghosts and stupid mythological gods for Lord knows what reason. We'll take revenge for Gerhard and for Stefan. I won't stop until I do."

"Well, let's get out of here first - shall we?"

Ben looked down. He'd been worried that Ellie would break under the stress of the situation, but this deep, simmering pit of pure rage was worse.

"Time for everything else later." He pulled her to her feet and pressed a kiss down on her forehead. "Let's summon these stupid mythological gods and see if they can't help us out of here."

THE ESCAPE

Ben paced at the far end of the sarcophagus, thinking as he walked and turned. He returned to Ellie, pulling her down to sit on the floor of the coffin. He positioned them until they sat crossed-legged, knee-to-knee, hand-to-hand.

"Focus on your familiar, Ellie, like we did in Black Cat Books." He rubbed his fingers across the fleshy part of her palm at the base of her thumb. "Close your eyes. Try to clear your head and focus on Khepri."

After several minutes of calling Khepri's name in her head, Ellie gave up in disgust. "It's not working." Ellie reached across the sandy, cold granite base of the tomb, through the darkness, searching for Ben's hand. "I can't feel the scarab. It glimmers in the distance of my mind and then fractures into tiny shimmers and dissipates."

Ben rubbed her hand. "I know. It's the same for me - as if something's missing."

Ben linked his fingers and reached his arms up into the air, pulling up to release every vertebra. As he eased out of the stretch, he opened his eyes and stared over Ellie's shoulder, towards the other end of the tomb. He let out a gasp, leapt to his feet, and rushed towards Gerhard's body. In the darkness, he forgot Ellie was in his path and tripped over her, landing in a jumble of arms and legs.

"Ouch! Bloody hell, Ben! That hurt." Ellie rubbed her elbow, which had been the recipient of a rather hard blow when Ben landed on her.

Ben extricated himself from the pile of limbs, hitting Ellie in the side as he did so.

"In the name of all that is merciful, will you be careful, you lumbering ape?" Ellie slid away from him, turning onto her stomach to rise onto her hands and knees. "Ye Gods! Ben, look at Gerhard."

Ben eased his way to his feet. "Um, yeah! Why do you think I ran towards him?"

"I have learnt not to question your motives as they are rarely based on logic or reason." Ellie dusted herself down and moved towards Gerhard's body.

He was as they had left him. On the cold stone floor. Still. Silent. Dead. Yet, his skin had an otherworldly glow, a blue translucency that bore no place on any human on Earth. It was so slight that the duo might have missed it except for the beacon of blue light focused around his head wound. As they moved closer, they saw the light was focused, like a spotlight, on Gerhard's wound. As they watched, the wound sealed, millimetre by millimetre. The skin closed, scabbed, and then healed, leaving fresh, clean skin - free of any scarring.

Ellie peered across at Ben, who was illuminated by the eerie blue glow. He was staring at the proceedings, mouth agape. He lifted his eyes, eyebrows raised. He reached for her hand, squeezing it. Neither uttered a word as the light completed its work on Gerhard's head wound.

The concentration of light moved down Gerhard's head until it focused on his mouth. As it stopped there, his mouth opened and Sobek emerged, smaller than a penny coin. He moved to Gerhard's chin and made a tiny gesture, almost like a bow. From there, he moved across Gerhard, towards Ben, growing as he moved, until he finally came to rest at Ben's feet. He was the size of a small iguana when he bumped his head against Ben's leg and lay down for a snooze. Ben leaned down and gave him a scratch under the chin.

Ellie nudged Ben, who looked away from Sobek and saw Khepri making his way in little scurries up Gerhard's body. As he entered Gerhard's mouth, Ben turned away, squirming. Ellie gave him a sharp crack in the ribs with her elbow, and he looked back to see the blue glow again shoot across Gerhard's skin as Khepri made his procession inwards. The spotlight flowed down his body until it settled on his chest.

Ellie leaned into Ben and whispered, "Are they hurting him? Should we do something?"

Ben turned to her and raised an eyebrow, "Well, a nasty, great beetle just entered our dead friend's mouth and worked its way down to his heart. That doesn't sound great, does it? But wait, he's DEAD. So, it's pretty unlikely they can do anything that puts him in a greater predicament than he's in at the moment."

She moved away and then swung her hip at him. "There's no need for sarcasm, Ben. It was an honest question!"

"Sorry, Ellie. That was unnecessary." He rubbed his eyes. "This whole situation is bizarre and, if I'm honest, more than a little frightening, but that doesn't make it okay to take it out on you." He reached for her shoulders and turned her towards him. "We're in this together. Come what may. It seems our little buddies are trying to help Gerhard, so we should leave them to continue their work. They can't make him worse after all, can they?"

She nodded as she slipped her hand into Ben's and watched Khepri toil.

The light continued to beam in blue rays from Gerhard's chest for a while before it pulsed, at first imperceptible and intermittently but gradually becoming clearer and stronger. The light's intensity grew until a pulse of light flowed lightning-fast across Gerhard's entire body, from the farthest tip of his snowy white hair down to his toes. It was so bright, it burnt itself onto Ellie and Ben's retinas.

Darkness followed, so shocking for its depth and utter blinkering effect.

Ellie fumbled around, searching for her rucksack, which she'd abandoned in the shock of Gerhard's death. When she found it, she delved inside, muttering to herself until her fingers touched the cold, cylindrical metal case of her torch. She pulled it free and turned back towards Gerhard just as Khepri emerged from his mouth and flew to her shoulder. She froze for a second, then turned the torch on and focused its beam upon Gerhard's lanky frame.

A shimmer of pale blue light floated above the body, sweeping down in a caressing touch as it swirled gently around him. Ellie knelt down and peered at Gerhard's face. "Ben, come see. His face seems different."

Ben joined her and leaned over Gerhard, and as he watched, he saw a deep crease around Gerhard's eye puff up and smooth out. This process repeated across the plains and valleys of Gerhard's features, tautening and resurfacing as it progressed. Ellie grabbed one of Gerhard's hands and saw an age spot fade and disappear before her eyes. His fingers plumped up and straightened. Ben leaned even closer, hovering just inches over Gerhard's face.

An eye opened, blazing in its azure intensity. "Are you planning on kissing me, my dear boy?"

Ben and Ellie scrambled backwards until their backs hit the wall of the tomb.

Gerhard sat up. "Oof, I feel like I've been cranked through a mangle." He looked across at the other two, his eyes blazing blue. "What's the matter? Cat got your tongue?"

Ellie leaned forward, shuffling towards him. "Gerhard, it can't be. You're dead..."

Stretching his head from side to side, he replied, "Well, that would explain the aches and pains away! Although, I didn't envisage heaven like this." He grimaced as his hand came away from his head covered in congealed blood. "Did you hit your head as well, my dear?"

Ben shook himself out of his stupor and rushed to Gerhard's side. "No, don't get up yet. How are you? Try moving your legs."

Gerhard's eyes flicked back and forth between them as he stretched out each of his lengthy limbs. "Well, all seems well except a rather horrendous headache. We need to stop worrying about me and focus on our predicament. Shouldn't we try to escape this cavernous burial chamber?"

Ben reached for Gerhard's hands and peered straight into his eerie eyes. "Ellie wasn't confused, Gerhard. I don't know how to sugarcoat this, so here goes. You died. In our arms, as a matter of fact, and you remained so for over forty minutes. We tried to resuscitate you but failed. So, imagine our surprise right now."

Gerhard turned to Ellie, who gave him a gentle smile and nodded.

"So, how am I lucky enough to be alive and well?"

Ben gestured towards the scarab still perched on Ellie's shoulder and the snoozing crocodile at his feet. "You owe it to our friends, Khepri and Sobek, who somehow healed you. Prepare yourself for one more shock..."

Gerhard tilted his head quizzically. "A greater shock than being resurrected from the dead?"

Ben coughed and adjusted his collar. "Well, yes, possibly. They didn't just resurrect you. They've shaved a few years off at the same time."

Gerhard's eyes widened. "Did you say I appear younger?"

Ellie moved over, sat next to Gerhard, and put her arms around him. "Gerhard, you look around fifty years old now, and your eyes have changed colour. They are now a shockingly intense shade of blue."

"I see, *ja*. This is all a little overwhelming." He rubbed his nose and looked down in quiet contemplation. "*Ja*, well, it is what it is. It will take some absorbing and consideration, but the fact remains we are still in a perilous situation, so for now... how do you say? Ah, yes. We should sidebar this and focus on getting out of here."

Ellie glanced sideways at Khepri, who had remained pinned to her shoulder like an old-fashioned brooch. "I don't suppose you have any ideas tucked under your wings?" The scarab rotated, shaking its elytra and creating a gentle hum. All three of them burst out laughing.

"It seems our little buddy, Khepri, has a sense of humour," Ben chuckled. Gerhard got to his feet with a little help from Ben and Ellie, who tucked her arm around him to offer a support. The only light now available in the sarcophagus was the beam of the torch that lay discarded on the floor and the soft blue glow of Gerhard's eyes and Khepri.

Ben squatted down to retrieve Ellie's torch and shone it around the tomb. "Any ideas, anyone?"

Gerhard saw his discarded backpack, dusty and blood-stained but still in one piece. "Ben, it's time to share our misadventure with Ellie. The statue has an undeniable pull for me. I believe it to be fundamental to our current quest."

"Guys, what misadventure?" Ben's faced tightened, and he turned to get Gerhard's bag. "Ben! I asked a question. What misadventure?"

"Well, less of a misadventure. More of a friendly borrow. Misadventure is so overstating it." Ben flared his eyes at Gerhard.

"Oops! Yes, sorry. My English can be so faltering sometimes."

"Dish the dirt now, or so help me, God..." The scarab jiggled again. "Not you, Khepri. Another God."

"Now, Ellie, don't have a conniption. We know, techni-cally, it was wrong, but as we fully intend to return it, then no harm done. And anyway, no one even realises it's missing - so no bad. What's one statue between friends, anyway?"

Ellie backed Ben against the wall, thrusting her finger into his chest as they moved. "Are you telling me you have what I think you have? Because if that statue you brought with us from the UK is not the replica you purchased but rather the priceless, original Gayer-Anderson cat taken from my godfather's collection, well, I won't be held accountable for my actions." She turned on Gerhard. "And you, the sensible, rational Gerhard, sanctioned this theft. That's what it is, you know. Grand larceny. You've stolen from my nation. You've put Bertram's position in jeopardy, which he has dedicated his every waking minute to build. I'm with thieves. Common thieves. So, what do you have to say for yourselves?"

Ben looked pleadingly at Gerhard.

"*Liebling*, that sounds so bad, but we had our reasons. I believed the statue to be a critical key to unlocking this mystery. I forced my will on Ben after much persuasion. He didn't have any choice other than to satisfy an old man's whims."

"No, nope. Don't think I'm going to fall for your elderly gentleman routine. I bet you took all of ten seconds to get Ben on your side, if even it was your idea. You should have asked me."

"You would have said no."

"Yes, I would. Because it's wrong on every level."

"Be that as may, we have the statue here, and I need to see it. It has an overwhelming draw, and that must mean something. We have little else to make sense of here, do we?"

Ben passed the pack to Gerhard, who opened it with shaking hands and pulled the statue free. Gerhard nearly dropped it in his haste to free it from its protective wrappings. As his fingers touched the green patina of the statue, he let out a large, almost purr-like sigh. The blue glow from his eyes brightened and flowed down his face, across his chest, and down his arms until it radiated all around the statue, returning his eyes to their natural green.

The statue shimmered and then stretched in his hands. It jumped free and landed with a soft thud on the granite floor. It bowed down, stretching through its back with its rear projected up towards the tomb lid. As it limbered up, it peered around, seeming to familiarise itself with the location before sitting down to give its paws a thorough washing.

Khepri lifted off Ellie's shoulder with a whir of his wings, circling her head before settling itself down next to the statue. They were both joined by Sobek, who lumbered across from Ben and slumped down to the left of Khepri. The three familiars turned to each other, forming a circle, and appeared to be communicating with each other as blue flashes and wisps flew from one to the other.

The statue remained aloof except for its tail, which whipped from side to side as it appeared to listen to the other two entities. Khepri lifted into the air and dive-bombed Sobek, who lashed out with his tail to send Khepri whirling through the air into the side of the sarcophagus. Khepri buzzed threateningly and flew at Sobek.

"Oops, someone's getting a little hot under his collar," Ben murmured from the side of his mouth. Bastet turned to him, raised her eye, and then sprang between the feuding familiars. Landing with a graceful swing of her tail, she put a paw on each of her allies and shook her head. They turned their backs on each other and quieted.

The cat coughed and spat out a large, blue fur ball, except this was lit from within and each of the filaments of "fur" were individual lights that swirled within the ball. The cat turned to Ben, Ellie, and Gerhard and gestured towards the sphere. As they watched, it expanded until it filled half the space of the tomb. A large gateway appeared, opening into a black, gaping abyss. The cat, scarab, and crocodile formed an orderly line and entered the sphere, pausing only to gaze back at the trio.

Gerhard patted Ben on the shoulder. "They want us to follow them. Realistically, they are our only hope of escape, so we should do as they want. They are the only things around here not trying to kill us, and that speaks volumes towards their intentions."

He offered his hand to Ellie, who nodded in return and stepped towards the gate. The air shimmered as they crossed the gateway into the sphere and settled back into a semi-opaque blue barrier behind them. Within the sphere, there was only the reflected light from its walls, which cast deep shadows across the faces of the trio. The familiars radiated their own subtle glow as always.

"Now what?" Ben asked.

"I suggest we settle down and watch. It strikes me we are mere passengers in this vessel. I'm confident that Bastet is a steady hand at the helm."

"Gerhard, you are asking us to put our lives in the hands of miniature god-lets from another belief system that have been pulling our reins, whether we wanted them to or not, since this entire mess started. Where in your logical mind does that sound like a good idea, for Pete's sake?"

Gerhard reached into his waistcoat pocket and took out his glasses cloth. He eased his glasses down his nose and removed them, enfolding the lenses within the cloth and polishing both sides with small, precise movements. "My dear boy, where does any of this fit into a logical algorithm? There is no logical explanation. Where logic doesn't exist, chaos rules, and the first rule of chaos is to find a pattern. The only consistent pattern we have is the involvement of these little creatures and ourselves. I think we should follow that to the end to find the answers we seek." He returned the glasses to his nose and folded the cloth into a uniform square, which he returned to his waistcoat. "Since my little foray with death, I find I am more strongly linked to Bastet than I was. I can't say we are communicating exactly, but I understand her intent, and I trust it."

Ellie jumped in before Ben could answer. "I'm with Gerhard on this. Without the familiars, Gerhard would be dead. He would be a cold corpse laid out on the floor. They have saved our lives on more than one occasion now. We need to trust them."

Ben looked from one to the other and raised his hands, palms up, to shoulder height. "Okay, but we need to remember we don't understand their motives for helping us. That's all I'm saying."

As the trio debated, Bastet had sat grooming, keeping an eye on the proceedings. Now she rose onto all four paws and stalked around the sphere. Khepri and Sobek joined her, distributing themselves equally around the perimeter. As one, they turned and walked towards the walls of the sarcophagus, stretching the blue, shimmering skin of the sphere as they moved. When they reached the granite walls, Khepri and Sobek settled while Bastet moved towards the final corner of the tomb. The sphere now fit the sarcophagus like an internal skin from floor to ceiling, coating every wall.

Bastet returned to the centre of the coffin. With a shake of her fur, a huge blast pushed the skin upwards, lifting the granite slab that had sealed the sarcophagus. The skin lifted from the floor, forming a floating, balloon-like rectangle topped with a lid of several tonnes of granite. The bubble floated up, lifting the trio and familiars with it, and moved away from the body of the sarcophagus until it landed in the catacomb hallway.

Khepri took flight, flying up to the skin closest to the granite slab. With a shimmer, he separated the bubble into two, pulling the one with the granite lid back to the sarcophagus, where it settled down in place. He reappeared, walking through the sides of the tomb a few seconds later, and rejoined them in the sphere.

"Well... that was awesome. Freaky but awesome," Ben said, walking towards the Serapeum exit. As he walked, the sphere expanded to keep him within its perimeter. Ellie hurried to pick up her bag and pack away the first aid kit she'd dropped when treating Gerhard. When both Gerhard and she had collected all their possessions, they hurried to catch up with Ben and the familiars, who had already followed close on his heels.

"Do you suppose the gas has gone? It's got to be at least an hour since they released it," Ellie said.

"I suggest we don't wait to find out.," Ben replied, nearly tripping as Bastet wove around his feet.

Gerhard chuckled. It was a deep, hearty laugh. "Bastet finds you amusing, Ben."

Ben stared down at the cat rubbing against his trouser leg. "Oh, great! That's me, the feline comedian. But how do you know what she finds funny?"

"I feel what she feels. It's odd because I feel amusement without it being my own. It's a little like watching a film where you can experience what the character feels without it being your emotion."

Ellie looked up from the door she'd been studying. "It's still locked and sealed, so let's hope our friends can pick locks. Not that they would have seen locks in Ancient Egypt, but still, let's hope."

"They did, actually, Ellie, but a lot more rudimentary than ours. Theirs were..."

Ellie held up her hand. "Not the time to nerd out on Egyptology, Ben."

"Um, no, I guess not. Right, jump to it, little deities. Let's blast this door to dust!"

The three familiars turned to Ben as one, and Bastet gave him a look of disdain. Khepri took off, flying straight at Ben, only veering off at the last moment to fly to the door and settle on the lock. The scarab contracted down until he could enter the lock and disappeared for some time, emitting little chirps occasionally.

CLICK.

The sound of the lock freeing echoed through the chamber. Khepri re-emerged and flew back to join the gang.

"Useful little guys, aren't they?" Ben said as he moved to open the door.

"Wait!" Gerhard whispered. "They may still be out there. I suggest we listen and see if we can hear them or ask Khepri respectfully if he can do a foray through the keyhole to see if they are still outside, waiting for us."

Ben moved away from the door with a curt nod. "Good idea."

Both Ellie and Ben crouched down next to the door with their ear to the wood. Khepri seemed unimpressed with their request and remained still next to Sobek. After more than five minutes of absolute silence, they ventured out.

As Ben reached for the door, Ellie said, "You know, Uncle Mourad will be here soon. Maybe we should wait for him. He's well-connected within the government and could help secure protection for us."

"I hate to say it, Ellie. but the only people who knew we would be here today were Professor Mourad, Walid, and the driver. We can't count out his involvement."

"Rubbish. Uncle Mourad is like family. I have known him my entire life. I've spent time with his family. His kids were like brothers to me. He wouldn't do anything to endanger me."

"Ells, it doesn't have to be him. It could be a leak in his office, but until we know for sure, we have to treat everyone as suspects. We're talking about our lives here. We can't take risks."

Gerhard raised his hand before Ellie could spit her response at Ben. "He's right, my dear. We have to take all sensible precautions. We should go see if we can find this location for Bastet and then rethink our plans. It's no insult, just sense."

Ellie looked from one to the other with big, fat tears unshed in her eyes. "He wouldn't betray me. You'll see." She turned, opened the door, and stepped around the metal drums of ammonia which lay scattered across the Serapeum's entryway. Gerhard retrieved his jacket, putting it on as he followed Ellie.

They made their way up the ramp to Rashid's little shack, peering around as they walked. Lying, limbs akimbo, like a shaken rag doll was the still form of the ramshackle caretaker. Forever silenced by three shots: one to the head, execution-style, and two to the chest. Blood had trickled down into sand, creating dirty red rivulets snaking away from his body, alive with the buzz of endless flies. Ellie ran to him, shouting in desperate Arabic. He didn't respond. He couldn't. His time had passed.

Ben reached for Ellie, passing her backwards to Gerhard. He knelt and examined the body. "This is recent. Blood's still oozing from the wounds. Whoever did this is sure to be close by. We need to move now." He jumped up and ran back to Ellie. "You know this area better than us. Where is this temple that Bastet showed us? Focus now, Ellie," he said as tears poured down Ellie's face. "We can't do anything for Rashid now, but we can make certain he didn't die in vain by surviving to help his family. Think, Ellie..."

Ellie gazed at him without focus, lost in her thoughts. "There are only two places: the main temple at Saqqara or the Abwab el-qotat."

"I've never heard of that," Ben said.

"No, you probably know it as the Bubasteion. It's an old cemetery of nobles that was later rededicated to Bastet. It's of the same period as the Gayer-Anderson cat. I don't know which is more likely, but maybe the Bubasteion as it was actually dedicated to Bastet."

"Okay... how do we get there?" Ben urged.

"It's straight across there." She pointed across the desert. "To the right of Teti's complex. We should cross the sand rather than take the road to avoid the gunmen."

Ben turned to Gerhard. "Are you able to run?" Gerhard nodded his confirmation.

They set off at a brisk pace, clearing the Serapeum complex, crossing the road to the open desert. In the distance, a sepia dust storm sped towards them, following the twists and turns of the compacted dirt road.

A car screeched to a halt, belching its passengers out of its gaping doors. Three masked men in sand-coloured camouflage fatigues sprinted towards them, armed with heavy duty machine guns.

"RUN!" Ben screamed, grabbing Ellie's arm to haul her behind him.

Gunfire exploded with deafening rattles from behind them. All three threw themselves to the ground and turned helplessly towards the gunmen. The heavy volley of fire bounced from the sphere's clear walls, rebounding the bullets back towards the gunmen, who weren't expecting it. Their own bullets shredded them before they even registered that they hadn't hit their targets. The bodies shuddered as multiple rounds hit them, each man's bullets returned to claim him.

Silence was deafening as the desert absorbed the guns' reverberations. The wind blew, lifting Ellie's hair across her eyes. Gerhard turned on his back and watched the white puffy clouds gliding across the blue sky. Ben's eyes remained glued on the scene, which was painted in a rich Technicolour.

A red wash across a yellow scene. Death, in all its colour, scent, and sound. Final. Chilling.

MOURAD ARRIVES

The Mercedes turned in the little dusty road, scattering the neighbourhood chickens in its wake. Grubby toddlers clad in diapers and tee-shirts ran barefoot alongside, shouting greetings with glee and waving at the immaculate gentleman in the back of the expensive car. They passed verdant strip fields of okra, cotton, and wheat being tended by wizened old men in faded galabiyas. Young girls were harvesting crops into large woven baskets on the backs of camels and donkeys. Their colourful jewel-tone dresses shone brightly against the vivid green foliage in the early morning sunshine.

Walid turned from the passenger front seat. "I couldn't be sorrier, Dr. Mourad. I don't understand how this fool has gotten us lost again. He took us directly to the site this morning with no problems. I'll talk to Human Resources when we get back and make certain we're never given this idiot again. The foreigners must wonder where we are. Even our Serapeum can only hold so much interest."

"*Malesh, habibi*. Don't fret yourself. He's new and nervous. We're all prone to mistakes when we first start a job. As long as he learns from his errors, then there's no need to involve HR. The poor man's got a family to feed, and our colleagues can be draconian."

The driver caught Mourad's eye in the rear-view mirror and gave a subtle nod.

"As you wish. I'll try Madam Ellie's phone again. Maybe it's back in coverage now." Walid turned to the front and fiddled with his mobile. Sighing, he returned it to his pocket and watched the scenery fly past.

They turned right, through the Saqqara gates, and pulled to a halt outside the ticket hut, which was tightly sealed. A scruffy guard sat slumped on what remained of an old plastic garden chair, greyed and chipped by the passage of time.

Mourad lowered his window with a press of a button. "What is the meaning of this? Asleep on the job! Good Lord, man! Half the treasures of Saqqara could be carried by this very chair, and you'd be oblivious. Why isn't the ticket office open?"

The guard jumped, falling from his perch into the sand. Scurrying to his feet, he stood to attention and saluted at Dr. Mourad. "*Pasha*! I'm grievously ashamed. May the Lord strike me as I stand here in front of you..." Before the guard could go into the poetic and endless diatribe of excuses honed to perfection by Egypt's lower classes, Mourad silenced him with the universal gesture of forefinger to lips.

"I'm not interested in excuses. Open the complex at once, and tidy yourself up, man. You're representing Egypt, and I, for one, don't want her to be represented as a tired, lazy, and work-shy idiot. Now jump to it."

"*Pasha*. I have orders, delivered by a courier this morning, that the site remain closed to tourists today. I've already turned away three busloads of foreigners."

"But that's preposterous! Upon whose command?"

"Yours, Dr. Mourad."

"I did no such thing. Open this complex immediately. Walid, get on top of this. Who ordered it, and how did they get my stamp to sanction the order?"

Walid scrambled to fish out his mobile and tapped at the screen urgently. "Yes, Dr. Mourad, sir."

The guard saluted as the car eased away, taking the road to the Serapeum. They pulled up just before the entrance, behind a car idling in the road with three doors hanging open.

"I'll get them to move," Walid said as he pushed open his door. He walked to the driver's side of the car. "It's empty, and the engine's still running." He turned towards the Serapeum and saw a pair of legs splayed out awkwardly next to Rashid's hut. As he ran towards the hut, he called back, "Come quickly! Something's wrong." As he rounded the hut's corner, his legs gave out as he saw the carnage wrought upon Rashid.

Mourad ran to join him, stopping abruptly when he saw the body. "*Ya khabar esswed.* We belong to Allah, and to Him we return. Walid, my friend, pull yourself together. There's nothing to be done for this poor fellow. We need to focus on Ellie and her friends. Quick! Let's go find them."

They ran down the steep slope to the entrance of the Serapeum, dodging the metal drums strewn in their path as they ran. The open door swayed in the wind.

"Ellie. Ellie!" Mourad shouted as he ran.

Walid grabbed him. "What if the people who killed Rashid are in there? We should call the police."

"You call the police. I have to find Ellie."

Mourad flew through the large wooden door, stopping to let his eyes adjust to the gloom. He turned to the left, running and calling for Ellie, covering his nose with a finely tailored handkerchief from his suit pocket. He'd circled the entire Serapeum.

"Walid, come help me search. I can't find Ellie or either of her friends. Come! Now!"

They both checked, searching every catacomb, alcove, and sarcophagus.

"Where can they be? They must be here somewhere! Keep searching. Jump to it. Look again."

Walid cleared his throat. "Sir, we've looked everywhere. They aren't here. I think we must accept that something has happened to them or, by some miracle, they've escaped."

Mourad peered around desperately as if he expected Ellie to separate from the wall and walk towards him. "They can't have escaped this. They can't." He moved to stand in the door, gazing up the ramp into the far distance. "Ellie, where are you?" he murmured.

THE MELD

A whirl of dust rose twenty feet into the air, capturing empty plastic bags and other detritus, growing as it swept across the desert floor to the right of the trio. They ran as fast as the pitted sand dunes allowed, heading towards a raised plateau some distance in front.

Gerhard stumbled as his foot disappeared into a deep crack in the desert. He looked back over his shoulder as he dragged his foot free. "There's another car on the horizon - hurry!"

They zigzagged across the flat plain, trying to use any of the archaeological dig craters or small, scrubby bushes to provide cover from the road. While the trio huffed, tripped, and gasped across the difficult terrain, the familiars glided effortlessly. The sphere remained a reassuring presence, embracing them as they struggled to reach their target. Saqqara's complex stretched out to their side, glimmering sleepily in the sun's hot sheen.

Bastet's statue galloped away from them, as if chased by the hounds of hell, towards the rising cliffs of the

Bubasteion. Bursting free of the sphere, the cat vanished into a small crevice in the cliffside.

"Oh, my God! Uncle Bertram's priceless statue has just disappeared into the dirt," Ellie puffed out as she sprinted to reach the crevice.

"Come on, Ells. You must admit that's kind of poetic. From dust he came, and to dust he returns," Ben said. He stopped to bend, placing both his hands on his knees, as he struggled to recapture his breath.

"Stop faffing around and come help me dig it out. We can't leave the Gayer-Anderson cat buried in the side of the hill."

Ben held up a finger as he chugged down great lungfuls of the hot air. "That statue will come back of its own accord, Ellie, since it's possessed with the spirit of Bastet."

Gerhard joined them, lowering himself to the ground and groaning as he pulled the rucksack from his back. He rummaged inside until he found his water bottle, from which he took a big swig before offering it to the other two.

"This much excitement is a little rich for an old man's blood. Although, I found that run easier than I expected. I wasn't that far behind you fine young people."

"You're certainly not as puffed as Ben appears to be," Ellie stated.

Ben crossed his eyes at her and studied Gerhard. "The change in you is remarkable, Gerhard. You're pumped. I mean, you're still the same build but more defined some-how. Younger."

Glancing down at himself, Gerhard nodded. "I'm not sure what 'pumped' means, but my joints and muscles are looser, as if the slowing of age has been eased a little. Jolly useful for our little sprint back there. Do we need to explore this Bubasteion, do you think?"

"Um, guys!" They turned as one to Ellie. It seemed the Bubasteion was coming to them.

From every crevice and hole, from behind every rock and around every corner, came cats. Feral cats. Spirit cats. Black cats. White cats. An endless stream poured towards them. Most appeared to be composed of the same blue light of the familiars, but there was a smattering of live cats. At the bottom of the cliff was the statue, standing alert and proud. It gazed towards Gerhard, who jumped to his feet and walked towards it.

The procession of cats continued to pour down the cliffs like a feline wave. The cats formed an orderly line when they reached the statue. Silence reigned. So many cats, yet not a noise was heard as they continued to form an ever-lengthening queue. When the last cat arrived, the flat basin at the base of the cliff was full of cats, all sitting and watching Gerhard. He couldn't have put a hand between them, yet silence reigned.

Bastet stood and turned to face the cats, who, as one, lay their left leg down to the earth and bowed, deep and long. As they returned to their seated position, Bastet tipped the top of her head to the right and nodded before turning back to Gerhard and bowing down to him as all the cats had done to it.

Gerhard nodded back and then turned to Ellie and Ben with a shrug. No one said anything. The atmosphere was too majestic and spiritual to sully with words.

They watched the proceedings in awe as, one by one, each cat moved towards Bastet and was absorbed into the statue. Bastet expanded and glowed ever more brightly, incandescent in her glory with each spirit she consumed. Time stood still. Even the wind quieted in the presence of such solemn piety. And so, one after another, the cats melded into the ever-growing Bastet until the energy radiating from her was palpable to all. Bastet was all-powerful, all-knowing, and not from the earthly realm.

It must have taken an hour for the cats to surrender their energy in sacrifice to their god, yet it seemed far shorter. Within the sphere that surrounded them all, time may have stilled its ever-moving race. Finally, the last cat made its way forward, a tiny kitten with long silver hair and big, earnest eyes. Bastet nudged the kitten towards Gerhard, who bent to pick up the little furball. All that remained were Ben, Ellie, Gerhard, the kitten, and the three familiars.

Bastet's form grew taller and slimmer. Her rear legs extended as her back straightened, and her paws lengthened into elegant fingers. With a final shake, she stood tall. A beautiful human female form stood before them, with shiny black hair that poured down her back. Her ample curves were covered in a diaphanous, emerald green gown that flowed over her body, forming a slight train behind. Her face had a feline quality, and her eyes the vertical slit pupil shared by all cats. Upon her head, she wore the double crown of upper and lower Egypt in gleaming gold and platinum, dusted with priceless jewels.

She radiated such power and wisdom as to render Ellie and Ben speechless. They found it almost impossible to look at her. Every glance burned their retinas as if they were staring at the sun.

Gerhard, however, appeared mesmerised. Bastet beckoned him forward and took his hands as he knelt before her with his head lowered. She patted his head gently, and he rose to his feet. She moved closer, placing her hands on his cheeks, and stared into his eyes with such compassion and love. Neither spoke, yet an unconditional love and deep understanding formed a bridge between them. She leaned towards him, smelling of an intoxicating blend of jasmine and rose, and placed a butterfly-light kiss on his cheek.

With a final soft smile, she blurred, dissolving into a million tiny, glittering particles that rotated into an ever-increasing whirlwind of energy around Gerhard. The tendrils of energy buzzed and fizzed as they rotated faster and faster until Ellie and Ben saw nothing of Gerhard, just a huge tornado of blue, sparkling energy.

The silence exploded with a cataclysmic boom that shook the entire Saqqara plateau, rocking date palms and pushing all the scrubby grass flat. It threw Ellie and Ben several feet across the sand, covering them with a fine layer of silica. They crawled back up to their feet, sand pouring from their backs, and turned, searching for Gerhard, fearful of what they'd find.

Standing tall and proud in the epicentre of the explosion was Gerhard, smiling beatifically at them. Immaculate in his tweed suit and waistcoat, with a dapper, red spotted handkerchief tucked in his chest pocket, not a hair out of place, he could have just stepped from Saville Row. In his arms rested the little kitten, transformed from the streetwise, scrappy little scruff into a sleek, silver-haired, emerald-eyed beauty. Both radiated health and power.

Ellie sprinted towards Gerhard, arms and legs flying in her race to reach him. She flung herself on him, sobbing. "I thought we'd lost you again. Oh, my God, Gerhard, don't do that to me again. Are you okay?" She turned him around, fully checking he was unwounded, and then fell to her knees, shivering. "I can't take much more of this."

Ben reached them and grabbed Gerhard in a full hug. "Man alive - I was sure you were a goner this time. What the hell happened?"

"Relax. I'm fine. Really, I am. I'm more than fine. I feel

invincible. The energy seemed to melt into me. I felt every particle of myself as individual elements. I saw things that make no sense - just disjointed images. Then my energy grew, swelling to a level I was sure would exceed my body's ability to contain, and it was. I felt something grow, like a new organ, and the energy centred there. I can't explain it, and I certainly don't understand it, but it's as if I now have an internal reservoir. All I really know is that we need to follow our familiars, and only once we have all melded fully with them will we understand this odd situation. I know I am Bastet's form on Earth, but for what reason, I cannot tell you."

He bent down to Ellie and wiped the tears from her face. "Hush now, *mein liebling*. I'm fine. Please stop your tears. Come give this old man a hug."

Ellie turned into his arms and wrapped her arms around his waist. "I.... I love you, Gerhard. Please don't die again."

He rocked her gently. "*Mein* Ellie, I'll do my best not to, little one, but it comes to us all one day."

A car raced across the desert towards them. The doors flew open before the car stopped. Dr. Mourad and Walid stumbled towards them. "Ellie - no, no, it's not possible. Ellie, oh my God, no!" Dr. Mourad fell to his knees, shaking his head.

Walid ran to the group. "Praise Allah you are okay. We saw Rashid and the other bodies and feared the worst. Then there was that massive explosion. Dr. Mourad has been out of his mind in desperation, searching for you. He couldn't believe you'd escaped. He's lost all sense of reason. *Al-hamdulillah* we found you alive. The police are coming. *Yalla*. Let's get into the car."

GUARDIANS OF THE ANKH

Not a rustle or a cough disturbed the silence in the room as its occupants shifted in their seats, eyeing each other, no one keen to maintain eye contact. The door flew open, hitting the wall behind it, leaving a deep indentation. Everyone shrunk down in their chairs, studious in their watching of the dirt floor.

"Explain to me, if you will be so kind, how the world's best-trained soldiers, armed with the latest wonders of warfare, are incapable of killing an old man, a linguist, and an archaeologist - none of whom have one iota of military training. Not only did they survive, but it seems they were able to lower our number by three. Amenirdis, thoughts?" Tjati spluttered as he circled the room, staring at each person in turn.

A young woman, dressed in black, looked up, her eyes huge. She shook her head, lost for words.

"Kawab, how about you? Did God smile upon the damned? Did our just and righteous cause lose God's support? Or was it the incompetence of an inept team?" Tjati turned to stare at the senior officer in the room, a man built to fight, aged to granite, and known for his fiery temper and zealot-like beliefs. "Nothing to say? I'm ashamed in front of my God and in front of all those brave men and women who have fought to prevent this day happening. On my watch, a meld has occurred, and now the old one is immune to all attacks. But may God smite me down if I will allow the other two to complete theirs."

He spun around, bending into the face of the person nearest him. "Eurydice, you will infiltrate the targets and feed information back to us." He raised his hand, stopping any response. "That, Eurydice, is a direct order! Your task is to infiltrate and disrupt. I will not tolerate further failure. Amenti team, you will be the backbone of our rapid response force. You will assassinate, on sight, both targets and anyone known to associate with them. This will end. Our job is to protect God's purity and preserve all that is good on earth. These people will not succeed. Now jump to it."

As a collective, every person jumped to their feet, young and old, keen to evacuate the room. They left to the percussion of chairs bouncing off walls as Tjati vented his frustrations.

PART THREE
BEN'S QUEST

REFLECTION

"**W**ell, thank all that is beautiful - you've finally answered your ruddy mobile. I've been trying to get you for ages. Our Dave is already having a snippety fit about me calling Egypt from our home phone. Do you know how much it costs? Do you? A bloody lot, that's how much. I'll be charging you."

Ellie tried to answer.

"Anyhow, I'm being pestered by that copper - the chief investigator one. He's being trying to get you. He has a lead he wants to discuss with you. I don't trust the police – never have – but I reckon you ought to call him back. I'll text you the number. Now onto important stuff - Shannon has finished one bedroom, and he needs a decision on colour. Now I've said to him that a nice, rich terracotta would be right classy, but he reckons you have something in mind. You know, the more I think about it, Ellie, the more I'm swinging to turquoise. It's such a jolly colour. You couldn't ever get depressed in a room painted in sea shades, now could you?"

Ellie stared out of the window of the police car as it

navigated the crowded back streets of Maadi, letting Charlie's inane chatter wash over her taut nerves. The everyday subject such a juxtaposition to her current situation. She wondered how her life had changed so much that a UK murder investigation seemed almost mundane.

"Jeez, Ellie - lost your tongue?"

Ellie chatted for a few minutes until the car pulled up at her parents' house. "I have to go now, Charlie. The police are dropping me home."

"Wait, the police are dropping you home! What the hell is going on, Ellie? Ellie, don't you hang up on me, so help me, God."

Ellie murmured her goodbyes and hung up swiftly.

It had been a long and difficult afternoon. Walid had called the police, who'd arrived and tried to make sense of the scene they found. They had taken the trio, Walid, and Professor Mourad to the Saqqara station for questioning. With Ellie providing translation, they questioned each person, trying to clarify what had happened.

All three told the same story. Someone had locked them in the Serapeum, and they'd succumbed to the gas as it seeped into the chamber only to awake sometime later by the open door. When they stumbled out of the tomb complex, they'd run to Rashid's hut to get help but instead found him slaughtered. They'd tried calling for help, but there wasn't mobile phone coverage, so they ran to the highest point to pick up coverage. Halfway to the clifftop known as Abwab el-qotat, they'd heard the trill of machine gun fire rattling across the desert behind them. They'd sprinted for cover, reaching the slopes of the hill as a huge explosion ripped across the plain. Shortly afterwards, the esteemed Professor Mourad Soliman and his assistant, Walid, had found them.

The police tried different questioning angles to find inconsistencies in the story but gave up, realising all five witnesses' stories corroborated one another. So, they'd agreed, reluctantly, to take the exhausted foreigners back to their home.

Ellie thanked the young policemen for their help and turned to make her way to the door. She was looking forward to a light supper, a shower, and a good night's sleep.

~

The bell shrieked throughout the house, screaming for attention. It repeated its peals as the person at the door leaned on the buzzer.

"Hold your horses," Ben murmured as he walked to answer it.

A whirlwind in black forced past him, screaming as she ran down the hall. "Ellie, *habibti*. Where are you?" She turned and pointed a finger in Ben's face. "What have you done with my Ellie? Where is she?"

Ben backed away, both hands raised to his shoulders. He shouted, "Ellie, there's someone here to see you - rather urgently, so it would seem."

Ellie came out of the kitchen, drying her hands on a tea towel. "Mama Aida! What are you doing here?"

"What am I doing here? My poor heart weeps. You come home at last, and do you call your Mama Aida? No! I get to hear my Ellie is in Egypt from the lips of another. Never in all my life did I think such a sad day would come to pass. It freezes my poor heart."

"Well, I..."

"No. Elena, you will not make excuses. Oh, what a day. I come overjoyed with anticipation to see my Ellie, and a strange man opens our door. Not a family member in sight to chaperone you. You will destroy your family's good name. Well, thankfully, Mama Aida is here to put all these wrongs right. Now come hug your Mama and welcome me. Did I teach you no manners?"

Ellie obeyed, glancing across at Ben, who stood with his mouth open in shock. "Ben, this is Mama Aida, my nursery nurse and moral champion. Mama, this is Ben, the student I mentioned on the phone. You'll meet his Uncle Gerhard soon. He's upstairs, taking a bath at the moment."

"Oh, no. It gets worse. So, you have *two* men under your roof and no chaperone. Thank God I came. Right, give me five minutes to get settled, and I'll sort this out. No one will ever question Mama Aida's ability to chaperone her Ellie."

After reorganising the house to have the men sleeping in a hastily prepared dormitory in the dining room and a single bed erected outside Ellie's door for herself, Mama Aida sat down to begin her interrogation of the men.

"I understand that you," she said, nodding at Ben, "may have fluid morals, but I'm shocked by you, sir," she said to Gerhard. "You seem like a fine gentleman, and yet, you've allowed my Ellie's reputation to be sullied by staying on her own with two men. Is this the action of a gentleman? May God strike me down if I'm wrong, but I will get answers!"

Ellie watched the proceedings with a degree of humour and a sprinkle of consternation as the two men received a verbal bashing and interrogation of which the Russian KGB would be proud. Although she tried to step in occasionally, she was firmly ejected by an indignant Aida. Finally, she lapsed into silence and became a spectator in the newest sport of "out-debate an enraged, protective Egyptian mama", a sport both men were sorely ill equipped to take part in.

"Mark my words, Ellie. These two are up to no good. I've been talking to Mahmoud, and he saw that young American climb down the bougainvillea just a couple of nights ago. Mahmoud is a nosey sort. He lacks my respect for privacy, so he followed him, and guess what he saw? This Ben character left the house in the dark of night to have a secret assignation with none other than Sam Gamal - the worthless ragamuffin that broke your precious heart!"

"No, Mama, you're mistaken. Ben wouldn't do that."

"Elena, don't allow your sweet, trusting nature to lead you down the path to heartache again. I warned you before, and you didn't listen. Please, my darling, mark my words. These two are using you. Wasn't it Ben who led you to Gerhard? They are working together, possibly with Sam, to get you here to Egypt. Talk to Mahmoud yourself. He will tell you."

Mama leaned down, pushed Ellie's disheveled hair away from her face, and placed a gentle kiss on her forehead.

"Mama Aida is here now. I'll make it all right, my little Ellie."

RESEARCH

The argument had cloaked the house in a dark, suffocating presence, which Gerhard was doing his best to ignore. The row had escalated over two days with neither Ben nor Ellie speaking to each other after the initial explosive quarrel. Gerhard was bemused that Ben had met the erstwhile husband, despite his advice to the contrary, and wasn't surprised Ellie had reacted with such volatility. Still, they had a mission to complete, and they'd delayed it long enough.

Mama Aida had left the house for the first time since she stormed on to the scene, and it gave them a chance to talk about their plans - if only he could wrangle the two opponents around the table.

"Meine lieben - unless you two want to spend your remaining years in each other's presence, we need to define our next steps. We've wasted enough time in anger. Put it behind you, and for goodness' sake, let's focus on our predicament. Sit!"

Gerhard pulled two chairs out from the dining table

and gestured at them. Ellie unwound herself from the sofa and took the furthest chair. Gerhard frowned at Ben and barked, "Move now - *mein Gott!*" Ben leapt up in shock and moved to take his place at the table.

"While you two have been skulking around the house, I've been doing more research. It seems likely that Kom Ombo would be our target destination for Sobek. There are loads of mummified crocodiles there and a temple dedicated to him. For Khepri, it's less clear. I haven't found mention of any temples dedicated to him. Ben, I want you to undertake as much research as you can into locations dedicated to the worship of Sobek. Ellie, find out what you can about the cult of Khepri and where, if anywhere, we can go to connect with him."

Ellie whipped around. "I'm sure that would suit you both to have me busy following leads that go nowhere while you plot behind my back. I will not be manipulated by either one of you anymore."

Gerhard rested his chin on his folded hands and peered at her over his glasses' rim. "*Mein liebling*, where has this come from, tell me?"

"You both lied to me about the Gayer-Anderson Cat. You used me to gain access to a priceless artefact, which you then stole. What do I know about either of you? Ben's a close friend of my worthless ex-husband, a fact he failed to share with me. I can't trust you both."

"So, we planned this elaborate plan, the destruction of my premises, and murder of my dearest friend all to steal a relic so well-known, it would be impossible to sell and to help Ben's friend gain access to his ex-wife. Are we both so intellectually challenged that we would consider this a plausible plan?" Gerhard removed his glasses and polished them as he watched Ellie's reaction.

"Sometimes, it's the stupid plans that work best as no one questions them. I should never have trusted either of you. I know not to trust men, but I allowed your gentlemanly old-world charm to disarm my natural caution. It's not something I will do again."

"For Pete's sake, Ellie. What in God's good name are you talking about? Has your brain addled? So what? We used some wacky hallucinogenic to get you to see the visions. How did we get you to see what you did, huh?" Ben ran his hands through his hair. "Could you be anymore paranoid? Believe me, I'd be happy to leave and never see your face again if I could. What can we do to win your trust? Get killed by the raving lunatics trying to murder us? Okay, so I screwed up by meeting Sam behind your back. I was wrong and I'm sorry. But get your head in the game. We're sitting ducks here, and I, for one, don't want lead pellets up my rear."

Gerhard watched Ellie's face as warring emotions flickered across it. "Elena, you don't have to trust us. Do all the research yourself or double-check our research, but are you willing to bet your life and ours on a lack of trust?"

The front door cracked back against the wall as Mama Aida huffed down the hall with bags full of groceries.

Ellie studied them in silence before nodding her head and leaving the table.

Gerhard blinked as the sharp rays of the sun found the solitary gap in the curtain and poured down on him in his rather uncomfortable camping cot. Across the makeshift dormitory, Ben was snuffling in his sleep, shaded from the sun by the banquet-sized dining table. Gerhard rotated his shoulder, releasing the knots. As his awareness swept away the grey fog of sleep, he remembered his previous night's dream. Jumping up from the cot, he grabbed his pillow and threw it at Ben, who snorted in surprise and peered at Gerhard blearily.

"What the heck, Gerhard! I was having a doozy of a dream."

"No time for dreaming, my friend. We have a trip to plan."

Gerhard moved to the living room, sat down on the overstuffed, dusty sofa, and composed a text message on his mobile phone.

Ellie, Ben, last night, I had a vivid and photo-realistic dream. I'm worried about involving anyone else in our problems, so to protect Mama Aida, I thought I'd text you the details.

Gerhard smiled wryly. It was as much about loosening Mama Aida's influence over Ellie as it was about her protection. Still, he couldn't risk another life being ended prematurely. Much as the old busy-body was a constant and loud thorn in their side, he knew her actions came from a deep and abiding love of Ellie, something he felt had been sorely missing from her life.

In the dream, I was leading the three of us across a desert plain shadowed by looming mountains. The three deities were floating above a large river, probably the Nile, led by Bastet.

Bastet and I turned and saw the Bubasteion in the distance, far behind us. Bastet transformed into her human form and manifested a small sphere of the blue energy in her hand. She turned to Sobek, bowed low, and handed him the sphere. She left Sobek and Khepri and took my hand, guiding us to the back, leaving Sobek and Ben to guide the group.

When I woke, her paw print was embossed on my hand. It's time, my friends. We must pursue Sobek's trail. For her safety, Mama Aida mustn't know of our plans. Now how can we get down to Kom Ombo?

The gentle ping of a text confirmation followed Gerhard pressing the send button on the next step of their path of discovery.

~

Ellie awoke to the soft chirp of her phone informing her she'd received a message. She'd had a disturbed night, worrying about Ben's betrayal and Mama Aida's accusation that the two men were using her. Their denial had seemed genuine, and once her emotions had calmed a little, she saw the logic of their argument. But Mama Aida had sown the seed of doubt, and her brain wouldn't stop worrying at it.

She read the text repeatedly. She had a choice: trust the guys and protect Mama Aida or continue fighting them and potentially put Mama Aida in the firing line. It wasn't even a choice. After losing Stefan, there was no way she would ever allow Mama Aida to be put at risk. It looked like they were going to Kom Ombo. But how?

After several hours of debating the different routes open to them, they were no closer to finding a foolproof way of escaping Cairo unseen by the mysterious group intent on killing them. But Ellie had an idea - one she didn't want to share with anyone. If the guys were cohorts with Sam, he wouldn't be any the wiser. This way, she could grab back control.

Later that night, after saying goodnight to everyone, Ellie retrieved the rope ladder she'd kept hidden in her window seat when she was courting Sam and lowered it to the ground as quietly as possible. Avoiding all the bougainvillea thorns that had so tormented Ben's late-night rendezvous with Sam, she climbed down to the ground and slipped unseen through the gate.

Cairo is often called "The City that Never Sleeps", but Maadi is a quieter dormitory suburb, so Ellie made her way to Road 9, the pumping social heart of Maadi. She soon hailed a cab and instructed the taxi driver to take her to Mohandeseen. Ellie watched the streets pass by, full of families having impromptu picnics next to the Nile in a desperate bid for some breeze to escape the hot, still night air. Poor families sat on the pavement at the side of the bridge, eating the treats that the street hawkers offered whilst engulfed in the exhaust fumes of the cars that crawled across the traffic-choked bridge.

Cairo had never made sense to her. In a country so full of space, of vast desert plains and scrubby valleys, why over twenty million people made it their home and business place, she'd never understood. There are other, smaller cities: Alexandria on the Mediterranean coast, Suez at the mouth of the canal, and the tourist cities of Hurghada and Sharm El Sheikh. Yet, over twenty percent of the country's population lived cheek-to-jowl in the polluted, noisy, and chaotic streets of Cairo. Egypt embraced the concept of urban spread but with its own definition, which meant to build more suburbs of Cairo rather than develop new cities.

As they neared their destination, Ellie wondered what reception she would get after such a long and silent absence. It was with trepidation she crossed the floating pier onto the houseboat's deck. She raised her hand to knock just as a deep, booming bark inside rocked the door. The door opened, and a black shadow rocketed towards Ellie, nearly landing her on the wooden decking.

"Elbi, down, boy."

A slimy, wet tongue washed Ellie's face as she bent to greet the dog. "You remember me, handsome fellow?" Ellie glanced up at the shocked face of her oldest friend. "Hi, Kareem."

He stared at her, unblinking, before he rushed forward and wrapped her in his bear-like embrace. "Ellie, I can't believe my eyes. I don't hear from you in years, not even a card to tell me you are alive and well, and then you rock up in the middle of the night at my front door. *Al Hamdulillah.* Come in, come in."

Ellie followed the Rottweiler and Kareem into the oriental interior of the houseboat. Dark wood flooring and walls were complemented with luscious wall coverings in a rainbow of colours and geometric designs. Large, comfy floor cushions replaced sofas and chairs, except for a wooden chaise longue that looked like it might have once been part of the old-fashioned ox-drawn plough favoured by the humble farmers of Upper Egypt. Large, brass-engraved trays rested on folding wooden supports and held little bowls of nuts and oriental sweets. A shisha pipe scented the air with the delicate perfume of apples as the smoke wafted lazily across the room. Old, wooden sculptures of various pharaonic, Hindu, and Buddhist deities dotted the alcoves around the room.

"Wow, this place has changed - very bohemian," Ellie said as she circled the room, touching an odd item here and there.

"Things change if you leave them long enough, Ellie," Kareem said as circled back towards her. "I host my tours here for the first two days before we cruise, so I thought I'd decorate it to start their Egyptian adventure in style. It's staging, really, but I've grown to like it. Doesn't hurt my chances with the ladies either," he admitted wryly.

"I bet it doesn't," Ellie acknowledged. "How are you, Kareem? How are Aliaa and Tante Azza?"

A shadow crossed Kareem's strong features. "I lost my mother last year. Her breathing had become very difficult, and she declined until living was too much for her. She's at peace now, God bless her soul."

Ellie sank down onto the cushions with tears in her eyes. "I'm so sorry. I had no idea."

"How would you? When you vanish without a word, with no forwarding details, it makes it hard to inform you. I'm fine now, but it was a tough time. Aliaa had just married, so at least I didn't have to worry about her future. She's expecting her first child in a couple of months."

"Aliaa, a mum? Wow, she's just a baby herself."

"She's twenty now. Not so young," Kareem said, adjusting the bowls of sweets into a more symmetrical pattern. He turned on his heel and bent down in front of Ellie "What happened, my friend? Where did you go? Why didn't you tell me you were leaving? I grieved for you. I searched everywhere, but no one would tell me anything. One day, we were laughing over mint tea, and the next day, you'd vanished. I lost my two best friends in one swoop. Can you imagine how that felt to go from the Three Muske-teers to Han Solo?"

Ellie grabbed his hands. "But Sam stayed here. I had to go. There was no choice. The betrayal was too great to bear, but Sam didn't leave you. I thought a swift, clean cut was the best for all."

"Ellie, Sam went mad. He was certain I knew where you'd gone. He attacked me when I didn't tell him anything and put me in hospital. He was crazed. Obsessed with finding you and understanding why you'd left. Then he just withdrew from everything except work. You took the best of him with you when you went. He's a husk. I haven't seen or heard from him since that night. I hear the odd things from people he works with, but I lost his friendship the night you left."

Ellie stared at him, aghast. "I'm so sorry, Kareem. I didn't expect that reaction. I thought he'd rub along okay until he moved on to someone new. By then, I hated him so much, I didn't care about his feelings, but believe me, I didn't want to hurt you. I'm so, so sorry."

"Well, time heals, and I wouldn't be a good Muslim if I didn't forgive slights. It's good to see you again, Ellie. Very good, indeed." Straightening, he smoothed down his trousers and linen top and offered Ellie mint tea.

Elbi entertained Ellie while Kareem prepared the tea, demanding stomach rubs and fetching a pile of toys for Ellie to throw for him. Each time Ellie threw something, the Rottie gave her enthusiastic licks before trotting off to retrieve the toy. Ellie stroked him, smiling at the dog's antics. "He's still as soppy as ever, I see."

"Yep - just a little more arthritic now. All the tourists love him. He's a true ambassador for the breed, just a gentle giant."

They chatted over the tea, catching up on the years they'd missed until Ellie felt she could raise the favour she'd come to ask.

"Kareem. I need to ask a favour. Do you still have *The Thebes*?"

"Yes, of course. Actually, I was meant to leave on a trip tomorrow, but my passengers got delayed by an Alitalia strike. Damned inconvenient. It took me ages to get all the permits from Mogamaa."

"I hate to ask this, and I wouldn't except I'm in a terrible bind. Can I borrow her for a trip to Kom Ombo and maybe Luxor? It shouldn't be more than a week-long trip, and I'd take care of her as if she were my own."

"I'd let you if I could, but the government has the river regulated. You need permits to travel, and it takes days to get the permissions. Then I must captain the boat and register at every stopping point along the way. It's not like the good old days. There's so much fear of terrorism."

"You just said you have permits. We could use those. Kareem, I wouldn't ask, but my life literally depends on this. I've got myself into a difficult situation with some very dangerous people. Believe me, I want to share all the details, but I can't. On Mama Aida's life, I swear I can't. For your safety, you need to know only the bare basics. Please help me, Kareem. You're my last hope."

Kareem stared at her for some time. "You have one hell of a nerve, Ellie. You walk out on me without a word and then expect me to jump headfirst into whatever you've got yourself into, no questions asked?" He sighed and patted Elbi's head. "Okay, you've got a deal, but I'll be armed if they are as dangerous as you claim. I can't manage the boat and guard you without backup."

"Oh, you'll have backup. I'll have two men with me, an American and a German. Just one more thing, Kareem. This must stay utterly secret. No one must know, not even Aliaa or your present floozy. Everyone must think you are going on a normal cruise with your pre-booked clients."

They sat chatting for a while before Kareem offered to drive Ellie home.

The car lights faded into the distance as they drove away. The man raised from his crouch beneath the shadowed window, stood, and walked away accompanied by Elbi's excited barking. As he walked, he contemplated everything he'd heard.

KOM OMBO

After a day spent avoiding the ever-seeing eye of Mama Aida, the three had hidden their bags in the garden and settled down for the night. Ellie tucked away behind the bedroom door protected by the ever-vigilant, elderly yet still fearsome Egyptian nanny, and the men were in their makeshift dormitory downstairs.

They'd decided to meet outside at two a.m. and had agreed a circuitous route to the mooring of *The Thebes* to make sure they weren't followed. Now they just needed to wait and listen for the steady snores of Mama Aida. Ellie would use her long-trusted ladder to meet the guys. Each of them planned to take taxis in different directions, changing cabs as often as possible before meeting at the pier.

Ellie had asked Kareem to do a little shopping for the trip, which included items of disguise and burner phones armed with data packages to help them continue their research whilst travelling down the Nile.

The final and hardest task for Ellie had been a letter for Mama Aida. She struggled to draft the letter, wanting to protect her old nursery nurse from any anxiety whilst also ensuring she knew nothing about their plans. Ellie knew the people chasing them would show the old lady no mercy and wanted to get Mama Aida to return to the safety of her village home.

She ended up scrawling a missive claiming the police had asked them to return to the UK to confirm new details about Stefan's murder. Ben booked tickets in their names to confirm the story and left printouts of the tickets scattered on the dining room table. Ellie asked her to close the house in the morning and return to her own home. Charlie, after a little persuasion, agreed to support their story should Mama Aida contact her.

The clock ticked down to their rendezvous time. Each minute dragged ever longer. Aida's every snuffle or movement amplified the suspense. The journey was on.

Gerhard offered his hand to help Ellie take the final step down from the rope ladder, which swayed against the house. She brushed the Bougainvillea twigs and dried leaves from her hair and grabbed her mobile from her back pocket.

"I sent you text messages from my mobile earlier detailing your routes - ignore them. I was laying a false trail." She pulled two index cards from her shoulder bag and passed them one each. "This is the actual course you should take. I've calculated each route to allow us to be within our boundary perimeter but spread across the city. Each location has many alternate entrances and exits, which should allow us to lose anyone if we're followed." She passed each of them a bulging plastic bag. "I've given you a range of jackets and hats in here - change your appearance between each leg of the journey. We can't risk them finding us on the Nile. We'd be sitting ducks, so take every precaution to cover your steps. Good luck. See you at the end point."

With that, she left the garden and turned towards Road 9. The guys followed in intervals.

Cairo thrives on hustle and bustle, so it was easy to hail taxis from the streets.

Ben travelled to the old border town of Helwan, across the water towards Saqqara, and into the up-market business and residential area of Mohandeseen before crossing over into the island of Zamalek.

Gerhard stopped at the old military Citadel and Mosque before changing cars and heading to the tourist bazaar of Khan El-Khalili, with all its spice stores and jewelry shops. From there, he changed again, moving to the old Abdeen Palace and finally to their meeting point.

Ellie went directly to the airport, where she changed taxi and visited the colonial suburb of Roxi. She changed and drove to the Nile Ritz-Carlton Hotel, which she entered via the Nile-facing entrance. After enjoying a coffee, she exited via the Tahrir Square door and walked to the front of the Egyptian Museum, where she got a taxi to Nile City Towers, a large shopping and business complex. She again used an alternative exit and hailed a cab, which took her across the Imbaba Bridge, into Mohandeseen, and back to Zamalek for her final taxi change at the Cairo Opera House. She was last to arrive at the wharf in Zamalek where Kareem moored *The Thebes*.

Kareem had already shown the two men to their berth and was waiting on the dock for Ellie. "Strange partners you have, Ellie - an elderly gentleman and a loud American! Are you sure you don't want to tell me what the hell is going on? I'd certainly feel more comfortable helping you than depending on these total strangers to protect you. All this cloak and dagger business is worrying me. It's not like you to be involved in subterfuge."

Ellie grimaced, tucked her hand into the crook of his arm, and walked across the gangway. "I wish it were that simple, Kareem. I don't understand what's happening or even why it's happening. But one thing is certain - I have no choice other than to proceed with Ben and Gerhard. But I feel much more comfortable having a friend close at hand." She stared across the dark stretch of water. "Just be careful, Kareem. These people are dangerous and have already killed. Your ignorance is your only protection. I won't jeopardise that."

The days passed slowly on *The Thebes*. They took turns sailing the boat, so they could travel around the clock. This meant that they didn't need to register with the police, which was a legal requirement at every stop otherwise.

Ellie furiously researched everything she could find on Khepri, which was precious little, hindered by the often weak or unreliable data network. One afternoon, she became so infuriated by the combination of slow connectivity and limited information, she threw the mobile into the Nile, much to Ben's amusement.

The charm of the old-world dahabiya sailboat captivated Gerhard. He'd interrogated Kareem about its history and restoration into its current incarnation as a six-berth passenger cruiser. The teak-paneled dining room and lounge had a regal gentleman's club meets the orient feel that just begged passengers to sit down and enjoy the passing scenery. The berths, whilst bijoux, were adorned with beds that cuddled their sleepers in a cloud of comfort and were dressed in rich umbers, scarlets, and deep greens that complemented the cinnamon beauty of the wood-scented rooms. After seeing the perfectly equipped kitchen, Gerhard opted to became the galley master, preparing all the meals. His culinary offerings were the highlight of days otherwise cloaked in boredom and anxiety.

Every evening, they gathered on the deck to enjoy the sun setting. The crimson sky bathed the Nile in hues of pink, and it amplified the green of the rushes and fields against the pink-tinged, dusty yellows of the surrounding hills. The local farming families worked in their fields, harvesting in the cooler evening temperatures, and shone like precious stones against the crops in their colourful galabiyas. When they passed through towns or villages, they adopted the persona of tourists, snapping photos and waving at the locals. Kareem insisted that to do otherwise would break their cover story.

The change in tempo and constant vigilance against unseen attack caused tempers to flare, and Gerhard did his best to keep Ellie and Ben apart. He acknowledged that they needed to have an argument to clear the air but wanted to preserve the fragile amnesty until they'd uncovered their mission in Kom Ombo. Kareem was a great calming tonic for both Ellie and Ben, who'd formed a firm friendship with the Egyptian guide out of Ellie's sight. He was a peaceful and happy soul and made it difficult for anyone to stay angry for long.

Each day, they expected an attack and were on full guard at all times, but the days passed peacefully.

"You know, it would be easier if they just attacked us. At least the dark deed would be done. All this waiting and not knowing is driving me bonkers," Ben said one evening as they watched the sun-gilded Nile pass by.

"I think we've slipped their net. All that taxi-hopping

may have paid off," Ellie replied as she sipped a glass of chilled white wine.

Gerhard pondered her words and watched a white egret at the edge of the river stalk its prey. "Still, it might be wise not to drop our guard yet. As long as we keep moving, the only way they can hurt us is to shoot from the riverbank or try to board the boat whilst we are moving. Laying mines in the river would be too random and could cause the wrong boat to be hit, so I don't think they'd try that. So, we should have notice of either attack. Especially with our friend here," he said, patting Elbi's head. The dog gave him a lick and settled down at his feet. "I'm concerned about the lock though. If I were orchestrating an attack, that would be my target point. We're essentially sitting ducks. We need to consider how to protect our passage through the lock, *ja*?"

Kareem walked up behind them and grabbed the local flatbread to dip into the babaganough dip. "I think I may have a solution. I know a couple of felucca captains that have helped me sail *The Thebes* occasionally. Maybe I can ask one to sail it through the lock while we hop off and go cross country. We'll meet up again farther upstream."

Ellie shook her head. "I don't want to jeopardise any more innocent lives. What if they don't confirm who's on board before opening fire? I won't risk another life," she said, moving over to Elbi and burying her face in his scruff.

"*Habibti*, you needn't fear. You know how these river men live. Gossip is the source of their happiness. I'll plant an elaborate false trail with them that will have these enemies of yours chasing their tails better than Elbi. Trust me, I wouldn't risk them if I thought they were in any danger."

Ellie gave him a wry smile. "They do love to gossip, don't they?"

THE ELOPEMENT

The next day dawned sunny and fresh. After another stunning breakfast prepared with Gerhard's normal culinary precision, the four-man crew adorned their well-worn and rather stinky galabiyas.

The jolly felucca captain recruited by Kareem was called Tarek. His height was nearly matched by his girth, and every time he smiled or laughed, he flashed tarred stubs where his teeth should be. He'd been delighted to provide some old clothes for them, especially when he received ten times what they were worth in payment. He struggled in vain to contain his mirth when he saw the motley bunch leave the saloon and cross the deck towards him.

"Oh, my dear lord, her groom will turn and run for his life when he sees her dressed like that," he spluttered to Kareem. "Still, once they've eloped, she'll scrub up okay." He nodded at Gerhard and Ben. "I'm amazed her father and brother are supporting this elopement. She must have one in the oven, eh?"

Ben snorted under his breath and got a firm elbow to the

ribs from Ellie. They continued playing the role of Italians, so they had agreed not to talk in front of the captain, who was unaware that two of them understood what he was saying.

Kareem had told the captain that Ellie – or Valentina, as he'd dubbed her – was returning to elope with her Egyptian boyfriend, whose family was against the union. He asked the captain to take the boat through the lock while he guided the nervous bride and her family to a local solicitor to perform an Orfi marriage. He'd explained that the groom's family would stop at nothing to prevent the wedding, hence the need to disguise the group as local farmers. The story touched Tarek's sentimental side, and he'd swallowed it hook, line, and sinker.

So, as the sun flirted with the horizon, they crossed the plank onto the riverbank of the hidden little cove they'd moored in to pick up Tarek. He'd left his donkey and trap as transport for them. Kareem leapt up onto the front seat, picked up the reins, and helped Ellie clamber up next to him. He instructed Ben and Gerhard to lie down in the back with their arms over their faces as if protecting their eyes from the gentle sun whilst napping. Kareem passed Ellie a basket full of gaily-coloured reed strips and told her to keep her head down and appear to be weaving the reeds into baskets.

"*Yalla!*" he said, flipping the reins to encourage the donkeys to move. And so, they plodded down the little dust track that began their journey to Esna.

After several uncomfortable hours of travelling and waiting for *The Thebes* to clear the lock and with no more excitement than Gerhard spotting a rare bird, tired and despondent, the four travelers re-embarked *The Thebes*. Kareem questioned Tarek to see if he'd experienced anything unusual, but it seemed he'd had a very peaceful journey. Kareem told him the sorry story of Valentina's fiancé leaving her standing at the altar, or solicitor's office, in this case.

"Don't be sad, pretty lady," Tarek said in heavily accented English whilst patting her hand in a fatherly fashion. "Egyptian men can make horrible husbands. Just ask my long-suffering wife, God bless her soul. You've had a lucky miss today."

Ellie schooled her face to appear heartbroken and moved towards the door.

"Her boyfriend probably found a younger tourist with a better passport," he said under his breath to Kareem in Arabic. Ellie's step faltered before she continued through the door, slamming it behind her.

"Old, am I?" she muttered to herself as she pushed past Ben to grab the first shower.

Kareem helped fit Gerhard's shemagh before moving on to adjust Ben's. The headdress completed the disguise. He passed them both the dark aviator shades preferred by many of the rich Arabs, which they put on, and before him stood two reasonable facsimiles of rich Saudi Sheiks. The fact that both Ben and Gerhard shared the same swarthy skin tone helped a great deal. Ellie came into the saloon dressed from head to toe in a black abaya and matching black headdress with just a thin slot cut to allow her to see. Kareem flitted around, adjusting the lay of a coat or the folds of the headdress, until he was satisfied.

"*Khalas* - not even your own mothers would recognise

you. Now are you sure I can't come to act as your tour guide?"

Gerhard stepped forward and patted his shoulder. "Thank you, my friend. You have already helped way beyond the call of duty, but alas, this next chapter is ours and ours alone. Please be vigilant, and should anything seem untoward, please take *The Thebes* and yourself to safety."

Kareem appeared uncertain. "Well, okay, if you insist. Ellie, remember to walk behind the men, and guys, carry yourself with arrogance. Remember to disappear among the tourists. You need to carry this disguise off perfectly. You must appear egotistical, aloof, and have a certain swagger. Ellie, you're meek, quiet, and docile - God help you!"

"Now that, I've got to see," said Ben, dancing away from the jet-propelled handbag Ellie swung at him.

Ellie turned to Kareem and walked into his arms. They hugged a little longer than necessary and then Ellie turned and, with a wave of the hand, showed that Ben should lead the way. She didn't look back.

Kareem had moored the boat just a short walk down river from the lauded Kom Ombo Temple. So, they strolled along the riverside corniche, playing the role of rich and spoilt tourists. Ben pulled the travel guide from his pocket and pointed to pictures of the complex. They moved a little further along, and there it stood as it had for more than two millennia, staring across the glinting Nile, a golden stone temple dedicated to long-forgotten gods. A relic of its time, it was achingly beautiful.

"Wow," muttered Gerhard in awe, forgetting his role for a second as he allowed the majesty and power of the ruins to wash over him. He took out his camera and took a range of photos of the temple and his companions. They bought entry tickets and made their way up the ramp to the imposing front.

Ben's eyes flicked around, watching for any sign of danger as they walked between the towering, golden stone columns of the vestibule. Every surface was carved with reliefs of the pharaohs and hieroglyphics telling their stories. He noticed paintings of flying vultures adorned the ceiling. Normally, he'd have stopped and studied everything, but for now, his archaeologist's sensibilities took second place to his primordial sense of survival.

The sun lay beams of light in their path, and the columns created deep pools of shade - perfect hiding ground for would-be assassins. Sweat droplets ran down his neck as he forced himself to wander around and point at random carvings to maintain their tourist veneer. They'd decided the most probable location of their next meeting with the familiars was the sanctuary dedicated to the worship of Sobek. It was at the rear of the complex, so it was vital they continue their disguise to reach it.

They ambled along, admiring a detailed carving of Sobek in one frieze. Ellie made them pose next to it to take photos. As they moved towards the rear of the complex, they broke into two groups as agreed earlier. Ellie and Gerhard veered to the left, visiting the Sanctuary of Horus the Elder, while Ben pottered around the Shrine of Hathor before appearing to search around for them and entering Sobek's Sanctuary to the right.

Ben allowed his eyes to adjust to the deep gloom in the enclosed sanctuary before moving around, examining the decorated walls. He ran his hands along the etched walls, fascinated by the artistry of the long-dead stone masons who had used shadow to accentuate their work. There was a deep peace within the Sanctuary, a level of silence and spirituality that evicted the modern world.

Unfortunately, the pulse of energy that normally preceded the appearance of the deities was absent. Ben used his mental link to call to Sobek as he'd done before, but the connection remained dormant. Scratching his head, he took a deep breath to centre himself and ponder his next steps. Sobek might be a pain in his ass, but the little fellow had been a powerful dude in his time and had his own temple.

Ben decided maybe he needed to pray to Sobek. Perhaps his familiar had ego issues. Realising that the ancient Egyptian prayers had been ritualistic and full of sacred offerings, Ben decided he'd have to do a more modern take on the process. He imagined wafting incense around the room and the laying down of valuable scented oils and colour pigments in offering to Sobek. He bowed low and walked backwards, away from the centre of the room, where the statue of Sobek would have once stood, whilst praying for his help.

Nothing. Silence.

He glanced around to make certain no one had been watching him, then walked towards Horus the Elder's sanctuary, where Ellie was chatting in Arabic. Gerhard was nodding as if following Ellie's endless jabber. Even Ben had difficulty following the Saudi dialect that Ellie was using. She appeared to be on a tirade about the Ancient Egyptians following false Gods.

She turned to Ben and asked in Arabic, "We thought we'd lost you, brother. Anything worth seeing over there?"

Ben shook his head and replied, "Nothing different to here, little sister." He gestured for them to leave the sanctuary and took a path out towards the external courtyards.

The ancient Egyptians had mastered acoustics, and Ben knew that conversations within the walls were projected, almost as if by loudspeaker, to other areas of the temple. The high priests had used this facility to listen in on the private prayers and confessions of Egypt's high society. When they were back at the front of the complex, they huddled around Ellie as she pretended to show them her photos and whispered to each other.

"What the hell can we do now? There was nothing in the Sanctuary. This isn't the right place! I'm sure," Ben confided to the group.

"You told us last night about the museum dedicated to the mummified crocodiles - that might be worth checking out. Oh, and I just saw a sign for a crocodile pit - just over there." Ellie said, pointing towards a key-shaped structure cut down into the sand to their side.

Some Egyptian visitors walked towards them, so Ellie again reverted to Arabic. "This is a lovely shot of you, Papa. Look at the sun just lighting your face," she said, pointing at the camera screen. They were edging towards the crocodile pit when Ellie spotted something. She lifted her camera. "I'm taking a panorama to show Mama tonight. I hope she's feeling better."

She rotated, holding the camera in front of her so she had a full view of the surroundings, her peripheral vision being impaired by the headdress. Every person in the panorama was Egyptian, and most appeared to be watching them. There wasn't a foreign visitor in sight.

She stopped and showed the guys the image, whispering, "We have a problem. We're surrounded!"

Ben flicked his eyes around, estimating forty people in the immediate vicinity. He scanned the area, searching for cover. They were standing in a huge, open area with just a tiny temple building far in the back, columns left over from a long-vanished building, and a couple of oddly shaped pits. Nothing that would offer any cover, and the only clear exit was blocked by a tour group of Egyptians. They were trapped.

The flight or fight instinct kicked into gear. He felt the energy surge from his core, powering his muscles for action. His mind flicked through ways to protect his friends. The options were limited, and none appeared to have a favourable outcome. The group was becoming encircled by the pseudo-tourists when Ben finally felt the spark of Sobek and saw the faintest wisp of blue energy radiating from the belly of the crocodile pit.

Ben closed his eyes to centre himself and took a large breath. "To the pit - RUN!"

Gerhard and Ellie didn't stop to question Ben's instructions and instead picked up the hems on their gowns and sprinted. The wisps of energy unfurled like a fern leaf, reaching out towards the trio as they hurtled towards the key-shaped pit. The Egyptians surrounding them reached into pockets, jackets, and bags and withdrew weapons.

Time slowed as they raised the guns. Ben glanced sideways to see Ellie stumble and fall, tripped by the Abaya. He twisted to go back and help her, his arms pumping to propel him. He saw the puff of sand as she hit the floor and the other where the bullet sank into the gritty ground just to her left. He reached her side, tugging her to her feet and pulling her with him towards their goal.

The blue wisp grew larger and formed into a tentacle that swept some the gunmen off their feet. Gerhard had reached the barrier around the pit and hurdled it, like a man possessed, and ran down the steps before he wobbled to a complete halt at the sheer drop.

Ben pushed Ellie over barrier before climbing it himself. A hand grabbed him and pulled him backwards. As he toppled, he shot his head back and hit his assailant with a brutal headbutt. The man fell back, clutching his nose, out of the fight temporarily, but there were others right behind him. Ben jumped to his feet, preparing to face the assembled firing squad. Then the tentacle wrapped around him, lifting him clear of the barrier and throwing him into the bottom of the pit, knocking both Ellie and Gerhard to the base.

They lay in a jumble of arms and legs, winded and frightened, looking up at an array of weaponry that would have made Al Qaeda proud. Every gun pointed straight at them, and as they wriggled around, searching for an escape route, they realised they were trapped at the bottom of a deep pit. The first click of the safety release echoed around the chamber, amplified and sounding like the last death rattle. This was it. They were about to be killed, having no clue why they'd even been targeted.

Ellie crawled onto her hands and knees and pulled herself upright. "Wait! Tell me why you are targeting us! What the hell have we done to be hunted down? Why us? Tell me, in the name of all that is merciful!" she beseeched them in Arabic, turning and looking them all in the eye. "Cat got your tongues? Brave enough to chase me with a gun but not to tell me the truth before killing me?"

A dark man with leathered skin and a dusty turban rolled around his head spat down at her. "It's not what you've done but what you can do in the future. It's who you are - filthy infidels. The House of Scarabs will not rise - so help me, God."

The man jerked as another man hit him around the head whilst shouting, "*Khalas*, enough. Fire!"

The pit amplified the sound of each shot to a level of rolling thunder, which deafened the three trapped within it. A barrage of fire concentrated into one small area. Each bullet slowed and hovered in midair until there appeared to be a spherical umbrella of bullets floating over Ben, Ellie, and Gerhard's heads. The gunmen couldn't believe their eyes and continued to open rounds into the shaft, unable to see the protective sphere thrown up by the three deities who stood next to their hosts.

Ben turned to Sobek, who had taken a human-sized form. "Okay, you've got me here. Let's get this over with, so we can get back to normal life."

Sobek lifted his crocodile head, stared Ben in the eye, and with a nod, grabbed Ben's hand. The other deities gestured that the trio should form a circle with Sobek, linked by hands. When the circle was completed, the trio felt their bodies fall to the dusty floor. When they looked down, they realised they were no longer in their bodies. Just a sheer silk thread of energy tied them to the motionless forms.

Sobek pulled their hands, and they floated up the shaft, through the sphere, and over the heads of their attackers, leaving their unconscious bodies protected by Bastet and Khepri. Like balloons with trailing strings, they floated up and away - over the dusty roofs and streets, over the patch-work of emerald fields, over the sandy plains and crumbling mountains, ever farther from their empty bodies.

THE MELD

S obek landed in a sandy valley two miles south of Kom Ombo. As they touched down, they tried to stand, but without the weight of their bodies, gravity could not anchor them to the ground, so they floated in the breeze.

"That was amazing. It was like being a bird but with none of the effort of flying. Did you see the views?" Ellie said, buzzing with excitement.

Bent doubled, with his hands on his knees, Ben looked green around the gills. He grated out, "Never again."

Gerhard studied their surroundings for any indication of where they'd been taken and why. They'd touched down in a dry desert basin with nothing but sand and crumbling rock formations, the largest of which had a large rectangular doorway carved into it, through which was a room. The cruise ship-shaped rock stood, like an iceberg in open water, anchored on the basin floor.

Finally, he said, "Ben, can you sense from Sobek if our bodies are safe with Bastet and Khepri?"

Ben raised himself up and peered at his familiar. "He's

oozing tranquility at me, so I guess so," he answered before fixing a hard stare at the crocodile-headed man in front of him. "Dude, no more astral projections or whatever the hell that freaky journey was. Not cool, man. Not cool at all."

Sobek nodded slightly and turned to walk towards the formation. The trio sighed and followed him. Although the hill appeared small from a distance, it towered above them as they moved closer. The doorway was halfway up the side and a sheer climb up crumbling stone that would have been hazardous if they'd been on foot. Their ethereal forms made the ascent easier, allowing them to float up behind Sobek.

As they reached the door, Sobek gestured for them to wait as he entered and was swallowed by the darkness. After a few moments, he reappeared in the doorway and gestured for them to follow him.

They entered a room lit only at the opening by a golden rectangle of sunlight. The pitch-black room was pock-marked with deep vaults cut into the sides, long enough to hold fifteen-foot coffins. Each of the burial chambers was illuminated by a phosphorescent green glow. Four further passages were carved deeper into the hillside, and they each emitted the same light. In the centre of the room was a slightly raised plinth, which Sobek approached. As he walked up and centred himself on it, a shaft of light shot in from the doorway, illuminating his features. His croco-dilian head was both fearsome and awe-inspiring. Ellie shuddered and turned to study the deep vaults more closely.

Some chambers still contained the wrapped mummies of long-dead crocodiles, preserved by the skill of the pharaohs' priests. Inside every chamber was a small, trans-parent crocodile that appeared to be curled in sleep. It was these forms that emitted the eerie green glow. It struck Ellie that these were the souls of the crocodiles held in stasis within their burial place.

As she turned to share her findings with Ben and Gerhard, the light that illuminated Sobek fractured into hundreds of individual rays. Each flowed to a chamber, merging with the glow of the occupant before transforming into a bright blue energy that washed the crocodile in its healing warmth. Each of the crocodiles awakened, yawned, and then turned to face the exit of their vaults. As Ellie watched, they grew, some reaching twelve feet and more. She jumped back as one yawned, showing a mouthful of dagger-like teeth.

One by one, each of the crocodiles slithered out of their holes, snapping at each other as they made their way to the foot of Sobek's plinth. Pandemonium broke out. The larger crocodiles consumed the smaller ones with just a bite. Many scuffles between equal-sized individuals ended with one ripping the other limb from limb and consuming their spoils. The room became a bloodbath as a battle for supremacy broke out within the enclosed environment. From the sounds echoing down the passages, the same thing was happening throughout the Necropolis.

Ellie leapt into one of the vacated chambers, and Ben and Gerhard followed suit. None of them wanted to risk their ethereal forms. Sobek watched on with the same tranquility he'd projected to Ben earlier.

The room grew quiet as the winners from the four passages joined the main room's victor to have a final fight for supremacy. As each crocodile had won a fight and consumed its opponent, it had taken on their strength and the strengths the adversary had won in their own battles. So, the final five were monstrous in both size and strength. Each wore the scars of victory like medals on a general's chest.

The walls shook as tails whipped into them, causing huge structural cracks. Bloody limbs freshly ripped from their owners splattered against the walls. The sound of hisses and snarls shook dust from the old, carved-out ceiling, raining debris down onto the dueling monsters. Gerhard averted his eyes, unable to stomach the sight of more bloodshed and injury.

Finally, the room was empty except for one huge monster of a crocodile, battered and scarred but the final survivor of an epic battle. It padded over to Sobek, favouring its left leg and with part of its tail missing, its victory determined but not without significant personal cost.

Sobek bent to the crocodile and touched its head in a gesture like the knighting of a lord. As he stepped back, his form morphed into a full, twenty-foot-long Nile crocodile. Sobek opened his gaping maw and bowed down low. The other crocodile looked around the now vacant room before stepping into Sobek's mouth to be the final victim of the great sacrifice.

The trio remained fixed in place, stunned by what they'd witnessed, before scrambling out of the burial chamber and walking, somewhat hesitantly, towards Sobek, the God of Crocodiles.

"That is a spectacle I never wish to experience again," Gerhard murmured, taking cautious steps to avoid the blood pools and body parts that covered the chamber's floor. "Quite horrifying."

"Jeez, Gerhard, the understatement of the century. My stomach threatened to revisit breakfast more than once."

Ellie and Gerhard woke, heavy in their bodies. They stared

up from the bottom of the shaft, able to see the Egyptians peering down at them but unable to move their bodies. Ben's soul hadn't rejoined his body and stood to its side. Sobek, in his vast form, took up most of the bottom of the pit.

Ben glanced down and saw water gurgling in from a hole in the wall and rising fast. He struggled to help his friends, but without the use of his body, he couldn't do anything. Ellie and Gerhard strained to break free of the paralysis to warn Ben about Sobek's approach, for the crocodile was prowling up behind him. Too late, Ben turned and saw Sobek's open mouth descend on him. Ben's soul was consumed within the essence that was Sobek.

The crocodile, in an almost perfunctory manner, turned to dine on Ben's body, swallowing him whole.

Gerhard called upon Bastet to break free of his binds. He bent down and scooped Ellie into his arms, shaking a little under her weight. There was nowhere to go, no way to escape the shaft. They had a heavily armed militia above them and their friend's killer behind them. He circled the pit, keeping his back to the wall and his eyes upon Sobek, who was undergoing a rapid growth spurt. His body now encircled the entire shaft, nose to tail. Gerhard realised this made the crocodile far less agile in the small space, which could give them a chance to outrun him. Ellie, still locked in her body, stared up at Gerhard with huge eyes.

The energy in the pit changed, amplified by the souls of Sobek's sacred crocodiles. Sobek pulsed with light, which grew brighter and intensified into a dazzling ring around the bottom of the shaft. The light gave a final blinding pulse before exploding upwards with tremendous force. The explosion blew out the top of the pit and everything near it, killing many of the Egyptians instantaneously and injuring most of the rest.

Gerhard had thrown himself to the floor, using his body to protect Ellie, and as most of the force of the explosion had gone up, they were unhurt. Ellie pushed free of him as soon as the rubble settled. Blinded by the light, they rubbed their eyes, blinking furiously. As their eyesight returned, they saw Ben standing quietly in the epicentre of the explosion, staring into space.

His meld with Sobek was complete.

Ellie and Gerhard ran to him, staring in awe. Unlike Gerhard, Ben had limited physical changes. The meld had enhanced his musculature, so he appeared stronger, and he had a few grey hairs at his temple, but his transformation was at a personality level. He projected a gravitas that had eluded him prior to the meld.

He stood. "Let's go while the going's good."

THE GUARDIANS OF THE ANKH

Tjati lowered the phone onto its receiver and stared into the distance. There was an inevitability to the call. Yet again, his plan had failed. He removed his glasses and rubbed the indentations on his nose. The weight of his task felt heavy on his shoulders.

He remembered the conversation he'd had with his predecessor when the role was passed to him. The old man had been so sad that he hadn't been able to fulfil his duty and end the House of Scarabs. He'd told Tjati of all the things he'd done to find the members of The House of Bastet and The House of Sobek, and how they'd always slipped through his widely flung nets. The only solid lead he'd found was the location of the members of the House of Khepri. He'd deployed a policy of observation as he believed, as did their seers, that the House of Khepri would attract the other houses like bees to honey.

Tjati had considered his predecessor's counsel wise and followed the same approach. He stayed close to the family members of the House of Khepri, deploying undercover spies to ferret out intelligence on their plans. Yet, in the thirty years he'd headed the Guardians of the Ankh, he'd come to believe the Westons knew nothing of their heritage or great power. That belief comforted him. Still, he'd remained vigilant, always employing tactics to isolate and marginalise them.

He exhaled. Maybe this was all his fault. If he'd taken less notice of the advice, he'd have received and just obliterated the family earlier. The House of Scarabs wouldn't be so close to fulfilling the role outlined for it over three thousand years before.

I can't be the Tjati that failed. I can't be the one to allow this monstrosity to occur. The good Lord knows I've tried my hardest to be His true and loyal soldier.

He fell to his knees, a solitary tear trailing a path down his freckled cheek, and prayed as he'd never prayed before.

PART FOUR
ELLIE'S QUEST

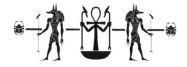

LUXOR-BOUND

"**K**areem, set sail now," Ben wheezed as he leapt onto the boat, running to release the mooring lines. "Quick - they'll be here any minute."

Ellie ran to help release the lines. Gerhard kept watch on the quayside, turning to spring on board as the boat drifted from the riverbank. Kareem directed the boat into the river's deep channel, ditching the sails in preference for the speed of the motors.

As the boat eased away from the centre of Kom Ombo, heading into the rural countryside, they saw a crowd running towards the quay. A buzzing hive of anger, emphasised by the wild gestures and shouts of the crowd, was left in their wake. A shot reverberated through the air, missing the boat and lodging into the bank with a puff of dust. They cranked the engine, and the boat surged forward, moving out of range.

Kareem eyed their bedraggled outfits and dirt-streaked faces. "A great success, I take it?" he said with a raised eyebrow. "So, that's the mob you're running from?"

Ellie nodded, sinking onto the bench next to him.

He watched her for a second before wrapping her in his arms. "Come here, *habibti*. Thank God you're okay," he murmured as he dropped a kiss on the top of her head.

She resisted for a moment before relaxing into his familiar embrace. With a large breath, she pulled back and looked into his eyes. "How long can we outrun them in *The Thebes*?"

He rubbed her back, shaking his head. "We can't outrun anything on the river except a felucca or a rowing boat. The motor's for emergency use. It's not powerful, and there's no wind for the sails. I'm sorry, Ellie, but now they've seen the boat. It's so recognisable, it's not safe for you."

She nodded, suppressing a sob, and leaned into him, pressing a long kiss on his cheek. "You have nothing to be sorry about. I've abused your friendship and brought trouble to your door. I'm so sorry." Ellie turned to Gerhard and Ben. "We've got to protect Kareem. Ideas?"

"Ellie, I'm a grown man. You don't need to protect me. I'm armed and have contacts at every point down this river. I'll be fine. They want you, not me!"

"You don't understand!" she shouted. "They have connections everywhere. We know nothing about them. It's like fighting a ghost with a sword. One of your bloody connections could be with them, and they've killed! Do you think they wouldn't torture to get information to help them find us? For God's sake, we don't even understand why they are chasing us, but they are relentless, and they won't stop until we stop them. They're deluded." She turned desperately to Gerhard. "Tell him. Make him see reason. TELL HIM."

Gerhard opened his mouth to reply, twisting his head to one side. Then he turned as a flotilla of small motorboats appeared from the bend in the river behind them.

At least ten small boats with large outboard engines roared towards them, as well as one large pleasure boat at the rear. Kareem grabbed his gun from the floor of the cabin and jumped outside. Before anyone could react, he was firing rounds of ammo at the incoming vessels.

Ellie watched helplessly as he gestured for Gerhard and Ben to grab the other guns he'd brought on board and join him. Kareem had done his years of military service and knew his way around the gun, as did Ben and Gerhard, to Ellie's surprise. She, however, had always been fervently anti-gun. This was the closest she'd ever been to one. She ran to the wheel of the boat and manoeuvred it to hide the vulnerable sides and present only the stern to the vanguard of the attackers.

The air was heavy with the reverberation of gunfire. Shots dislodged shards of *The Thebes*'s wooden hull, which flew like shrapnel, embedding in the upholstered seat of the captain's chair behind her.

"Don't fire on the pleasure boat," Ben screamed. "It's firing at the smaller boats." Ellie tried to see but ducked down as the window behind her shattered, raining down splinter-thin shards of glass. No matter how she tried, the boats were gaining on them and flanked both sides of the boat. Three men couldn't compete with the overwhelming gunpower of the other side.

"Gerhard - behind you!" Ellie screamed as a thickset Egyptian man with one eye clambered on board, pulled out a knife, and lunged at him.

Gerhard turned and grabbed his attacker's forearm to stop the knife. As his hand touched the man's dirty sleeve, a blue glow spread up the sleeve and around the Egyptian's flowing gown, wrapping itself tighter as it engulfed him. The man looked to Gerhard in shock before gasping and falling to the floor, staring up from a sightless eye. Gerhard stumbled backward, escaping the truth at his foot. He'd killed the man with just a touch. His eyes met Ellie's before he straightened, ready to face the next man already making his way on board.

Ellie searched around, desperate for inspiration. She saw the lamp rocking with the sway of the boat, turned back to the wheel, and swung it to the far left. As the boat turned, it banged into the boat to its left, knocking the people trying to board into the dark and fast running waters of the Nile. Still, it was hopeless. They were so outnumbered.

She saw Ben sprinting towards her, horror streaked across his face, his eyes focused behind her. She dropped to the floor as he raised his gun and shot where she'd been moments before. A man smelling of hot days in the sun fell on her. Blood splashed her face. Ben dragged her up as her would-be assailant grabbed her ankle. Ben kicked him and delivered a punishing punch to the wounded man's face. Where the blow made contact, the blue mist expanded, wrapping the man in its deadly grip. As his life stuttered to an end, he released her ankle. Ben stared in disbelief, unable to process what he'd just seen. What he'd just done.

"Your touch will kill them. I saw Gerhard do it," Ellie shouted over the rumble of the fighting. She bent and retrieved the gun and gave it to Ben, pushing him towards Kareem, who was surrounded by three men. "Go help him."

As the fight progressed, Ellie lost sight of Gerhard, who'd taken to reaching over the side of the boat and grabbing anyone who tried to board. It was an effective defence strategy, with bodies falling into the gaping mouth of the Nile at every touch.

Ben and Kareem were fighting back-to-back but overwhelmed with the volume of attackers. Ellie saw someone climb the sail and raise his gun to fire at the two men. Before she could shout a warning, he fired. A screen of shimmering blue energy flew up, and the shot bounced back at the man, killing him. As it deflected the attackers' targeted shots, the fight evened out until just one man stood on deck and empty boats bobbed on the current of the Nile.

Ellie peered at the pleasure boat that had come to their rescue. Haloed against the burning sun, it was little more than a dark outline. She saw an arm, silhouetted against the sun, raise and wave at them. The engine rumbled on full throttle as the high-powered boat raced towards them.

Kareem turned his gun from the prisoner to the fast approaching boat. "No offence, but we don't know who you are. Show yourself before I unload this gun into your hull."

A man stepped out of the wheelhouse into a pool of sunlight.

"Sam?"

THE ALLY

Ellie gasped and grabbed the boat's rail. Kareem leapt from the deck onto the other boat and grabbed Sam by both arms, staring at him for a moment before pulling him into a back-slapping hug. Ben stared, open-mouthed, looking from Sam to Ellie, who were staring at each other.

"What the hell, man! It's so good to see you. We wouldn't have made it without you distracting them. The old military service skills came through, huh?" Kareem slapped him on the back again before pulling him in for another hug. "Damn, it's good to see you again!"

Sam nodded, never taking his eyes from Ellie.

Ellie nodded briefly before turning away and walking to Gerhard's side. "We need to get information out of this guy. More may be coming, and we should be elsewhere when they arrive." She ignored Ben's gaping stare and walked up to the sole survivor of the attack. "What's your name?" she asked in Arabic.

He spat at her, phlegm dripped down her cheek.

"Oh, I wouldn't have done that if I were you. Did you

notice how my friends can kill with just a touch? I'm curious if I can do it... shall we try?" She reached towards him, and he jumped back, avoiding her touch. "Don't fancy that, huh? I'll repeat the question. It's a simple one. What is your name?"

"Hossam," he mumbled.

"Hossam, now we are getting somewhere. You see how this works? I ask a question and you answer. Now what is the House of Scarabs?" Ellie asked, leaning close to stare into his eyes.

"You are," he spat back. "The three of you are the House of Scarabs – or will be, if we don't succeed."

"Succeed in killing us, I suppose?"

He nodded.

"What organisation do you represent?" she asked with her finger trailing through the air next to his cheek.

He pulled back again until his back was against the shining teak wall. "We are the Guardians of the Ankh," he stated, lifting his chin and staring into her eyes. "And we will not fail. Kill me – it doesn't matter. There are many others who would take my place to serve such a cause. Who would gladly die to stop you."

Ellie shuddered at the mania in his eyes. He was a fanatic in its truest sense. Why did he hate them so?

"Tell me, Hossam, why is the House of Scarabs so bad? What have any of us done to stir such hatred?"

"You're heretics. Your existence is an insult to my God. You will wreak such evil on this world. You will not make it to Karnak. We will stop you."

He surged towards her and wrapped his fingers around her throat, closing her windpipe. She fought back, struggling to take a breath. She pulled at his fingers, trying to release them to let air pass. He was a large man and well-trained; her efforts achieved nothing. Kareem and Sam jumped back onto *The Thebes*, rushing to help, as Gerhard moved forward and raised a fingertip to the man's straining hands.

Hossam's last conscious act was to squeeze tighter before the life flowed from his body and he released Ellie. She fell into Ben's arms as she struggled to reclaim her breath.

"Gerhard! Why? We needed to know if any more are coming. We could have learnt more," she croaked.

"*Nein, mein kleiner liebling*, we need you alive more than we need that information. There will be more; we know that. We will not be safe until you've met Khepri. It's clear we must make our way to Karnak. We got that from him. Ben and I appear to be virtually impervious to danger now. You're not. We must move on. Come now, let's not waste time."

"Elena! My Elena, are you okay?" Sam said, running to her side.

She looked up "You. Are. Not. Welcome. Here. GO!" She pulled free and walked away, towards the lounge. Sam grabbed her arm. She pivoted, slapping his hand away. "I am not your anything. You gave up the right to call me that the first time you touched that woman. Go now. We have enough problems without you adding further complications."

"Elena, I didn't..."

She shook her head, "Don't deny it. Just don't. Why are you here? Did you tell him where we were going?" she said, whirling to point a finger at Ben. "Or maybe it was you?" she shouted, glaring at Kareem.

Sam walked up behind her, stopping a few feet away, "Neither told me anything, Ellie. Ben said you wouldn't listen to him and to move on. I haven't seen Kareem in months, years. When you visited his houseboat, I followed and listened in at the window. I heard what you were planning and decided to follow, hoping I'd get a chance to talk to you. So, I borrowed the boat from a colleague, and here I am. No one plotted against you."

"Grand marital drama. I get it, very important and all that, but maybe not now, whilst we have these Ankh guys trying to kill us. Priorities, peeps!" Ben said, earning glares from both Ellie and Sam. "Only saying," he said with a shrug of the shoulders. "Jeez, don't shoot the messenger."

Gerhard nodded. "He's right. This isn't the time."

Ellie glanced from one to the other before nodding. "Okay, well, I guess we need to get rid of these bodies and clean the boat, so..."

"Ellie," Kareem said, turning her to face him. "I've seen things today that will take time to absorb, if I ever do, but the fact remains you are my oldest friend. You must get away from here, and fast. For God's sake, leave me to scrub the boat down. I'll continue towards Luxor. Who knows? I might even distract them. Just promise me you'll explain all this when you can."

She nodded mutely.

"My prayers will be more ardent tonight. Of that, you can be sure," he said, wrapping her in one of his huge hugs. "Be safe, Ellie."

"I think we should take one of these speedboats," Ben said, peering down at the boats that surrounded them.

"It's too far to travel to Luxor in that. You'd need to refill the tanks, and you'd stand out like a sore thumb in the remote villages between here and there. I'll take you in my boat," Sam said.

"No! No way. Absolutely not!" Ellie spat out at him. "We'll take our chances with the speedboats."

Kareem stepped forward, blocking Sam from Ellie's sight. "*Habibti*. Elena, honey, put this to one side, in the name of God. Sam's right. Your only chance of avoiding notice is to go on his boat. The two of you can fight this out another time. In fact, you should. But for now, backbench your emotions and allow logic to prevail. Those men were not messing around; they mean to kill you. Save your life to fight another day. Please, honey. It's your only hope."

Gerhard and Ben kept their own council, just watching the drama play out. Ellie turned to them. "What do you think?"

"That's a loaded question if ever I heard one, Ells," Ben murmured, shifting from one foot to another. "If I answer it, you'll say I'm siding with Sam. You need to find the truth yourself."

Gerhard nodded in agreement. "Ben's right, Ellie, my dear. The path of greatest wisdom is often the one of most discomfort."

Ellie stared towards Kom Ombo, watching the white egrets wading among the reeds at the river's edge. The gods were mocking her, forcing her into close quarters with the one person she couldn't bear to be with. She sighed, strengthened her shoulders, and gave a bleak nod in their general direction.

The men rushed to clear the deck of the bodies, throwing them overboard. Ellie went below to pack the necessities, placing the Gayer-Anderson cat on the dining table with a note to Bertram. She trusted Kareem would make certain the statue found its way back.

At the last second, she penned Kareem a letter. She wasn't sure she'd make it through the coming days, and it felt right to say how sorry she was for involving him, for hurting him when she'd run away all those years ago. She'd boxed her emotions in ice for so long, she'd forgotten how important he was. As Sam had been her heart, Kareem had been her roots. She owed him a goodbye.

When she finished, she brought the paper to her heart before tucking it under a cushion, where he wouldn't immediately find it. She couldn't risk him trying to save her. She wouldn't risk his life. This was her battle. She'd fight it alone.

She went back upstairs, hugged Kareem briefly, and left *The Thebes*.

GUARDIANS OF THE ANKH

Dressed in white galabiyas, the two men dug around the foot of the mammoth columns, affixing the explosives to the foundation stones and then covering their exploits with a thick layer of sand.

"I don't feel comfortable with this, Hazem. Do you? I mean, this is our heritage."

Hazem looked down at him. "As long as it pays well and doesn't end in my death, I couldn't give a shit."

Aboud stood and observed the frenetic activity around him. He'd known most of the guys since his special ops days. He'd joined up with a passion for Egypt and a burning desire to serve his country. Yes, things had changed, and now he had to make his income selling his specialist skills to the highest bidder. But that old fire still had hot embers, and he couldn't equate the huge purse he'd get from this job with destroying one of the world's – and Egypt's – greatest treasures.

What did they know about the client? Yes, he was an esteemed and well-known man, but this action went against everything Aboud thought he knew about the guy. What would drive such a man to destroy something he so clearly loved?

Shaking his head, he knelt back down to lay the next ring of explosives around another of the three-thousand-year-old columns.

Tjati studied the bustle of people moving in military precision and felt the familiar ache in his chest. He'd lost so many trusted comrades, he'd had to resort to hiring ex-military resources, and it didn't sit well with him. Members of The Guardians shared his philosophy. Their families had been associates of the order since it began; they were steadfast. These mercenaries were just bodies for hire. They had no loyalty to anything except a deep and golden bursa, and that worried him profoundly.

Command central was an ageing, yellowed canvas tent erected on the scrubby land in front of the Scarab's statue. This was where he believed the fight of his life would take place if he didn't stop the trio from reaching Karnak. He stared at the temple, gleaming in the early morning sun, proudly watching over the Nile as it had for thousands of years. He prayed to God that he could spare it, that he would find them before they reached here. His role as Tjati took precedence over his own personal desires, so he would destroy it if he had to, but he prayed it wouldn't come to that.

The flap of the tent opened to allow Eurydice to enter. Gone was her usual disguise. Instead, she stood in camouflage fatigues, an elderly woman washed in sorrow but with the glint of determination of a true zealot.

"Is it done yet?" he enquired.

"The explosives will be in place within the hour. We have ten members of the Guild with remote detonators to ensure that unforeseen fatalities will not stop the mission." She handed him a small, pocket-sized box. "Here is yours. To set off the explosives, you lift this safety cover and press the button. The explosions will occur instantaneously, so make certain you are away from the hot zone before you press it."

"That may not be possible."

"No," she acknowledged. "Probably not."

"Come, Eurydice. Let us pray together. Our God will hear our prayers today and bless our righteous mission." She rolled out her prayer mat to face Mecca, and he dropped to his knees in the dirt. The Muslim and Christian prayed together, side-by-side, to save their unified view of the world.

They'd spread maps across the campaign table. Tjati and Eurydice, oblivious to the vicious heat under the canvas canopy, perused the maps, trying to define the most likely route the trio would take. They had spies at every point along the Nile, on every route from Kom Ombo to Luxor. However they were travelling, be it by car, airplane, helicopter, train, or donkey, if the trio were heading to Luxor, they would find them.

The satellite phone rang, the loud pealing startling them before Eurydice jumped to answer it. She murmured quietly before turning with bright eyes to Tjati.

"We've got them. They swapped boats. They are on a smaller boat with Sam."

Tjati nodded, turning to reach for his combat bag. "Tell

them to keep the boat under constant scrutiny but not to intercept it. I will head up this mission." He sorted his bag whilst Eurydice ended the call.

With the heavy bag on his shoulder, he turned to Eurydice. "I need to know I can depend on you, as my second, to complete the mission should I be unsuccessful. I need your troth, Eurydice. Under the pure gaze of God's eyes, you must promise me to finish the job our families committed us to so many generations ago."

Eurydice's watery old eyes gazed up into his hawk-like stare. "I swear my troth to our cause to complete the final mission of the Guardians of the Ankh, to destroy all members of the House of Scarabs and their descendants. I swear this troth under the merciful and true witness of Allah. May He be merciful upon us." She lowered her head and kissed Tjati's hands. "I have lived a long life, all of it dedicated to the service of the Guardians of the Ankh. I have forgone a family, a husband, and my true place in society, hidden and invisible within it. This I have done, and this I will do. You can trust in me, Tjati, as I trust in you. Complete your mission, and we can celebrate tonight *inshallah*."

He stared down at her for some time before patting her deeply lined cheek and leaving the tent.

HEALING

The inky blackness of night had long since wrapped the land in its sleepy embrace. The star-clad heavens provided the night's only light, which twinkled on the Nile's dark surface as the gently lapping waters provided the evening's soundtrack in an otherwise silent movie.

Sam hummed to himself as he guided the boat towards their final destiny. He'd spent much of the previous hour observing Ellie in snatched glances. Ben and Gerhard had retired for the night, leaving the first watch to Ellie. She'd gritted her teeth, but in an act of stoicism, she'd been performing her duty whilst ignoring him. He didn't mind; he was contented for the first time in years. Her proximity was a balm to his long-tortured soul.

"For God's sake, stop humming that damn song!"

"I'm sorry. I wasn't aware I was humming anything," he answered softly.

"Well, you were, and I hate that song. 'Angel of Mine', my foot."

"It was your favourite. You chose it as our first dance."

"Yes, another thing our brief union destroyed," she snapped at him before turning back to her lone vigil at the stern.

Sam looked down at the helm and scratched his head. The beauty of the night was swallowed by the bitterness of the comment. He turned and studied her. The Nile breezes played with her flaming titian locks. On the surface, she had changed little. Her skin was a soft, creamy alabaster, and she'd still fit in the elegant dress she wore on the day they married, yet her eyes told another story. They were cold and empty. She now wore a shield that aged her.

His Elena had been a passionate and open soul. This woman was the exact opposite. He wondered, as he had so many thousands of times before, what he'd done to bring his world crumbling down. He spun on his heel and put the boat into autopilot to navigate the long, straight stretch of the Nile.

"No, damn it. Enough is enough. I did nothing except love and adore you. Yet, you dare to point your finger at me in accusation. I wasn't the one who abandoned us – *you* were." He pushed his fingers through his dark, wavy hair. "I loved you beyond life itself. You were my best friend. My very heart. *Khalas*, Elena. I will take blame when it's due, but you did this, not me."

Ellie turned very slowly to face him. Her face was a vista of ice.

"Oh, no, Sam. We are not going there. I refuse to debate this subject with you. It's pointless. I know the truth. I've accepted it, and your empty protestations of innocence hold no sway with me. It's so far in the past, it's covered in a layer of dust an inch thick." She dismissed him, turning back to face the Nile.

He tore across the boat and grabbed her by both shoulders, shaking her. "How can I protest my innocence when I don't even understand the accusations against me? You didn't even have the decency to tell me what devastating action I took to force my wife to abandon me, our home, our life. Did I suffocate you with love? Did you tire of me?" He shook her again. "God help me, I will have the truth this time, Elena. I will not go to my grave riddled with doubt and pain. You will tell me."

"Oh, that's right - intimidate me. That's just typical. Go to hell, where you belong," she spat before wrenching free of his hold.

He watched her move away. His cheeks clenched as he took a deep breath.

"You're right. I'm sorry. I shouldn't have shaken you." He moved close behind her, breathing in the scent so unique to her, a clean, floral perfume that reminded him of happier times. "I swear, as God is my witness, all I've ever wanted was for you to be happy. Your happiness has always taken priority over mine. If you can tell me you're happy now and mean it, then I'll accept this torture as the cost I must pay. But you're so far from happy..." he said, rubbing his hand down her arms. "I find I can't bear it."

Ellie stiffened but didn't move away. She watched the waters eddy and part around the boat's hull, a dark flow of energy. "Happiness?" she scoffed at him. "I haven't had a moment of happiness since you destroyed us, but I've found a certain peace. A satisfaction in what I've achieved. Happiness is overrated anyway. It's a temporal disturbance in life's flow. I find if you don't expect it, then life moves along easier."

He stepped closer and wrapped a length of her hair around his finger. "I've missed you... us. Until my dying day, you will always be the only woman I've loved. The only woman I've wanted. Since you left, I've not so much as looked at another. No one matches you. They can't and they never will. My beautiful Elena..." He kissed the top of her head, exhaling and fighting the urge to pull her into his arms, where he thought she belonged.

She turned and, with a volcanic burst of energy, slapped him. He pulled back, rubbing his cheek.

"You dare speak of love. Oh, your love was so deep, you took another woman to bed, to our bed! Well, save me from such love," she spat, her eyes blazing with hatred and anger. Sam stepped away from her, banging into the helm door behind him.

"What? I've never slept with another woman since we met. I don't even think I physically could, truth be told. Where the hell did you get that notion? I swear on the only thing precious to me—your life—I didn't sleep with anyone. You must believe me."

"Believe you? Never! You know something, you didn't just end our marriage that night, you killed our child. I was pregnant, Sam. Pregnant. While you were salivating over some harlot, I was growing our child. You want to know what love is? Do you? Love is when your body fails to thrive without its nurturing touch. My heart broke, and my body couldn't sustain my child. You killed our child just as much as if you'd taken a knife and stabbed it."

Sam stared at her, aghast. His legs crumbled as tears poured down his face. His sorrow rendered him mute as he rocked back and forth. A silent blanket wrapped the boat.

He remembered the day she'd left. She'd run downstairs barefooted, her hair flying behind her, and leapt into his arms, laughing as he exhaled under the strain of her unexpected weight. She'd covered his face in kisses before capturing his mouth in a passionate kiss full of longing and love. He'd responded ardently, unable to resist her.

"Come back to bed. We have something to celebrate," she'd mewed in between increasingly passionate kisses.

He'd glanced across at the wall clock and moaned. "Oh, God, I'm hosting that seminar, and I'm already late. Don't tempt me, you minx." He'd caressed her cheek and kissed her once more. "Shall we reconvene at five p.m.?" he'd murmured into her hair.

"You'd better believe it, and maybe again at six," she laughed with a teasing grin. He'd growled in frustration and bemoaned the seminar's timing before easing out of her arms, picking up his old, battered briefcase, and leaving their home. When he'd returned that night, full of excitement and ardour, he'd found an empty house. Her clothes were gone. Now, at last, he understood why.

He sobbed as he imagined their child running and dancing between them. A darker version of Elena. He imagined their happy home, which, by now, would have had a brother or sister for the lost baby. He imagined Elena softly cradling his child as it nursed at her breast, her head bent, watching it as she sang a gentle song. The loss he felt at losing Elena was nothing to what he felt now.

He lifted red-rimmed eyes to her steely gaze. "I didn't know."

"How could you? You were too busy fucking your bitch."

"Elena, I swear to you, there has never, ever been anyone but you. I'm begging you to believe me. I swear it on our child's life."

"Ah, well, that's just it. Our child had no life," Ellie said, brushing her hair from her face with a sigh. "Sam, please, no more lies. I saw the photos with my own eyes. Stop the pretence. It's all in the past, and I can't talk about it anymore. It's opening old wounds."

Sam stared at her, unable to process what he'd heard. Confusion wracked him. How could there be photos of him when he'd done nothing? His breath came in deep gasps as the old panic attacks he'd only recently overcome returned with a vengeance.

"I... I..."

He grasped his throat, unable to claim the surrounding air. He was locked in the horror of a misunderstanding of such vast dimensions, he didn't know how to unravel it. His face reddened as his body refused to breathe.

Ellie heard him gasping and turned to see him collapsing onto the deck. She ran to his side. "Sam, are you okay?" He shook his head, unable to get words beyond the block in his throat. "Is it asthma?" He shook his head again as she continued to run through a list of possibilities.

He pointed to his pocket. She pulled a large paper bag from it with a look of confusion. He grabbed it and brought it to his mouth, trying to breathe steadily in and out, as the doctors had taught him.

She sat on her heels as understanding crossed her face. "A panic attack? You never had those."

"Only since you left," he replied when he regained control of his breathing. "God, Elena. To think what you went through alone. What you've carried ever since. I should have been there. It was my responsibility to protect you, and I failed. I'm so sorry."

"It was your responsibility to be faithful as well," she whispered, the wind knocked from her sails. "The photos are graphic. They leave no doubt. How I've wished I could wash those images from my mind, but they play back, especially at night as I try to sleep. Your body, all slick with sweat, crawling over hers. Your hands stroking her face, just as you'd always done to mine. I see them and I hate you. So, Sam, give up on this great innocence act. The photos proved what a fool I'd been to love you so utterly. I'd poured everything into us, into our love, our marriage. When I left, I had nothing because my life made no sense without you. But I've carved out a new life. I've learnt to trust no one. To live solo. It's time you did the same."

Slow claps echoed around the boat. They both turned to see a man clapping, slowly. "Bravo. What a heart-wrenching tragedy. Romeo and Juliet you are not though."

He lowered his hands and reached for the machine gun swinging on its shoulder strap. Sam and Ellie both gasped as the man walked from the shadows of the boat's bow and into the gentle lamplight.

BETRAYAL

"Mourad? What are you doing here?" Sam asked.

"Oh, my dear boy, I would have thought the gun made that question redundant. I'm here to kill you. Well, to be accurate, I'm here to kill Ellie and her cohorts. You are collateral damage. I'm saddened by that, but a mission is a mission. God's work trumps all others. I know you'll understand."

Ellie stared blankly at him, unable to process his appearance. The elegant, gentle, scholarly man she'd known and loved her whole life stood before her in military fatigues with a gun. It made no sense.

"Uncle?"

"Now, Ellie, my dear, there's no need to make this more difficult than it needs to be. Don't think this is something I relish. It's not, but unfortunately, all our efforts to keep you away from the other members of the House of Scarabs have failed. Throughout the generations, we have chased your families, pushing you ever farther apart. But you had to be the one to unite them. I never wanted to kill you. Allah knows I've had my chances to kill you and your mother over the years, but I was trying to follow a moderate policy. Now I will go down in history as the Tjati that failed to stop the partial meld of the House of Scarabs. I have no choice now. You must die. The House needs all three pillars to fulfil its destiny. By killing you, I end the House of Scarabs. Well, and killing your mother, obviously, but that's in progress as we speak."

"NO!" Ellie screamed, fighting Sam to get to Mourad.

"I know. It's terribly sad. I'll miss the old girl more than you can imagine. She's one of my best friends and a damn fine archaeologist, but well, you've forced my hand."

"Mourad. For God's sake, what the hell are you talking about? What is this 'House of Scarabs'? You know Elena. She's a peaceful, God-fearing woman. Just tell her what to do. You'll do it, won't you, Elena? Please, Mourad, let's work out a solution where this 'House of Scarabs' isn't an issue," Sam pleaded, pulling Ellie behind him as he spoke.

Mourad shook his head from side to side. "It's far too late for that, Sam. That boat has sailed. She's absorbed the essence of Khepri, and he will push her to complete the meld. It's inevitable. She has to die. It's her, a short-lived human soul, or my eternal lord, God. There is no choice when faced with that option. Would you put her before your God, Sam?"

"Yes. Before anything."

"You would face eternal damnation for her? It didn't take much meddling for her to leave you, did it? Some carefully manipulated photos, and she walked away. She didn't even trust you enough to listen to your side of the story. Seems she's not as loyal as you, huh?"

"YOU! It was you?" Ellie screamed. "You killed my baby!"

She grabbed the handgun tucked into the rear of Sam's trousers and leapt sideways, shooting wildly. Shots thundered into Mourad's chest, arm, and shoulder. His fingers on the machine gun's trigger tightened, letting off a volley of rounds that peppered the boat. Sam spun sideways as he tackled Ellie to the deck.

The silence was deafening after the thunderous gunfire.

Ellie struggled to pull herself free of Sam, sobbing hysterically. She looked across at Mourad, his arms outstretched on the deck as if Jesus on the crucifix. His face was permanently painted with a quizzical expression. She stared down at the corpse, unable to process this old family friend had caused so much of her life's miseries.

Sam gasped, reaching for his shoulder, which felt like he'd been run over by a lorry. He pulled his fingers away and saw blood coating them. Ellie turned slowly to face him. Her hair flowed wildly around her shoulders, like a flaming halo against skin whiter than Sam had ever seen, her eyes haunted. She'd never seemed more beautiful to him.

"Oh, Sam, I'm so sorry!" she sobbed, running to him. He opened his arms. She covered his face in wild kisses. "Can you ever forgive me? I should have trusted you." Her hands ran over his torso to his face. She glanced down and froze. "You've been shot!"

"It's just a glancing wound. It's nothing. Come back here and kiss me."

The drumroll of shots had woken Ben and Gerhard. As they raced up onto the deck, they feared what they would find. The Nile glowed an azure blue as sinuous fingers rose into the air, knitting together to form a perfect orb around the boat. The fingers crept under the fast-flowing water until they reached the three boats that were surrounding the river cruiser and worked themselves up the hulls of the boats, searching out life. When they touched the occupants, they slivered over them, wrapping around their throats and up over their heads. All the occupants struggled to free themselves, thrashing around the boats blindly until they fell, silent and lifeless, to the boats' floors.

Holes riddled the fibreglass body of the boathouse. A man lay, as if in religious reflection, in a pool of blood oozing across the deck. Then there was Ellie and Sam.

Ben smirked. "Don't mind us! Jeez, it takes a massacre on board for you two to get your act together."

"Ben, hurry. Help me get Sam below. He's wounded," screamed Ellie as she held her hands against his injured shoulder.

Gerhard eased Ellie to one side and pulled the fabric away. The wound was large and free-flowing. Gerhard pulled Sam forward and saw the bullet had gone clear through him, leaving a large but clean exit wound on his back.

"Well, at least the bullet isn't lodged inside. It seems to have missed his major arteries. Sam, can you move your arm?" Sam tried, wincing, as he lifted his arm to rest on Gerhard's shoulder before dropping it back down again.

Gerhard watched as the blood slowed to a trickle. "This will need stitching and immobilising to give it a chance to heal. Do you have any superglue on board, Sam?"

Sam nodded wanly toward the helm house. "I think there's some kind of glue in the toolbox in there. I saw it when I was rooting through it, looking for a screwdriver the other day."

Ben sprinted to retrieve it while Gerhard dispatched Ellie, who gripped Sam's hand as if her life depended on it, to find clean cloth and the first aid box from below deck.

"What happened, Sam? That's Professor Mourad, is it not?"

"Yes," Sam said, spitting the whole story out as the others tended his wound. Ellie stood away from the group, watching Gerhard dress the wound with his normal efficiency, her eyes flicking to the grotesquely posed corpse of her old family friend.

"I killed him. I killed Uncle Mourad. Oh, my God," Ellie sobbed, rubbing her hands furiously on her trousers. "Daoud and Alex! How will I ever explain what happened to their father? Tanta Mariam depends on him. What have I done? I murdered him..." She grabbed the antibacterial wipes from the first aid box and scrubbed her hands. "How will I ever live with this?"

Sam struggled to his feet with help from Ben and moved to her side. "*Rohi*, my soul, you didn't murder him. You protected us. Me," he whispered as he pulled her to him. "He gave us no option. May God bless his soul."

"No. I could have talked him down. I should have tried. He made me so angry. I shot him in anger. That's the truth."

"Oh, my darling, yes, you did, and you'll learn to come to terms with that over time, but you had no other option. He was a zealot. His religious convictions blinded him. Honey, he was seconds away from killing us. Luckily, you got the first shots in," he said, dropping a kiss on her head and wrapping his arms tighter around her, wincing. "The blame lays solely at Mourad's feet."

He gestured to Ben and Gerhard over her head, to dispose of the body as he rocked Ellie in his arms, whispering words of comfort. She didn't notice the gentle splash as they eased Mourad into the Nile to join the carcasses of horses, donkeys, and many of his comrades in recent days.

REUNION

Ellie stretched and smiled as the sun played on Sam's sleeping face. The soft slap of the waves sounded through the hull, creating a gentle lullaby in the cosy cabin. Ben and Gerhard had insisted they'd take the rest of the night shift to give Sam a chance to rest. For once, Ellie hadn't argued with them.

She and Sam had taken the double berth and spent much of the night holding each other as they talked about Mourad's betrayal and mourned the loss of their child together. It had been cathartic for Ellie. She'd woken feeling lighter than she had in years. Even with the craziness that surrounded her, she felt at peace.

Sam mumbled and turned in his sleep, his head falling into the crook of her neck. She stroked his wavy, black hair. "I do believe I may have found my way to heaven," he croaked, nestling into her neck and leaving a long trail of kisses from there to her waiting lips. "Morning, sexy woman."

She beamed at him as she leapt up and straddled him.

"Morning yourself. I find I have a hearty appetite. How about you?" she said between passionate kisses.

"Hmm, now you come to mention it, I find my hunger is aroused too," Sam answered, taking proceedings into hand as he pulled her down to him.

Sometime later, they emerged, laughing and holding hands, onto the deck to find Ben at the helm and Gerhard preparing a makeshift breakfast.

"You two slept well?" Ben smirked. "Don't they both look refreshed and perky, Gerhard?"

Gerhard shook his head slightly and smiled at Ben. "Leave them be. They don't need your teasing after the night they've had."

Ben goofed, "I'd say that's exactly what they need after the night they had! So, the ice maiden melted at last," he said as he winked at Sam, who put a protective arm around Ellie.

"It took a little Egyptian warmth is all," he replied, laughing.

Ellie elbowed him in the ribs and cuffed Ben around the head. "She still has claws, so quit riling her," she snapped and then laughed.

Gerhard had prepared huge, fluffy omelettes dripping in butter from their depleted supplies. They each grabbed a plate and ate silently, enjoying every unctuous mouthful.

Ben wiped his plate clean with bread before sighing with satisfaction. "I needed that. Thanks, man."

Gerhard smiled and threw the tea towel at him. "You're washing up, then."

Ellie followed Ben into the galley and made coffee whilst Ben grumbled as he made his way through the dishes.

"Seriously, Ells, it's good to see you happy. Sam's a great guy and a very lucky one."

She turned her head and stared at him. "Did my ears hear right? Did the illustrious Ben Ellis just give me a compliment? Let me grab my phone, and you can say it again, so I can catch the moment for posterity."

Ben flicked bubbles at her and laughed. "Nope, never going to happen."

They carried the drinks on deck and sat sipping the coffee as they watched the green fields pass by. "It's odd. We're on our way to face God-only-knows-what for God-only-knows-why, and yet, I feel content," Ben said.

Gerhard nodded. "The calm before the thunder."

The other three laughed, spitting coffee everywhere. "The calm before the storm, Gerhard," Ellie said, leaning over to give his cheek a kiss. "I think maybe we should discuss the hot potato on the table," she continued.

"From everything we learnt last night and earlier, it's fair to say we are the descendants of this 'House of Scarabs' group." They all nodded. "Mourad and Hossam seemed certain it – and so, by default, us – is evil." More nods. "Could they be wrong? I mean, I don't feel evil. I'd never do anything to hurt anyone willingly, and I can't imagine either of you doing so either. I guess the big question is should we stop? Maybe run. Make certain that this final 'meld' doesn't happen," she said, fidgeting on her seat.

"Our choices are limited, *liebling*," Gerhard answered. "Can you imagine Khepri allowing you to stop? We'll find ourselves compelled to complete the meld. They will push us towards our final destination. I think we can only manage the outcome, not the journey."

"And you're happy with that? With some damn cat god jerking your strings?" Ben said, scowling at the Nile as he spoke. "I'm an archaeologist. This should be a dream come true for me. But I'm so over it right now. I'm being played by a frigging crocodile."

"No, of course not. Very far from it, but I'm being realistic. We haven't had a say since we first met. They have pushed and pulled us to this point, and I don't see a practical way of avoiding it. I'm merely assessing the data, not agreeing with it."

They looked at each other glumly. "So, onwards it is?" Ellie asked.

"As if we have any choice," Ben answered.

"I've been thinking about Karnak. There is no temple dedicated to Khepri or any link to him apart from the scarab pedestal. It seems it was dedicated by Amenhotep III, who also ordered the creation of 200 large stone scarabs that have been found across the breadth of the territory he ruled." She waited for them to reach her conclusion.

"The pedestal is our destination?" Ben said staring into space. "It's in an open arena. The perfect hunting ground."

"Yep. We're going to need some divine help and great disguises," Ellie agreed.

"I don't like it, Elena. Not one bit," Sam said, twirling the wedding ring he still wore. "You could be killed. If this Guardian of Ankh get its way, you will be. We need to go to the government and get you protection. It's crazy knowingly walking into an ambush. You've been lucky so far, but luck only lasts so long."

Ellie put her hand on his, stilling it. "You heard us. We have no choice. If we go to the government, we could be placing ourselves into the Guardians' hands." She stroked his cheekbone, cupping his face in her hands. "Believe me, *habibi*, I'd rather nothing more than to just walk away and leave this all behind me, but it won't go away. My mum's in danger. I must complete the meld."

He jumped from the loveseat at the front of the boat and twirled to face her. "Then I will come to protect you. Because *wallahi*, I swear to God, I will not stand by and lose you again. Don't ask me to!"

Ellie stared up at him. "Oh, honey, you're wounded, and we have the deities to protect us. You do not. Let me do this. Just this. Then I will return, and we can start anew. Besides, we need you to guard our escape route."

He closed his eyes, breathed deeply, and said, "So be it, Elena. So be it."

SUBTERFUGE

"Y ou stay close to Ben and Gerhard, you hear me?"
Sam said, pulling Elie's collar up around her
neck and securing the headscarf over her
flaming hair. He lifted her chin up with his fingertips,
placing a chaste kiss on her quivering lips before yanking
her into his arms and holding her head tight to his shoulder.
"Be safe, Elena, and go with God's blessings."

"That's the point in question, isn't it?" Her eyes glistened
with unshed tears. "But I promise I'll do my best."

They stared into each other's eyes, neither wanting to
take the first step apart.

"By the Gods, you two had better look after her. I'm
trusting you to bring her back, just as I've handed her off to
you, with not so much as a rustled hair on her head," Sam
said gruffly.

Ben wrapped him in a hug before cuffing him around
the head. "Don't worry, buddy. We've got this. Just focus on
keeping yourself safe and having this boat ready to blast off
when we return."

It was a sombre trio that stepped off the boat onto one of

the Nile cruisers tied in a long line away from the dock. They had moored next to the furthest boat and had to walk through the boats to reach the riverside dock. Walking through the luxurious receptions of the pleasure cruisers, all full of happy, sunburnt tourists, was a shocking juxtaposition to their situation. Life was going on as normal, with people laughing, toasting each other, and dancing, and yet, every step they took forward was a step towards death – if not theirs, then others'.

It had been a calculated move to dock in the chain of boats. They hoped the Guardians wouldn't risk the lives of so many foreign tourists and would bide their time. Gerhard had speculated that this would give them time to get to the Karnak Temple complex before facing their adversaries. It also helped to keep their boat hidden behind the much larger floating hotels.

They'd taken no chances though and were armed, as if fighting a war against a small nation, rather than a gang of rogue assassins. They tucked Ellie in between the two men so that any attackers would need to get through them first, as the Guardians had made it clear she was their main target. They'd donned new disguises, the holiday makers a little surprised to have a Roman Catholic nun and two priests walking through their receptions.

As they entered the last boat before the dock, Gerhard stopped them. "Although we met in the most peculiar of circumstances, it has been a great pleasure to know you both. You've rejuvenated me, and for that, I thank you."

"Oh, no, buster. You don't get to say the goodbye speech here. We will get to the bottom of this goddamn mystery, and tomorrow, we will have breakfast together and decide what's next. No one is dying. No one is saying goodbye," Ben said fiercely. "Now move your asses, and let's show these Guardian pussies what the House of Scarabs is made of!"

As they disembarked, they found a group of tourists formed at the end of the boarding bridge.

"Right, folks, we're going to enjoy the great temple of Karnak today. I'll do my best to bring the culture and history alive as we move around the various complexes. A few housekeeping rules today, okay?"

The group murmured their agreement.

"First off, follow the blue polka dotted umbrella as we move along," the tour guide said, brandishing a massive golfing umbrella in the air, "and make certain you keep up with the group. Please don't go wandering off alone. Secondly, you'll have free time to explore the delights of this wonder when we reach the famous scarab pillar. At that point, there is a basic café, and you'll have one hour to explore or sit and enjoy a cool drink and lap up the wondrous scenery. Please make certain you come back to the scarab promptly and we'll make our way back to the boat for the fancy dress party. Okay, everyone?"

The group nodded quietly.

"Come now, you can do better. Everyone excited?" the tour guide shouted, trying to get the boatload of English tourists to whoop and show a degree of excitement. They shuffled and murmured again as embarrassment consumed their English psyche.

"Quite so, very excited," said one man who held himself with the frame of a man used to marching in military formation. He'd decided to take one for the group and give the tour guide a satisfactory response. "Shall we proceed?" he suggested as he gestured towards the temple.

The tour guide, who introduced himself as Osman, was dressed in a flamboyant orange suit with a green shirt and tie, presumably to stand out and be a visible landmark to his group. He raised his umbrella, pointed in the general direction of the temple, and shouted, "Today's the day we will fight the tourists of Karnak and emerge victorious, my friends, enlightened by a vision of history so sublime, you'll remember this day forever. You'll tell your children and your children's children that today was the day you saw the most amazing sight of your life. That today was the day Osman enlightened you. Follow the umbrella, folks."

Ellie raised her eyebrows and smiled at Ben, who was trying hard not to laugh out loud. "I think he may have watched one too many Hollywood blockbusters," Ben said, "but he's right. Today may well be a day they live to remember, but not because of Osman's narration."

Gerhard chuckled. "Seems we've found our cover. Let's get lost in the middle of this group."

Osman proved himself a knowledgeable, if flamboyant, guide. He kept the party entertained, if somewhat embarrassed by his antics, as he acted out the battles and victories of the pharaohs who'd constructed the temple across its history.

"He'd be up for a Tony if he were treading theatre boards," a taciturn Northerner muttered under his breath to Gerhard as Osman writhed on the floor, acting out a poisoning.

The trio had kept themselves to the middle of the group and been busy taking photos and pretending to share them with each other. They scoured the shots for any clue as to the Guardians' whereabouts, finding no obvious trace of them.

The group moved through the second pylon, into the stone forest of the Hypostyle Hall. Columns reached up to the skies, towering fifty feet above them, creating a patchwork of shadows and light rays so far below on the floor. No one could help but be entranced and awed at the sight. As the surrounding tourists stared, Ben shivered, seeing the hall as the perfect trap. The shadows were hiding places, and the rays, a spotlight searching for the three of them. He searched around, combing the hall for any sign of the Guardians.

GUARDIANS OF THE ANKH

"**I**ncompetence! You dare to come here and tell me you can't find them," Eurydice raged, throwing the cup of water at the deputy in front of her. "We've lost Tjati and the entire support team. We are the last line of defence, and we will not fail. Do you hear me?"

Kawab shook the water off and took a deep breath before patiently explaining, "Eurydice, the temple has ten large tour groups and endless smaller parties wandering around the complex. It's like trying to find one sheep in a flock of thousands. Impossible. We must close the temple. It's the only way."

"How, pray tell, do you plan to do that? Without Tjati, we have no influence in the Ministries of Tourism or Antiquities. Besides, it will draw more attention here, which we can ill afford."

Kawab looked her firmly in the eye. "We'll expose one of the explosives and proclaim terrorist interest. The Guardians will swoop in as an anti-terror team and take control of the complex."

She placed her hands on the campaign table. They'd

reached a point of no return. She either threw everything she had at it, or they'd fail. She stared up at him. "Can it work? Do we have the manpower to control and search the people?"

Kawab nodded silently. "It is our only hope..."

Eurydice turned and faced the open flap of the tent, staring intently at the scarab pillar. "Make it so."

EXPLOSIVE FORCES

Osman had his group link hands around a richly decorated column to show the sheer size and magnitude of the architectural genius behind the temple's construction. Then, suddenly, a scream bounced around the hall.

"A bomb! There's a bomb at the base of this column."

The group froze for a split-second before they ran in all directions, a random wildness to the pattern of their fleeing. Screams echoed, joining new cries as hundreds of voices joined in a crescendo of fear. Some more infirm visitors fell in the chaos and were trampled under the feet of the panicked crowd.

They abandoned one old lady in a wheelchair at the base of the column, pleading for help. Gerhard bent down to her. "Madam, may I be of assistance? Would you allow me and my colleagues to push you to safety?"

"Oh, Father, thank you. Yes, please hurry." The woman beamed at them. "You're my guardian angels. Saved by God's own people."

"Sister Theresa, you push this dear woman, and Father

Patrick and I will clear the path for you," Gerhard said to Ellie.

She nodded and grabbed the wheelchair handles, pushing the woman towards the side exit that opened to the sacred lake. She shouted across at Gerhard, "Should we meet at the café as Osman instructed us, Father Ernst?"

Gerhard pulled a wounded old man to his feet and dragged him along towards safety. "Yes, Sister Theresa. That would appear to be a prudent course of action. We should deposit our friends there before undertaking more of our dear God's work."

Ben scowled at them but also bent to help people to their feet and get them out of the hall as quickly as possible.

Ellie's trajectory faltered as bands of men dressed in black ghosted in and out of the columns, armed to the back teeth with belts of ammunition and machine guns strapped across their chests. She shouted to the others to hurry. They cleared the hall and broke out into the outer courtyard leading to the sacred lake. Ellie saw the café to the left and ran as fast as she could, encumbered by the weight of a wheelchair across uneven terrain.

"Stop there, Sister," said a muscular man with his gun pointing in her direction. "You need to move towards the exit in an orderly fashion."

She smiled meekly. "I'm offering God's sweet hand to this poor woman, who has been separated from her loved ones. She's organised to meet them here, should they get lost. It's terribly important she stays put. My colleagues and I have been helping the wounded."

"That's all well and good, Sister. However, you are within the blast zone. We must clear the area. They have ordered me to move everyone to the car parks, where we will process them and make certain they are returned to their respective groups. If you'd follow me," he said, gesturing along the side of the temple.

Ellie searched the area, looking for Ben and Gerhard. She spotted them easing some of the wounded down into chairs to the rear of the open-fronted shack that normally served coffee and soft drinks to the overheated visitors. It now resembled a triage post.

"Father Ernst, Father Patrick, could you come over here?"

Ben glanced up, his eyes twitching as he saw the armed guard so close to Ellie. He patted the hand of the man he'd just assisted into the chair and followed Gerhard, who walked sedately towards Ellie.

"What is the problem, my child?"

"You must leave the area, Father. I was just explaining to the Sister that this area is within the blast zone. I must insist that you evacuate now."

Gerhard walked towards him and smiled gently. "Surely, you're not asking a man of the cloth to abandon those in need? Why, that would be a dereliction of our duty to our dear Lord Jesus Christ and God himself. Thank you for your concern, my son, but we will stay with these poor souls until you get medical support or evacuation via stretchers." He smiled at the man and patted his hand. "Now be a good chap and gather your burly colleagues to go back into the temple and help the injured in there. Be a hero, my boy."

Aboud, the guard, watched his colleagues in the distance uncertainly before turning back to Gerhard.

"Come now, there are people in need. Isn't that who you signed up to help?" Gerhard said, pointing back into the temple.

Aboud closed his eyes, shook his head from side to side,

and then rolled his shoulders backwards. "Yes, Father. Yes, it is, and it's long overdue I did it."

Ellie and Ben watched in disbelief as the man pounded back towards the special ops soldiers and shouted orders for them to round up the wounded and to call for paramedics.

"Hmm, that could have gone either way. Seems I was in luck," Gerhard said with a grin. "Come on, let's move."

They returned to the café, smiling at the people inside reassuringly. "What the fuck are we going to do now?" Ben hissed as they stared out at the scarab statue on the top of the pillar some distance in front. "We're just a few feet away. Shall we run for it?"

Gerhard gave an indiscernible shake of his head. "It has snipers focused on it. Look at the tent behind and up there, on the top of the temple. It's far too risky for Ellie. She'd never make it there. I think we should..."

"Father Ernst! Father, come here. Hurry!" Gerhard turned sharply to his right and saw Aboud beckoning him with a desperate wave of his arms. "There's a man – he's in a bad way and asking for a priest. He wants the last rites. Hurry, now!"

"Jesus Christ! We're done for now," Ben murmured under his breath. "Now what?"

Gerhard raised a hand in acknowledgement to the soldier and said, "No matter what, we must stick together. Let's go see if we can give this fellow some peace and help others to get out of that damn temple before the idiots blow it up around our ears."

Ellie frowned slightly and asked, "Gerhard, do you know how to administer the last rites?"

Gerhard grinned wryly. "I have a rough idea, but we'll wing it, as you Brits say. They won't know."

Gerhard led the way as they crossed within metres of

the statue, towards the Hypostyle Hall. Ellie stared at the scarab that had caused them so much anguish. It sat atop a granite pillar not much taller than the average man. One side was flat, with hieroglyphics adorning the surface. The statue was a slightly incongruous sight, having neither the polish nor grandeur of the other statues in the temple complex, and sat alone on the lakeshore.

Visitors now trotted around it as the guides delighted in spawning the story that doing so improved your chances of finding love. She stared at the carved beetle that crowned the pillar, an ugly fellow that didn't seem to warrant all the troubles they'd faced. Just an ugly old bug stood on a plinth of stone.

Ellie didn't notice the raised stone in the paving and stumbled slightly, bumping into Ben. He grabbed her arm, helping her keep her balance as she tipped forward.

～

"What's that fool playing at?" Eurydice pointed out of the tent's flap to the guard blatantly disregarding his orders to clear the complex. Instead, he was encouraging a group towards the temple.

Kawab looked out to where his leader was pointing. "He appears to be beckoning to a priest."

"I'm not entirely blind. I can see that. Get your men under control, Kawab. Oh my God, we appear to have a religious convention. There's three of them."

Eurydice pushed past Kawab. She watched the nun stumble and one of the priests reach to help her. Eurydice spun to face her deputy.

"Tell me, since when a nun has worn jeans and mountain boots under her habit?" She spun around and grabbed her gun and detonator. "Get out of my way, man. I'm ending this now!"

Kawab watched as his leader ran, far faster than seemed possible for a woman of her age, towards the Hypostyle Hall, into which the false priests had disappeared.

He smiled widely, lifting the walkie talkie to his mouth. "Everyone to the hall. Targets spotted. Repeat, everyone to the hall."

He stepped out of the tent and walked calmly towards the job he'd trained for his whole life.

THE LAST RITES

Gerhard knelt at the side of the gravely injured man. There seemed little doubt he wouldn't make it. The man's eyes fluttered open when Aboud touched his forehead gently.

"Father Ernst is here to give last rites, my friend." He clasped the man's hand and nodded for Gerhard to start.

"Blessed is our God, always, now and ever, and unto the ages of ages," Gerhard intoned, forming a cross on the man's forehead. The man smiled weakly at him before staring up at a dust-ridden ray of sun that shone behind them. He beamed.

Aboud patted his hand, leaned across to close his eyes with great respect, and said, "Alas, he's passed away." They stared down sadly at the stranger who'd started the day excited to visit one of the world's greatest wonders and ended it dead on the dusty floor.

"I'm sorry for my part in this, Father," Aboud said, rubbing his forehead and studying his boots.

"It's not our past actions that measure our worth, my

son, but the learnings we take from them and how we apply those in the future."

Aboud nodded with tears in his eyes, looking at the injured around him. "Get these people out of here. NOW!" he screamed at his men, who scurried to obey his order.

"ELENA! Ellie! My heart's own love. Where are you?"

"Mama Aida," Ellie spluttered. She turned around to face the displaced voice. "Mama Aida, run. Please, God, there's a bomb in here!"

"I know. I planted it. There's one on each column. Can't be too careful, can we?"

Ellie blinked, staring. Speechless.

In front of her didn't stand the wizened, crooked old crone she'd known her entire life. This wasn't a peasant woman in a long, black galabiya. The woman in front of her shared the same face and voice but none of the characteristics or vocal patterns. She stood straight and tall, dressed in black military fatigues, with a belt of ammunition and the Guardians of the Ankh's preferred weapon of choice: a machine gun. A gun pointing straight at Ellie.

"NO... no," Ellie mewed. "Not you. Mama... no!" Her legs collapsed before the gun spluttered its first round. It swung her sideways as a bullet hit her shoulder. Another blasted into her stomach. She felt the weight of a body landing on top of her and hands dragging her behind a column.

Ellie saw Ben's eyes flooded with tears as he shook his head at Gerhard. She turned to see what they were looking at and saw Sam lying next to her on the hard floor. Her glorious Sam. The man she'd loved her entire adult life staring back at her, his black curls framing his sweet face.

He winked at her. "I'd do it all over again, my Elena,

knowing this day would come, to share just one day with you. It's been a ride, my love." He smiled gently at her.

"Sam," she croaked weakly, gasping as pain grabbed her. "Sam. I'm sorry, so very sorry."

His eyes fluttered shut for a moment. "Don't be! You've been my life. I love you, Elena, and nothing will change that. Just promise me to live. To move on and live."

A fine trickle of blood ran from his mouth across his golden cheek. Ellie tried to move to him. She fought to get closer but could only move her hand. She slid it across the floor, through the stream of blood, reaching until her fingertips touched his. He smiled and stared into her eyes as he took a breath... a final breath.

She stared, her brain slowing to protect her from the truth. He appeared so peaceful, as he had on so many lazy Saturday mornings during their marriage. Laying there looking at her with an expression of such love. His final expression of love.

Then it hit her. A weight so heavy thundered down onto her chest. She couldn't breathe. She couldn't speak. The pain paralysed her cognitive senses and her physical being. She was drowning in a tsunami of anguish that had taken her far away. Everything else receded – Ben, Gerhard, the danger they were in – everything. She was lost, staring at a face that would laugh, kiss, smile, frown no more, and all she wanted was to join him. To give her life force free rein to fade away as her blood soaked deep into the Egyptian sands.

From a great distance, she heard a voice screaming. "Why? Tell me why? Mama, I thought you loved me." She realised it was her own.

"But I do, child, more than I love anything on this earth. I only love God more, and it's His calling I'm answering. Do you have any idea how much I've given up to try to save you? I came from a good family. I have a degree in electrical engineering, and yet, since I graduated, I've worked as a maid and then a nursemaid for your family. I could have married and had children of my own. But from the moment I saw you, I knew I'd protect you with my life. You are the daughter of my heart."

Silence resonated louder than any gunshot.

"They ordered me to kill you, and I disobeyed every order. I thought if I could just make certain you never married or had children, then your line would die out, and the House of Scarabs would cease to be a threat. But then you ran away with that man," she spat, "and came back married. I knew I had to break you apart. I laid so many traps. So many opportunities for him to stray, and yet, he was as loyal as an old flea-ridden mongrel in a warm new home. I watched, feeding you contraceptives in your morning breakfast, doing my duty. Then he kicked me out – me, the woman who'd raised you, who'd kissed every scraped knee, who'd taught you to walk and talk."

Ellie shivered. She was so cold. She listened, unable to process the depths of deception.

"Argh!" Aida shrieked, "It's your fault, Elena. If only you'd stayed in England, none of this would have come to pass. Now I have no choice. You must die and me with you. I'm an old woman and ready to meet my maker, but you, you needn't have died. Elena, you're not evil, but you're the vessel of such evil. You're an affront to God, and so, you must die. You understand that, don't you, my Elena? You're a smart girl and always have been. I'm just sorry we have to leave such destruction behind us. Mourad would have cried to see this."

Gerhard had crept around the columns, following the

path of Mama Aida's voice. He saw her crouched low behind a column just to left of the one protecting Ellie and Ben. She reached into her pocket and pulled out a little box, innocuous in itself. Time slowed as she lifted the clear tab which covered part of the box, revealing a button. Her finger lowered towards the button, little sparkles of dust shimmering in its path.

Gerhard ran towards her, everything in slow motion. Each footfall puffed sand up as one fell after the other, narrowing the distance between them. Eurydice's head turned, her focus eagle-sharp, none of Mama Aida's rambling characteristics visible. Her hair falling across her cheek, the finger faltered for a second before continuing its inevitable descent. The corners of her mouth twitched into a serene smile as the button connected.

Each column was illuminated for a microsecond by a ring of sparks that radiated from the base, growing into a wave of fire. The pillars that had stood for several millennia crumbled from the base as a shower of stone and grit exploded out. They hung in midair before tilting and falling. The stone goliaths hit each other and split into gigantic meteors that exploded around the confined space, that contracted and then expanded outwards. Dust blocked the sun and choked the air.

Gerhard felt the first impact of the explosion but through a bubble of cotton wool. As Aida's finger hit the button, a sphere of energy puffed up around him like a balloon, wrapping him in a bubble that was tossed through the air as the explosion expanded. Missiles flew straight at him, but they hit the sphere wall and bounced away harmlessly. He watched the destruction of one of the world's greatest wonders.

When the dust settled, nothing remained standing.

Rocks were scattered far and wide but all he had eyes for was the other blue sphere sitting atop a five-foot-high remnant of a column. Inside it, Ben held Ellie limply in his arms. Even from that distance, Gerhard saw him shouting at her. She was ghostly pale.

The spheres dissolved around them. As Gerhard looked around, he saw a few of the soldiers picking themselves up from the ground. One man turned and saluted him. Aboud turned back to his men and organised them into a search and rescue team. Gerhard smiled weakly. After all the problems they'd faced, it was warming to see human goodness prevail. He lifted his face to the sky, circled his shoulders, and hurried over to help Ben.

Ben and Ellie hadn't fared so well in the explosion. They were both covered in cuts and scratches, their clothes shredded. A deep veneer of dust covered them, changing them into a monotone beige, the only colour coming from the deep green of their eyes. Eyes that stared at each other as Ben ordered Ellie to stay with them.

"Pass her to me, Ben. Ben, you can let her go now. Pass her to me." Ben didn't lose Ellie's gaze as he carefully transferred her to Gerhard before jumping down and retrieving her.

She screamed as he pulled her back into the cradle of his arms. "You stay with me, Ells. I haven't come this far to lose you now. You still owe me lessons, and I'm going to claim them - so help me, God."

The path to the scarab pillar was littered with boulders, rocks, and pits. Ben marched with determination. Every step judged. Gerhard trailed behind like an elderly footman. Ellie's gaze never left Ben's face as he swapped between blasting her and cooing endearments. He was all that was anchoring her to this plane, but his desperation was clear to her.

The dust billowed in whirls around them, coating the sun in a yellowy haze. She drifted, remembering the sand-storms of her youth. She remembered lazy days on digs, reading under a canopy for hours on end, and the paddock of yellow daisies she'd danced in with her grandmother. Everything was so peaceful.

Ben ran the last few steps and eased down onto his knees next to the statue. Ellie nestled in his arms. Her eyelids fluttered down, dark lashes fanning against her cheek. She sighed as Ben lifted her hand to touch the statue, an exhalation that didn't contract.

"Ellie!" Ben shook her. "Ellie, you will not go back on your word to Sam. We need you. I need you." He shook her, with silent tears washing a path through the dust on his cheek, until Gerhard stilled him.

"It's too late, Ben. She's gone..."

The two men held each other, with Ellie as she'd been in life – their centre.

THE OTHER PLANE

Ellie snuggled deeper into the cosy bed. Taking a long breath of the honey-sweet air, she opened her eyes lazily. She frowned at the unfamiliar setting.

It was a large, airy room bathed in the pink glow of the early evening sun. White furnishings and deep carpet offset walls of warm gold. Two over-sized comfy chairs – the type she loved to curl up in with a mug of cocoa and a good book – flanked a huge, white marble fireplace. Gauze curtains that fluttered softly framed the French doors, partially shielded by a large chaise longue. Beyond the doors was a beautiful Juliet balcony covered in a mass of white roses, which fragranced the entire room with their heady scent. The four-poster bed on which she lay was swathed with white, sheer fabric that rippled in the gentle breeze.

She gazed around for anything familiar. Slowly, so as not to attract attention, she crawled across the bed and eased onto the floor, her feet sinking into the soft pile of the white carpet. All she could hear was the summer buzz of insects flying and birds singing. No sounds of human activity. No roars of cars or hums of air planes overhead. No sounds of construction or music floating on the air. Just nature at its purest.

Her lips tightened as she saw she was wearing white yoga pants and an off-the-shoulder sloppy top. She knew the clothes were not hers and wondered who the hell had dressed her. She crossed on tip-toe to the window and glanced out, checking no one was around. Her mouth dropped at the vista.

She was in a vast building, a gatehouse for the largest gates she'd ever seen. Her balcony faced meadows and woodland that stretched far into the horizon. Meadows danced with an array of wild, abundant flowers and hummed to the happy buzz of bees. Trees in the woods stretched up to the skies, gigantic gladiators, proud and tall. The foliage was greener and the sky bluer. She'd never seen nature display such vigour or beauty.

Turning to her left, she studied the gates. They stretched up four stories high and shimmered and shifted. As she looked closer, she realised they were veins of water that twisted and moved, changing patterns, some geometric and others nature-based, all complex and achingly beautiful. The water reflected the colours of the meadows and forests in every twisting vein.

But where was everyone? There was no sign of humanity. Frowning in confusion, she padded across the floor to the door, eased it open, and peered into the corridor. It was empty except for a row of doors and a console table topped with more of the white roses. The corridor ended in stairs to the lower floor.

Ellie stepped out and looked around, puzzled. The perfume of roses was so familiar, it brought a deep ache to her chest. *Grandma*, she thought. *These were her favourite.*

She stepped over to the glorious display and bent to

sniff the soft petals. They evoked the memory of her embrace, the scent of her grandma's hugs. She picked one from the display and walked along the corridor, the rose's soft perfume surrounding her.

Ellie opened doors as she passed them, checking out the rooms hidden beyond. There were three further bedrooms, decorated in a more masculine manner, each with their own en-suites, and the most opulent bathroom she'd ever seen. It more resembled a waterfall, with water tumbling over a stone wall surrounded with delicate green ferns. Her fingers trailed through the water, and she smiled at the thought of showering there. The room beguiled her.

Although the rooms were gorgeous, she knew this was not her home. She grappled with her memory, trying in vain to grasp even the tiniest fragment. Nothing. She was adrift in a blank book.

"Come on, Ellie," she said to herself. "Keep searching. You might find some answers."

Downstairs, the grandeur continued, every room more breathtaking than the last. She wandered through a vast library with jewel-coloured, deep plush chairs. A vast dining room. A sitting room with a wall of glass that framed the meadow, creating a masterpiece of composition. The kitchen was every chef's dream, with a huge central island that could have sat an entire football squad.

What there wasn't was any technology or people. She sighed in contentment. It was peaceful and she felt safe, something she knew had been a rarity in her life. Laughing, she twirled and danced. If she had to be stranded some-where, it might as well be in her dream home.

Elle rustled around the kitchen, opening cupboards to find the provisions to make a light supper. She took her meal into the sitting room and enjoyed it as she watched the sun paint the meadow, in pink and red tones, in its dying moments. The sofas were so deep and tempting. She lay back, sinking into their softness, and let exhaustion capture her again in its slumberous embrace.

∾

She woke the next morning, stretching in contentment. A fawn and its mother were grazing in the distance, dew still fresh on the swaying grasses. She leapt up, full of energy, excited to explore. The need to see the gates up close nagged at her subconscious. She'd found the back door yesterday but hadn't discovered a front door yet.

"Nothing ventured, nothing gained, Ellie," she murmured to herself as she made coffee.

Half an hour later, she was scratching her head in confusion. She couldn't find the house's main entrance, and it made no sense that they would've built such a grand house with just a back door in the kitchen. Giving up her exploration in disgust, she opened the kitchen door and fell back in surprise.

In front of her was a large, rectangular lake, surrounded by ruins, with people milling around. The scene was familiar to her. Above it, piled up like the layers of a multi-story car park, was the same scene but with different people from an earlier time. Each layer appeared to represent a different time in the history of the complex. It went up as far as she could see, layer upon layer. Same place, different time.

Turning to her right, she saw a glass tower that housed the great gate, linking it to every plane. A large glass pontoon floated on a pool at the base of the tower. She stared, openmouthed, trying to make sense of what she saw.

It was layers of history, one above the other, yet running in parallel.

Something drew her to the tower. Peering up, she saw it was constructed of a continuous tube of glass, with not a joint in sight. As she neared it, a door slid open, allowing her to take tentative steps onto the pontoon before sliding shut behind her and merging back into the smooth wall of glass.

She was so close to the gate, she could touch it. Her fingers slid through the tendrils of water as they twirled around her hand, caressing it gently. The bottom of the gate released its form, allowing the water to swirl into the pool and lift Ellie up to the first level.

She turned to watch the level come into view, her eyes widening as she saw the white bun and rotund form of Elspeth, her grandma, come into view. She held the hand of a small child with a tumble of red curls and sun-kissed skin. The girl was finding it hard to contain her excitement and bounced from foot to foot, smiling up joyously at the man holding her other hand.

Sam.

And then it came back to her, hitting her with the velocity of a sledgehammer. She remembered the betrayal, the ultimate betrayal of Mama Aida. She remembered Sam giving his own life to save hers. She remembered the heat of the explosion as it rushed across her cheek. She remembered everything. She realised where she was.

As the doors opened, she sprinted towards the people she loved most. She grabbed Elspeth and smothered her in kisses. Sam swept her into his arms and kissed her in a way no man should in front of others. Ellie extracted herself and knelt in front of the girl.

"And who might you be?" she breathed out.

"I'm Amarine, silly. Everyone knows that – right, Gran?" she said, turning to Elspeth.

Ellie's eyes filled with tears as she stared up at her grandmother, who nodded gently. "Ellie, let me introduce you to Amarine Verity Gamal, your daughter."

"Oh..." Ellie said, glancing at Sam over their daughter's head. "Our daughter?"

Sam nodded, beaming. Ellie wrapped Amarine in her arms and lifted her, swinging them around as she showered the girl in four years' worth of lost kisses.

"My daughter," she sighed, closing her eyes as the girl cuddled into her, wrapping her arms and legs around Ellie and snuggling in. Ellie stroked the soft curls and lay kisses upon the sweet-smelling head as she felt the ever-present gaping hole in her chest fill and close.

Sam came up behind them and wrapped his two girls in his safe embrace. "Home," he whispered softly. "I'm home."

After some time, they realised they'd forgotten Elsbeth and turned back to her. She was smiling at them, her cheeks wet with the sheen of tears. "I've dreamt of seeing this moment. I've told Amarine every story I remember, but this little miss has been so impatient to meet you both."

Amarine slithered out of Ellie's arm and skipped to Elspeth. "Gran, does this mean I'm not an orphan anymore?" she asked innocently.

Ellie looked to Sam, her eyes full of tears. She closed her eyes and shook her head. So much pain, and for what? Why?

As her eyes swept around, many of the black-clad soldiers who'd been hunting her ambled aimlessly in the distance. "Oh my God!" she said, reaching for Sam.

"Don't worry, Elena. They can't hurt us now. The poor souls are lost and blind here," Sam reassured her.

"Yes, their penance for the damage they did on Earth is to wander, blind and deaf, lost in their own senses until the burn of regret takes hold and they fully repent," Elspeth explained, watching the men with a level of pity that Ellie had yet to feel.

Elspeth ushered them towards the café, so they could sit and chat. Ellie glanced around the shack. To her left was the woman she'd help rescue, sat in her wheelchair all alone. Her heart sank and guilt overwhelmed her.

"Oh, I'm so sorry," she said, walking over to the woman.

"Do I know you, my dear?" the woman answered with a sweet smile.

Ellie nodded. "I was the nun that left you in this café. Well, not a nun as such but dressed as one," Ellie said, adjusting the statement at Elspeth's confused frown.

The woman beamed at Ellie, leapt to her feet, and embraced her. "Oh, don't be sorry. You released me. You're my heroine. Without you, I'd have been locked in that body until I was unable to breathe for myself. You saved me that indignity. I'm so grateful."

The woman proved her point by dancing them around the café floor, much to Amarine's delight, who shouted, "More, Mommy, more!" The two women collapsed in giggles on the rickety old chairs as Amarine mimicked them. After a few minutes of chatting, the woman bid them farewell.

"Now I have to find my way home," she murmured.

"Just close your eyes and think of it. A door will appear, a door to your home," Elspeth explained. Ellie watched in amazement as a door materialised before them. The woman waved goodbye, opened the door, and stepped through into a comfortable sitting room. The door vanished.

"Wow, that will take some getting used to," Ellie said.

Sam and Elspeth shared a glance before smiling back at her. Ellie had been soaking up the sight of her daughter playing hopscotch in the sand and didn't notice the exchange.

They sat chatting for some time, enjoying the morning sun as Amarine flitted around them, a ball of energy. Ellie couldn't take her eyes off the young girl. Amarine was a perfect counterbalance of both Sam and herself. Her shining green eyes were a duplicate of Ellie's, right down to the crescent of amber, and her hair, although red, was a deeper chestnut tone, which bounced with Sam's curls. She laughed loudly and boldly, just as Sam did, and her features echoed his more chiseled features. Yet, the expressions that crossed her face mirrored Ellie's. Her skin was a milkier version of Sam's bronze hue. Ellie stared in wonder at the beauty of their creation.

There was a slight shimmer in the atmosphere as a door appeared again. "Maybe she wants her wheelchair back," she joked. This time, she caught the glance that passed between Elspeth and Sam. "What?" she asked with a frown.

The door opened, and the singularly most stunning woman she'd ever seen stepped through it. Ellie saw a court-yard with a fountain behind the woman before the door slammed closed.

"Hello, Elena. I have waited a very long time to meet you. Elspeth. Sam," she said, nodding at them.

"Kiya, Kiya," Amarine shouted, dancing around the woman. "Mommy came, just as you said. She didn't know my name. Can you imagine?! Oh, and she looks just like me," she said, swirling around in a circle. "She's almost as pretty as you."

"Oh, sweetling, if she looks like you, then her beauty far exceeds mine," Kiya answered.

Amarine studied her intently and then nodded. "True,"

she agreed. The adults laughed as she fluttered off, pretending to be a butterfly.

Ellie's eyes flitted from Elspeth to Sam before settling on Kiya. "Tell me," she said.

Kiya looked around the group, her eyes resting on Amarine for a moment before she said simply, "You have to go back."

"Go back where?" Ellie asked, glancing at Sam and Elspeth, whose sad expressions said more than any words. The realisation hit her. "Oh, no, go back to Earth? Leave them? No way in hell, or heaven, come to that." Ellie scrabbled up out of the chair, moving away from them. "Amarine, come here, darling. We have to go home now. I'll take you to Scarab's Rest. You'll love it there."

Amarine raised her eyebrow and laughed. "Mommy, I already live there with Gran and now Daddy. Kiya explained everything earlier, when she told me you were coming for a visit. You can't stay because you're alive, Mommy. We're all dead, so we can't visit you, but you can come back and visit us. Isn't that right, Kiya?"

Kiya smiled down at her gently before lifting eyes full of sadness to stare into Ellie's. "Yes, sweetling, perfectly correct."

"Sam," Ellie croaked. "No, I won't leave you again. I can't."

He walked to her slowly, as if approaching a nervous colt, and reached for her hands, pulling her into his embrace. "*Rohi*, my soul, my own love," he whispered into her hair, "you must. It's not your time. I understand now. You were born for great things. God has willed it so."

She pulled away and stared at him in utter disbelief. "I don't care. My family comes first, and I'm not leaving you."

"We are *all* family, my child," Kiya explained gently.

"For your greater family, the family of humanity, you must return. I'm so sorry. I know how hard it must be."

"You know nothing. Who do you think you are? You barge in here and order me about. Well, open that door and go back where you came from," Ellie said, thrusting her finger into Kiya's chest.

Kiya sighed and swirled her hand in a full circle. The three deities appeared behind Kiya: Khepri, Sobek, and Bastet, standing tall in their human form. With a large flash of blue, Ellie found herself once more contained within a blue sphere.

"I'm sorry to take her. I'd hoped it wouldn't come to this." Kiya said, sadly. "I'll bring her back to say her farewells."

DESTINY'S PATH

Ellie struggled pointlessly within the sphere as it glided towards the glass tower. She screamed every obscenity she knew at her four companions, who studiously ignored her as they entered the tower and descended in the lift. She turned and watched her family shrink into the distance.

Kiya walked, her hips swaying, as she guided the sphere towards the gate house. Ellie studied her in mutinous silence. Kiya's golden toga shimmered as it moved. She had calfskin sandals on her feet, and her ears, fingers, wrists, and neck were adorned with elaborate gold and garnet jewelry. Thick, black kohl highlighted her cornflower-blue eyes, and her hair was up at the front and raining ringlets down her back. She resembled a blonde goddess.

Maybe she is, Ellie thought.

Kiya walked around the house, having clearly visited before. She made a pot of coffee and then gestured for them to follow her to the library. When Ellie was last there, she hadn't clicked that the room was a direct replica of Bertram's. Kiya settled herself in the chair next to Ellie's favourite. She gestured towards the fire, which sparked to life, and poured two cups of coffee.

"We have much to discuss, Elena. I am more sorry than mere words can express that you are in this position. Much as I also regret the impact it has had upon my existence. But there you are - it is what it is, and we don't have time to dwell on it."

Ellie glared at her in silence, her arms crossed, her foot tapping.

"I can release you, and we can sit and discuss this over a nice coffee, or I can bind your mouth and show you why you must return. But be sure, the vision will not be pleasant. Which is it to be, my child?"

"I am not your child," Ellie spat back with venom.

"When you've lived as long as me, everyone appears as a child. I have seen life before me, and I see life not yet lived. Every soul in comparison is young. I apologise if it annoys you. Believe me, Elena, I am your friend. Now hurry. The coffee is getting cold. It is a secret pleasure I've taken from your time," Kiya said with a serene smile.

Ellie nodded up at the three deities standing behind the chairs, "What of them? They've been dragging us around like dogs on leashes and not said a single word. Are they about to get chatty too?"

Kiya chuckled, the sound of perfectly tuned wind chimes blowing in the breeze. "Oh, they can't talk. Well, only through me and my fellow seers. But I am their voice. It was to me they first voiced their prophecy all those millennia ago. It was I who selected your families to form the House of Scarabs, and it's I who have guarded you ever since via the power they granted me." She smiled up at them. "They are more than happy with my choice and thank you for your help," she said.

"I haven't agreed to help them," Ellie replied.

"Ah, but you will," Kiya said, staring into the distance. "You will do so much, my child. So much good." She turned back to look at Sobek, who'd stepped forward. "We must hurry. Gerhard and Ben await you. Ah, well, our little chat will have to wait for another time. I'll precis it for now."

She released Ellie from the bubble and passed her a coffee.

"Elena, I think you're aware the three of you together form the House of Scarabs. To forge the House, it was necessary you each complete a challenge in which you'd die and pass through the ritual of resurrection with the god you represent. That's because the gods were endowing you with their powers, the power of resurrection."

Ellie gasped, her eyes widening.

"It's bound to be a bit of a shock," Kiya said kindly.

"Bit," Ellie spluttered. "Resurrection, like bringing people back from the dead?"

"Yes, precisely so. The House of Scarabs is the key to the gateway from Heaven. Together, you can return anyone to life as long as a part of their body still exists on earth. They will return clear of illness and at their optimum age. You have much to do and to beware of, for these powers engender great greed."

"Hang on a minute. That sounds ghoulish. I don't want to be Frankenstein, raising bodies from their graves. It's horrific. No, I want no part in that," Ellie said, pulling away. "Everyone I love is here, and you want me to leave them to bring back dead people? No - no way!"

"It's too late. I'm sorry, but you are already Khepri's key. Now hurry. You have your farewells to say. I so wish your family could go with you. That was what I planned, but as

Sam pointed out, Amarine didn't ever fully exist, so she can't go back. She needs at least one parent here."

Ellie sobbed, shaking her head from side to side. Kiya patted her hand and passed her a perfectly pressed linen handkerchief.

"As the key, you can come and visit upon occasion. This house is yours. It's modelled on your dream house, I believe," Kiya said, smiling at Khepri, who nodded. "You can stay for two days - no more. And beware, as your body is at its most vulnerable during that time. It's the only time you can be killed, so plan your trips carefully."

Ellie stared at her, at a loss for words.

"Truly, child, I know we ask a lot of you, more than of Ben and Gerhard, but your role in the fate of humanity is crucial. Without you, two millennia of planning and work will come to naught. We have no choice. You have no choice. Our destinies were preformed long before our births." Kiya eased Ellie out of the chair. "We will talk again, my child. Remember I am always here, for you are my kin. Our purpose is to protect and support the House of Scarabs. We are at your service. Now go – hurry. You have but moments for your goodbyes," she said, gesturing at the door which had appeared next to them.

"But how? I mean..."

Kiya shook her head. "We don't have time, but it will become clear in due course. Go."

Kiya pushed her through the door, which slammed behind her.

"Mommy, you've been ages," Amarine said, pouting. "Now we have no time to skip together. I love skipping. Do you?"

Ellie grabbed her, pulling her into a fierce embrace. "Not as much as I love you, lollipop."

"Ah, you called me that when I was on Earth. I heard you. You used to say, 'Hurry and grow, lollipop, so I can meet you.' And look, I grew real big, Mommy."

Ellie stared at her, eyes wide. "Yes, I did. You were my secret lollipop. Mommy loves you so much, Amarine. Remember that when I'm away. And I promise you, I will come back to visit as often as I can." She covered her face with kisses and pulled her back in for a hug.

Sam walked up behind them and cocooned them in his embrace. "You are my everything, but I can't leave her. She will be the target of great interest here as the only child of the gatekeeper. Some may try to use her to get to you. She needs me. She's the only thing that could ever keep me from you."

Ellie stared into his chocolate eyes, saving the memory of his arms and the adoration on his face to return to when she was alone on the living plane. "I always knew you'd be the greatest dad. She's a lucky girl. Oh, but I'll miss you so much." She blinked the tears away, nodding at him as she turned. Elspeth blew her a kiss, and Ellie pulled her lips tight, swallowing the emotions that threatened to overwhelm her. "Keep them safe for me, Grandma."

"You know I will, darling. Now go make us proud..."

Ellie bit her lip, drawing blood, as she closed her eyes, willing the pain away. She brushed the tears from her face and knelt to stare into little green eyes. "I'm so glad I got to meet you, lollipop. Will you promise me to dance, to laugh, to play games, and to do your best to make Daddy laugh at least twenty times a day when I'm gone?"

Amarine considered the question before answering seriously, "Twenty times is a lot, Mommy. Could we make it eighteen instead?"

Ellie laughed and nodded. "Okay, that's a deal, Eighteen laughs." She got up and ruffled Amarine's hair, smiled at Sam, and rubbed her fist around her chest, as she'd always done to tell him she loved him when they were in public. He smiled with tears in his eyes and returned the gesture. He took Amarine's hand and walked back to Elspeth.

Ellie studied the group one more time, with tears pouring unchecked down her cheeks, before turning towards the gate. It shimmered and cleared as she unlocked it and walked through.

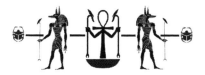

EPILOGUE

A ripple flowed across the desert plains, the agricultural green lands, the concrete jungles of the cities, and the fast-running waters of the Nile. It was a ripple unseen by the living, just a subtle blur that softened the focus for a second. Yet, it exploded through the realm of the dead, heard by everyone, understood by only a few who'd been waiting a millennium for its arrival.

They stretched like satisfied cats, moving towards the nearest gateway, in no particular hurry after having waited for so long. As they slipped through the barrier, the ripple's impact became felt in the living world.

The royal mummies reanimated in front of the startled gaze of thirty schoolgirls on a trip to the Egyptian museum.

In Luxor's Valley of the Kings, American tourists witnessed Tutankhamen's resurrection.

Nobles exited their tombs in Saqqara after several millennia of slumber.

A gentle knocking emanating from a sarcophagus in the storage repository of the British Museum shocked the young Egyptologist working nearby.

The ancient Egyptians had returned, ready to reclaim their heritage and positions. Innocents in a strange new world.

THE END

I hope you enjoyed my little tale. As an indie author, I totally depend on reviews to encourage other readers to take a chance on my book. I'd be so grateful if you'd spare a moment to leave one. It's easy. Go to my Amazon book page and click the *Write a customer review* button towards the bottom of the page.

Want to know more about this world and what happens next?

Sign up to my reader community list at www.hazellonguet.com/communitylp. I'll keep you informed about new releases and give you priority access to *FREE* short stories that explain the backstories of some of your favourite characters as I write them. As a thank you, you'll get a *FREE* copy of the prequel *House of Scarabs: Genesis*, which takes you 3,000 years back to the time of the pharaohs and explains how Ellie, Ben, and Gerhard's ancestors were imbued with the seed of the House of Scarabs. Grab your copy now at www.hazellonguet.com/communitylp or read on for a preview.

AFTERWORD

Evil comes in many forms, in both the unintentionally heinous acts done by good people and the rotten souls that rampage through life, leaving misery in their wake.

Can anyone be truly good or truly evil? When I first dreamt this story, I became fascinated with the concept that the Guardians of the Ankh were good people forced into terrible actions. The trio of the House of Scarabs were a kind, normal bunch but encumbered with powers that could unleash global chaos. Neither group were traditional goodies or baddies but a complex mix of both, which, honestly, is truer to life than the standard premise of good versus evil.

The book came sixty percent formed in one of my reality dreams - dreams so intense, painted in such rich shades and detail, that the barrier between dreaming and reality blurs somewhat. It fascinated me, and as a lifelong bookworm, I wanted to know the ending, but I was the only one who could uncover it, so I started writing. I hope my attempts have done the story justice. I have tried to be historically accurate but there are occasions where I've bent the facts a little to suit the story.

It's taken me an age (five years), as I went through a move across continents, and then another within the UK. I became a doggie mum to two Rottweilers, Magical Merli and Asha, the one-eyed queen of hope. Through it all, I kept slogging on with the story, sometimes with months of breaks enforced by home renovations or illness. I'm proud of the final result, but now the bookworm is whispering again, "But what happens next?" That, I will answer in the sequel – *House of Bastet*, coming out in 2019.

I hope you enjoyed *House of Scarabs*. It feels odd to put my baby out for everyone to judge, but if you liked it, I'd be so grateful if you could leave a review here. They help us bookworms find great new reads, and they help the independent authors find new readers.

The bookworm in me loathes typos or story inconsistencies, so I've worked day and night to catch the little blighters. I've set traps to find and eradicate those tricky little spelling mistakes and grammar goofs, but if you come across any, please let me know, and I will zap them with my magical editing wand. Email me at: contact@hazel-longuet.com.

Thank you for using your precious time to read my book, and I truly hope we meet again in the pages of another story or via one of my social media connections.

You can follow me on Facebook:
http://www.facebook.com/HazelLonguetAuthor

You can tweet me at: http:///twitter.com/HazelLonguet

Join my reader community:
www.hazellonguet.com/communitylp

Or visit my House of Scarabs' Pinterest board to see
locations, casting ideas and book covers:
http://www.pinterest.co.uk/hazell/house-of-scarabs-
inspirations/

Farewell... for now.

Hazel

If you are wondering how the story started, read on for the
opening chapter of the prequel, **House of Scarabs -
Genesis**.

GENESIS

PREQUEL TO HOUSE OF SCARABS

Faced with the extinction of their faith, the high priest of Egypt must take steps to preserve the

gods' knowledge for the sake of the pharaoh's immortality.

One vision rocks the foundations of the Egyptian belief system. The pharaoh's seer knows that their civilisation will perish and their faith fall fallow. Horrified at the implication, she shares the news with the high priest of Egypt. Only together can they plant a seed that will allow the culture to return and flourish. Her vision is clear. They must select a group of men who will carry the power of the ancient gods within them. They will form a secret organisation that will cross the plains and oceans to ensure that one day, the pharaohs can rise again and reclaim their rightful place as world leaders.

Nothing must stop them - not even the pharaoh.

The only problem is they have a spy in their midst who's determined to see them fail.

Genesis is the prequel to *House of Scarabs* and should ideally be read after it. If you like historical thrillers, quirky characters, and tales of mysterious ancient powers, then you'll love this novella.

Read on for a sneak peek at the first two chapters of Genesis or go to www.hazellonguet.com/communitylp to download it for *FREE* when you join my reader community.

For those of you who will never join a mailing list but still want to read the prequel, I've made it available to buy on Amazon from the end of January 2019.

THE SEER

The fountain of knowledge was bathed in sunshine, the water throwing glimmering lights around the walls of the courtyard. The fountain held centre stage, with four twisted old olives standing sentry in each quadrant of the famed courtyard of all knowledge. Except for the gentle trills of the dancing water and the distant birdsong from the gardens surrounding the temple complex, all was quiet. The day was young and the sun yet soft.

Kiya hummed softly whilst gazing into her scrying mirror. At only twenty years and one, she was young for her weighty role, yet everyone agreed that never had a pharaoh been so blessed with such a powerful and accurate seer.

Raiders had captured her family long ago and sold them into slavery. They were split amongst various owners and spread across the known world. Kiya considered herself one of the lucky ones to have found her way to the pharaoh's court.

When she'd come into her powers as a mere child of eight, the pharaoh's court considered her something of a child protégé. Her astounding accuracy saw her fly up the ranks until she'd taken the role of Pharaoh's Seer. She'd held the position for five years, and so far, had never seen something that didn't come to pass.

The early mornings were her favourite time, when the sun had yet to heat the air, the temple was wrapped in the silence of sleeping priests, and the birds were rejoicing the dawning of a new day. She could let her mind wander and enjoy a modicum of freedom before her duties pressed down on her.

She laid the mirror down with great care and wandered over to sit on the edge of the fountain, trailing her fingers through the twirling jets. The sun played with her honey-blonde hair, bringing fiery highlights into focus.

A movement in the water caught her eye, and she stared, immediately taken into a vision. As the importance of this vision became obvious, she held her breath, wishing that this was the one that broke her perfect record. Unable to process what she'd seen, she hurried back to the scrying mirror that rested on one of the devotional cushions scattered across the yard. She gazed into the depths of the polished metal surface, which clouded and again replayed the same vision, with the same details and same horrific outcome.

Dropping her precious mirror, she lifted the long white lengths of her dress and ran to gain the high priest's counsel. Telling the pharaoh what she'd seen could result in her own execution. Only the high priest could help her. She knew this emphatically, for the vision had shown her the path to take. The future never lied.

THE HIGH PRIEST

Haremakhet was particularly reflective that morning. Egypt had basked in a prolonged period of peace under the guiding hand of the pharaoh and his all-seeing seer. As a high priest, it had been a period of great reward. Less political wrangling gave him time to build the temple's brethren. He'd opened religious studies to more of his pharaoh's subjects. They lived in blessed times, a golden epoch.

And yet, today was different. Today, he felt the dark hand of fate hovering.

He swept the Holy of Holies with a worn broom almost bare of bristles. His assistant priests had tried to wrestle it from his hands more times than he cared to remember, and yet, he always returned to it. It wasn't his responsibility to clean the inner sanctums anymore; it hadn't been for years, but he felt closest to his gods when he was toiling in manual labour, serving their needs. It was a philosophy he insisted all his priests follow, but few embraced it as whole-heartedly as he.

He heard the soft tap of feet running through the

temple toward him. Surprised another was about so early, he turned to greet his visitor. He knew it was Kiya as the sun lit her fiery hair, which was so unusual within the kingdom. She was trying to show respect to the deities but was obviously in distress and hurrying through the rituals to get to him.

"Your Eminence," she said, flowing into a deep curtsy, her left arm across her chest as she bowed her head and bent at the waist.

"Your Omniscience," he replied formally, touching his head and heart and bowing back. "You appear in a rush, my dear. Is all well with you?"

"With me, yes. But not with our world, Haremakhet. The gods, praise be to them, presented me with a vision of such consequence that I fear our society is doomed," Kiya said. She looked earnestly at the high priest. "I seek your counsel, Haremakhet, for this is a prophecy of such import, yet I can't share it with our great pharaoh. The gods forbid it, and even if it were not so, I would be extremely fearful to report such loathsome news. He would surely kill me to remove the blight."

Haremakhet had never seen Kiya so riled. She was always the epitome of decorum and propriety. A woman of rare beauty, beguiling and serene. Her greatest quality was how unaware she was of her impact on others. As High Seer, she was destined to remain a maiden, her virtue intact. Only if it were so would the gods continue to bless her future visions. He'd often thought it sad but acknowledged the importance of her role to the entire Egyptian dominion.

"Do the gods, praise be to them, sanction my consultation, Kiya?"

She raised her cornflower blue eyes, eyes so startling and intense that people often had difficulty looking at her.

"Haremakhet, they demand it. The actions you and I take today will shake the world over three thousand years after we meet our makers. This is our destiny, to set theirs."

"Whose, Kiya?" he asked, bewildered by her trance-like reply.

"The House of Scarabs, Haremakhet. The Resurrectionists. Those we choose today will carry the secrets of resurrection forward to allow our great pharaohs to rise again. They must leave our lands and travel to new, unknown territories and carry that knowledge, protecting it until the time is right to start again. Our great gods will wither, and a new god will rise and be worshipped around the world. The ways of our people will be forgotten, lost to the desert sands. Our great knowledge will be lost, and civilisation will retreat, leaving our people illiterate and backward. Egypt will lose its place in the global theatre. Our temples will be looted as the people turn to their new god, a god so great he has no name. His followers will banish the other gods into the realms of myth and legend. Such is our future, High Priest, and there is no action I can recommend to change it. It is set and will happen. All I can do is guide you to ensure we respect the desires of our pharaohs, past and present, and give them the gift of regeneration. This is what we must do."

He stared at her as her words resonated in the echoes of the Holy of Holies. He said nothing. He wanted to. He wanted to shout at the gods for abandoning them to such a bleak future, for not fighting this all-powerful usurper. Yet, he knew that they were all-seeing and all-knowing. This abandonment, whilst extreme, must surely be for some long-term benefit that was too great for him to imagine.

"Kiya, the rituals of resurrection take twenty years to master, and only a few of the graduates are ever granted the powers by the gods. Every one of them is known and would be missed. How can we create this House of Scarabs without showing our hand?"

"My dear friend," she whispered, grasping his arm, "the gods will preside over the initiation. They will seed a latent talent that negates the need for years of apprenticeship. We must select the candidates from the brotherhood of priests that serve Khepri, Bastet, and Sobek. I know not why. We must make haste. Our preparations can't take long. The House must be formed when the moon is next full. Blessings be, Haremakhet. Tell no one of this, for if we fail, our souls will be subjected to the rage of Anubis in the afterlife."

"Wait. Kiya, I have so many questions."

Kiya smiled. "As do I, Your Eminence, but we have all the information deemed necessary by the gods to complete our task."

Her eyes glazed as she gazed into the distant corner of the holies. She shook her head slightly and turned back to him.

"Haremakhet, our son. You will live out a long and peaceful life serving us, as will more generations to come. Our demise is assured but not in your lifetime and not permanently—if you do as we request. Be good and be true. Offer wise counsel. You will bathe in our love."

Kiya's eyes cleared as she found his gaze. "It's time, Your Eminence," she said with a gesticulation of piety.

Touching his head and heart and bowing from the waist, he answered, "It appears it is, Your Omniscience. Gods' blessings go with you."

Kiya backed out of the Holies before rushing away.

The high priest studied the floor, watching a scarab beetle dart across the sandy surface. The light played on its back, turning the black body into an oiled sheen of purple, green, and blue. He closed his eyes and contemplated everything Kiya had shared with him. With a deep sigh, he picked up the broom and completed the temple floor, said his morning prayers in a whisper, and left to convene a religious council.

Download Genesis for FREE at
www.hazellonguet.com/communitylp
or
BUY it from Amazon.
Available from the end of January 2019

ACKNOWLEDGMENTS

Writing is a very solitary endeavour, and yet, no novel can make it to publication without the touch of numerous individuals.

Thanks to my amazing editor, Coral Coons of Briar Rose Editing, for her patience and gentle support. Any mistakes are resolutely mine.

Mai Gabr and Mohamed Gabr, you've been heroes helping me with my Arabic and German queries. Love you guys, and thank you for answering my crazed WhatsApp questions at all hours of the day.

My parents and sister have been my biggest supporters and cheerleaders. Without them, I don't believe the book would have ever been finished.

Phil and Sal, you're the best. Thank you for years of unswerving support and friendship.

Merli, my writing buddy and office partner. The best Rottweiler in the world. Rottweilers are amazing dogs, loyal, loving, steadfast and unfortunately massively misrepresented in the media. He's a big softy and melts my heart when I'm busy typing a scene and he rests his head in my lap, wanting nothing more than my attention. Rescue dogs are called this because they rescue the humans they move in with – that's a fact.

Finally, thanks to you for reading my book.

16171238R00215

Printed in Great Britain
by Amazon